COURAGE BAY SENTINEL, JULY

Fire Department On High Alert

The heat wave that has plagued Southern California shows no signs of letting up, and Courage Bay's emergency services are reporting an increase in heat-related call-outs. Linda Tate, a news photographer from KBTS television station in San Diego, is here to make a documentary on the city's emergency services, focusing on the smoke jumping team. Sean O'Shea, who heads up the unit, says the risk of forest fires is high and his team is on full alert.

Rare Virus Reported In Hospital's E.R.

As if a heat wave and drought are not enough, Courage Bay Hospital reports the emergence of a virulent respiratory illness among several walk-in patients in the past week. Alec Giroux, attending physician at the hospital's emergency department, says there is no cause for public alarm. However, the Center for Disease Control in Atlanta has been contacted and is sending specialist Janice Reed to monitor the situation.

Toxins Suspected In Courage Bay

Last night, Officer Robert Kellison of the mounted police patrol and marine biologist Melody Harper helped rescue an injured dolphin that had beached on the shores of Courage Bay. Harper, a former resident, is in the city to investigate possible toxins in the bay. Forest fires, rare viruses and now suspected toxins—for the city of Courage Bay, trouble has definitely come in threes.

Bobby Hutchinson is a multitalented woman who was born in a small town in the interior of British Columbia. Though she is now the successful author of more than thirty-five novels, her past includes stints as a retailer, a seamstress and a day-care worker. Twice married, she now lives alone and is the devoted mother of three and grandmother of four. She runs, swims, does yoga, meditates and likes this quote by Dolly Parton: "Decide who you are, and then do it on purpose."

Joanna Wayne and her husband live just a few miles from steamy, exciting New Orleans, but their home is the perfect writer's hideaway. A lazy bayou, complete with graceful egrets, colorful wood ducks and an occasional alligator, winds just below her back garden. When not writing, Joanna loves reading, golfing or playing with her grandchildren, and of course, researching and plotting out her next novel of intrigue and passion. She also teaches writing classes at a local university and is active in several writing groups. Writing is a passion for Joanna, second in importance only to her family. Taking the heroine and hero from danger to enduring love and happy-ever-after is all in a day's work for her, and who could complain about a day like that?

Kay David was born and reared in Texas. She has lived all over the world from the Middle East to South America. Drawing frequently on these exotic locations for her books, she sees the setting of a story as another character in the complex romances she writes. A graduate of the University of Houston, Kay has undergraduate degrees in both English and the management of information sciences. She also holds a master's in behavioral science. Kay lives on the Texas Gulf Coast with her husband of twenty-nine years, Pieter, and their globe-trotting cat, Leroy. She's hard at work on her next Superromance novel.

CODE **RED**

BOBBY **HUTCHINSON**

JOANNA **WAYNE**

KAY **DAVID**

H E A T
W A V E

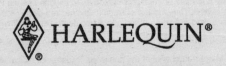

HARLEQUIN®

TORONTO • NEW YORK • LONDON
AMSTERDAM • PARIS • SYDNEY • HAMBURG
STOCKHOLM • ATHENS • TOKYO • MILAN • MADRID
PRAGUE • WARSAW • BUDAPEST • AUCKLAND

ISBN 0-373-83609-0

HEATWAVE

Copyright © 2004 by Harlequin Books S.A.

The publisher acknowledges the copyright holders of the individual works as follows:

LIGHTNING STRIKES
Copyright © 2004 by Harlequin Books S.A.

NO KNOWN CURE
Copyright © 2004 by Harlequin Books S.A.

WARNING SIGNS
Copyright © 2004 by Harlequin Books S.A.

Bobby Hutchinson is acknowledged as the author of "Lightning Strikes."
Joanna Wayne is acknowledged as the author of "No Known Cure."
Kay David is acknowledged as the author of "Warning Signs."

CONTENTS

LIGHTNING STRIKES
Bobby Hutchinson

CHAPTER ONE

LINDA TATE had always been terrified of heights, although she was far too proud and stubborn to admit it. She wished now she'd babbled it out to whoever would listen.

It might have saved her from this.

Knees quivering and adrenaline pumping, she clung to the sides of the open hatch in the Twin Otter, high above the earth. Her heart felt as if it was about to come crashing out of her chest as she listened to a final briefing from her spotter, who was pointing way down at the tiny plastic orange panel that marked where she was supposed to land.

Except that she knew she was going to die instead.

She only hoped that her treasured digital video camera and the incredible shots she was about to get would survive. She'd been too scared to eat anything, so at least her body wouldn't be covered with vomit. If there was anything left of her body when this was over.

As a television news photographer for KBTS, San

Diego's primary news station, she'd flipped a kayak while riding down a white-water canyon, been knocked cold and dragged through icy snow by manic sled dogs and gotten bucked off a horse at a famous dude ranch. Linda had come through every catastrophe smiling, albeit grimly at times, with film coverage that had won her several awards.

Sure, they were for best comedic news coverage, but they were recognition all the same.

That was before she'd enrolled in Rookie Training for Smoke Jumpers.

"You two don't have to go through the whole thing, but in order to tag along with a smoke jumping crew, you have to know the basics and be fit," her producer had assured her and Jacob Gibson, the reporter whom Linda accompanied on assignments. "You have to be trained as jumpers—we want the view from on high."

So ten days ago, she and Jacob had arrived here in Redding, the California training base for smoke jumpers. Even though they didn't have to, Linda had considered it a matter of personal pride to master the fitness qualification test—running a mile and a half in eleven minutes, then doing 25 push-ups, 7 pull-ups, and 45 sit-ups. Jacob had flunked on the running part, but further down the line he'd proved to be gifted at tree climbing. Go figure.

And he was also acing this final jump test, damn

his hide. He'd launched himself out of the door moments before. His chute was floating downward with him attached, and she absolutely had to photograph this portion of the training for the feature.

But was her job worth this? Ending up thousands of feet above the ground, with a lunatic at her side shouting, "On final," and then—*please God don't let me die*—"Get ready."

She felt the sharp slap on her shoulder that meant go for it.

She screamed as she let go, and suddenly her feet were over her head, aiming up into the blue California sky, and she was falling—one second, two, three, four—

"Uuuumph!" With a miraculous snap, the blessed parachute deployed, a patriotic red, white and blue curve above her, and sky and earth rocked before coming into focus.

The world went profoundly silent.

Dazed, Linda gulped in air, glimpsed Jacob over to her left and down, waving up at her and laughing, and belatedly she remembered her camera. She snapped off shot after shot of him and the other jumpers as she floated down, and she was actually laughing herself as the earth approached, which was probably why she forgot to turn into the wind, the way she'd been taught, before she hit the ground.

Instead of a graceful landing, the wind caught her

and she found herself sprinting like a demented track star for about a hundred yards, plowing up a final furrow of dirt and grass for another thirty before she frantically braced her feet and did a full face plant.

She lay still, ears ringing, tongue smarting where she'd bitten it. She swallowed blood and cursed, words her brothers had taught her and which she only used in extreme distress. The only positive thing she could think of was that she'd worn contact lenses and not her glasses. They'd have gotten smashed for sure.

"You okay, Lindy Lou?" The worried voice belonged to Jacob. He was puffing. She'd missed the patch by a long shot, and even after a week of daily torturous five-mile training jaunts, he still couldn't run worth a damn.

"No, I'm not okay." She was furious, and she was also lisping because of her tongue. "There's dirt down my neck, and my hands are all scraped." Linda sat up and rubbed sand out of her eyes, stripped off her gloves and, hands shaking, struggled with the snaps and buckles of her chute.

"That's it? Nothing broken?"

Jacob was kneeling on one side of her, and a medic was on the other. Ten of the rookies from the smoke jumping course were now ringed around, as well, anxious looks on their faces.

"Stop *poking* at me, I'm fine." She was royally pissed off at herself. And she wasn't the only one.

"*Tate*." The trainer now stood over her, arms akimbo, fierce scowl in place, voice raised to a dull roar. "What the hell did you think you were doing? You missed the patch by half a mile, and goddamn it, how many times did I stress turning into the wind on landing? And instead of taking goddamn *pictures*, did it dawn on you that you were supposed to be manipulating your goddamn *chute*?"

"Yes sir, sorry sir." She struggled to her feet and got rid of the chute, and the assembly gave a ragged cheer. She managed a grin and a wave in spite of the pain in her right ankle. Although there were a small number of qualified female smoke jumpers in the U.S., she was the only woman in this training group. Linda had vowed to prove that any female could do this and make it look easy. Well, she'd flunked the easy part.

But what the hell, she wasn't going to do *this* for a living, not in her lifetime. Today was her final day, and she couldn't pretend she wasn't relieved.

Relieved? Relieved didn't begin to cover it. Pathetically grateful came closer.

One of the other jumpers, a pilot himself, gave her a thumbs-up and called out, "When you're landing a plane, Tate, any landing you walk away from is a good one."

Hey, he was right. Her spirits rose. She'd looked death square in the eye and walked away. It made her feel proud and a lot less angry with herself. She straightened her shoulders and grinned at the guys, ignoring the trainer's ferocious scowl.

She might be limping, but by God, she was alive. And if she never had to jump from another plane, it would still be too soon.

CHAPTER TWO

TWO MORNINGS LATER, however, she was once again plummeting towards earth, only this time her chute wouldn't open. It was wrapped around her like the tentacles of an octopus—and the trainer, who was somehow beside her, was holding a ringing telephone.

"Tate," he was hollering. "How many times have I told you to answer the goddamn telephone?"

When it finally penetrated her sleep-drugged mind that she was having a really bad dream, she struggled out of the sweaty mess of sheets rolled around her, lifted the receiver and snarled, "What?"

She had to clear her throat even to get that out. God, she hated people who woke her up on the first day off she'd had in two really stressful weeks.

"*What?*" she repeated. "*And it better be good.*" This time her voice held a satisfactory degree of menace.

"Morning, sunshine."

Linda took a quick swig from the bottled water on

her bedside table and put her nose three inches from the clock so she could read the time.

"Gibson, it's not even seven yet. We're not leaving on assignment until tomorrow. *Why* are you persecuting me?"

"Because I happened to be in your neighborhood and I thought maybe you'd have breakfast with me. But if you're this grumpy, it's a bad idea. Bye, Lindy Lou."

"Hold it." Before he could hang up, she came to enough to realize that he wouldn't be calling her this early unless there was some sort of emergency. "Okay, I'm awake, and it's your fault, so stick around and face the music, Gibson."

He was her best friend, which meant he knew really well what she was like first thing in the morning, so he wouldn't wake her without a good reason. They'd traveled together enough on assignments to know one another the way married couples did. *Platonic* married couples.

"What do you mean, you're in my neighborhood?" she asked. Jacob's condo was in a trendy new development near San Diego's Old Town, and her apartment was close to the ocean, on the outskirts of La Jolla. Not exactly next-door neighbors. "Where in my neighborhood?"

"Sitting outside your building, actually."

Linda put on her glasses, got out of bed and staggered to the window with the phone. She pulled aside the heavy curtain and squinted out.

The morning was hazy, as mornings tended to be in La Jolla, but it was going to be another hot day. Big surprise there. Southern California was experiencing the worst heat wave in years, day after day of blistering temperatures with, the weatherman said, no end in sight.

Other states were suffering through similar conditions. Wildfires were already blazing in Alaska and New Mexico, Idaho and Montana. It was feared Southern California would be next, which was why she and Jacob were heading to the city of Courage Bay, a self-contained community that bordered the Pacific Ocean near Los Angeles. There, they'd profile the local fire department and the small, elite group of smoke jumpers who lived there.

Sure enough, Jacob's vintage turquoise Porsche was in her parking lot. He stuck his head out of the window and waved up at her.

"Okay, I see you," she growled into the receiver. "And I'm totally awake now. Come on up. You can make some coffee while I shower." She hung up and buzzed him in, then stumbled into the bathroom.

The hot water was therapeutic. Her short spiky hair, which some poetic suitor had once said was the shade of expensive maple syrup, required no more than a finger comb and a hefty dab of gel. Makeup was lip gloss and a swipe of eyeliner. She'd inherited her mother's good bones, skin and strong jawline. On the downside, she'd also gotten her mom's gene for extreme shortsightedness.

Linda's silver-gray eyes, framed by wire-rimmed glasses, were wide apart under arched brows. Her long, lean, exceptionally strong body was thanks to her father's Nordic ancestors, and she'd never regretted being almost six feet tall and having well-defined muscles. Growing up with three older brothers, she'd needed both strength and fortitude.

She pulled on well-worn, faded jeans, a hot pink sports bra and a shrunken orange Gap T-shirt. The rich smell of good strong coffee welcomed her when she got to the kitchen.

"Peace, comrade." Jacob handed her a steaming mug, and she propped herself on a high stool at the counter beside him. "I thought maybe pancakes?" He stirred a third teaspoon of sugar into his coffee. "There's a decent place not far from here."

"Pancakes, huh?" Linda took a deep, satisfying swallow. "Okay, Gibson, spill your guts here. How come you're not home in bed making out with Olivia?"

Olivia Browne was the hotshot pilot for the station's news and weather copter. Supersmart, capable, offbeat attractive but not beautiful, she wasn't at all one of Jacob's usual bimbo babes. Until now, the women in his life had come with senseless giggles and an expiry date, but Olivia had been around the better part of a year already.

Jacob had even admitted that marriage had crossed his mind, but he came to his senses when Linda pointed out that marriage was either incredibly courageous or totally insane of him—he'd divorced three times already, she reminded him, and wrote the same number of alimony checks each month. They'd agreed that the rule was three strikes and you gave up on the marriage bit.

"Ahhh, yes. Olivia, former light of my life." He tried for an offhand tone and failed. "She's leaving. Moving out today. She says it's over. She thinks I cheated on her. That mouthy, bitchy friend of hers, Mimi Desalvo, told Olivia she saw me with a redhead last week."

Linda raised her eyebrows and gave him a look. "And did she?"

Jacob sipped his coffee, ran a hand through his glorious head of thick wavy dark hair and avoided her eyes. "She might have. Yeah, she could have. I had lunch with that new computer whiz they hired at the station. She's a redhead. At least, she was last week."

"And?" Linda raised an eyebrow, and Jacob held out a hand, palm forward.

"*Lunch*, Tate. I was having trouble with my virus protection program, and I needed advice. Nothing else. No hanky-panky, no plans for any, scout's honor." He sighed and added, "What really gets me is that Desalvo was all over me at a party last month. I told her I wasn't interested, that I was in love with Olivia. And I am, worse luck."

Linda nodded. "Ahh, a woman scorned. Did you tell Olivia that?"

"Only about fifty-nine thousand times. But I didn't tell her at the time, so now she doesn't believe me. She says she can't trust me."

"Sounds like she can't trust Mimi either." Linda could understand women coming on to Jacob, and she could also understand why Olivia might have trouble believing him. Besides the great hair, he had all the right equipment to qualify as a stud.

Jacob was well over six feet, shoulders out to there, a six-pack where most guys developed a beer gut and, thanks to expensive dental work, a mouthful of white teeth. To say nothing of strong, rugged features, dark, thick-lashed green eyes and a dimple in the middle of a he-man chin. To make matters worse, he was also good-natured, kind and witty. He'd been blessed with everything except constancy and self-control where females were concerned. And before Olivia, he'd never exhibited either good sense or restraint when it came to bedding them. Quantity over quality, that was Jacob.

But she couldn't help feeling sorry for him. Neither of them was scoring in the relationship sweep-stakes. She hadn't even had a date in several months.

She tried to tease him a little, maybe get him to smile.

"You're a chick magnet, Gibson. I swear you sweat that stuff they sell by the eighth of an ounce in the back of magazines, that pheromone stuff that drives women out of their panties."

"Humph. It didn't work on you."

"Lucky for me I'd already built up an immunity." And lucky, as well, that she'd realized soon after their first meeting that Jacob was deeply insecure, that he needed female attention to reassure him, to make him feel good enough, and that a relationship with him would be fated to crash and burn. He'd come on to her—he did to almost every woman he met—but Linda had been able to turn his attempts at seduction into friendship.

Her three older brothers had taught her more than how to pass a football. They'd given her a Ph.D. in male behavior and the reasons behind it.

"You know, I had a friend at college who was a female version of you," Linda said. "She looked a little like Julia Roberts and she went through men as if they were paper tissues. I've often wondered what would happen if you and Gina got together. Want me to try and locate her?"

It was a test. She waited to see what he'd say.

Without hesitating, he shook his head no. "The only woman I want is Olivia."

That was both surprising and reassuring. "Good. I've lost track of Gina anyway."

"Yeah, I know what you mean," Jacob said with a heavy sigh. "I've lost track of half the people in my life. This job of ours isn't the best for nurturing long-lasting relationships."

He sounded morose, which was totally unlike him. Linda put a hand on his arm. "I'm really sorry about Olivia, Jacob."

He patted her hand with his, "Thanks, Lindy Lou. I really care about her. There's more to it than just sex this time. We can talk about things, she's smart, and she makes me laugh. And she has a career of her own that she loves, so she doesn't spend all her time waiting for me to come back from some assignment."

"I think she's pretty amazing. Anybody who spends their working day flying around in a copter impresses the hell out of me." Linda shuddered at the thought. "But you're not that bad yourself. Maybe she'll think it over and realize she's making a big mistake."

Jacob shook his head. "She told me up front there were no second chances with her. She's clear-cut and hardheaded."

"Well, lunch with some redhead doesn't qualify as a red-hot roll in the hay. Everybody does lunch with members of the opposite sex every now and then. I don't get why she's so freaked about it. Olivia doesn't strike me as narrow-minded."

"It's because of her age. She's five years older than I am. It doesn't bother me but it bugs the hell out of her. And I guess it makes her insecure."

"So she's what, forty-three?" Jacob was thirty-eight, exactly ten years Linda's senior.

"Yeah." Jacob absently stirred yet another spoonful of sugar into his coffee. He stared down at it. "It's come up before, but we've always talked it through."

"She's never been jealous of the time you and I spend together, has she?"

"Nope. She knows we're good friends, and she also knows that's all there is to it. I explained it to her early on. She likes and respects you."

"So what made her go ballistic about the computer geek?"

He dropped his eyes and his ears turned red. "I think it's because I lied about it."

"Ahhh. So it was the lying that got to her."

"Yeah. Pretty much."

"I can understand that. Lying gets to me, too."

"Damn, I'm such a jerk. After all the women I've known, you'd think I'd at least have learned not to lie. I get caught every time."

Linda had to agree with him there, but she didn't do it out loud. Instead, she said, "Those pancakes are starting to really tempt me. Let's go drown your sorrows in maple syrup, Gibson. And remember what you told me when I split with Andrew. You said, and I quote, 'Your heart's been broken before, and it's mended again. It'll mend this time, too.'"

"You know, I really hate it when you quote me to me."

"Think how I feel, having to hear the same tired stuff over and over. You do have a tendency to repeat yourself when you're not reading from a script."

"For that bit of slander, you get to buy breakfast." He gave her an affectionate punch on the upper arm, but he also smiled, which was what Linda had been aiming for.

"Let's go eat before you expire." He knew and respected her healthy appetite.

It was already hot outside.

Linda folded her lanky body into the Porsche and snapped her seat belt into place as Jacob started the engine. "Thank heaven for air-conditioning." She found the local news station on the radio. "It's already boiling in here. You should have just left the motor running."

"Yeah, great idea." Jacob grinned at her. "With the doors locked and the keys inside. You already tried that once, remember?"

She made a face at him. "How could I forget? All you guys made such a big deal out of it." Her mishaps had long ago stopped embarrassing her. "I was just trying to keep the van from getting stolen. All our equipment was in there."

"Yeah, it sure was. And a riot was going on outside, which made it kind of hard to get the story on film."

"So I screwed up on that one—everybody makes mistakes. Besides, we still got the footage we needed, thanks to that dear woman who had the bird's-eye view from her apartment and her video camera handy."

"You, Tate, have one hardworking guardian angel, is all I can say."

"Yup, I do. And I'm grateful."

Linda knew she had a penchant for the unlikely, the dangerous and sometimes the bizarre. And she also knew that despite her best intentions, things seldom went according to plan when she was filming. But between them, she and Jacob always managed to turn what could be career catastrophe into fascinating coverage. They were a good team. She just knew they'd do an exceptional job on this assignment.

"I can't wait to get to Courage Bay," she declared as they pulled into the parking lot of the restaurant. It would be intensive and physically demanding. And she wouldn't let herself worry about the jumping out of planes part.

"I'd feel better about going if Olivia wasn't leaving me," Jacob sighed. "You have any ideas on what

I should do to win her back?" Always the consummate gentleman, he climbed out and came around to open Linda's door. In a plaintive tone, he said, "You know, I don't think I've ever been dumped before."

Incredible as that was, Linda believed him. "Steep learning curve here, my friend. As to winning her back—I think you should keep telling her the truth, keep saying how you honestly feel. Flowers are good. Chocolate's always appreciated. Apart from that, think outside the box. Appeal to her sense of romance. Women like that. Write her letters instead of e-mailing. Don't stalk her or anything like that, but think up unusual ways to let her know you care."

Jacob nodded and his doleful expression eased. "Good thinking. At least Courage Bay isn't that far from here. I'll be able to drive back to see her when we get a break—unless there's a forest fire and we end up following the smoke jumpers and getting dropped to hell up in the mountains somewhere."

The getting dropped part made Linda's stomach tense. She knew the jump was inevitable, but that didn't make her like it any better. She deliberately focused on the bright side.

"Doing a documentary about firefighters and smoke jumpers really turns me on. They're so physically appealing, all those lovely biceps and glutes."

Jacob gave her a look, and she quickly added, "From the camera's viewpoint, of course. But they're also heroes, and the viewing public need heroes in this day and age. Yup, I have a great feeling about this one, Gibson. We're gonna do a documentary to die for."

Oops, bad choice of words.

CHAPTER THREE

IN SPITE OF that little verbal slip, the great feeling was still there the following morning as Linda tossed cotton trousers, underwear and bright-colored T-shirts into her worn brown leather backpack.

Packing was easy, because her clothing was chosen for function and comfort rather than style. Sturdy shorts and a lightweight olive green vest joined her toiletries and her grubby Adidas trainers. She added sturdy hiking boots and then sandals and one black jersey all-purpose tube dress that could take her out to dinner.

Her camera case was already stocked with extra batteries, a charger, videotapes, lens cleaner and her trusty roll of gaffer's tape—she'd used it to patch everything from a gash on her leg to a leaky canoe. There was an old adage that said it wasn't the camera that counted, it was the photographer, but Linda knew that much of the credit had to go to her compact digital video camera. She sometimes wondered how photojournalists had ever managed before the advent of video. They'd had to carry backbreaking equipment to do the same job she did with her digital. Most of her job involved live filming, but still shots for news coverage could be extracted easily from tape, making more than one camera unnecessary.

The familiar excitement about a new assignment escalated as she emptied the fridge of the few perishables and ran a load through the dishwasher. She had no dog, no cat, no plants to worry about. Take no prisoners—that was her motto, all right.

Mementos from her trips were scattered around the rooms—pottery, some Aztec art. A few black-and-white photos she'd taken of her family stood on the mantel, a few more of her photographs that she'd deemed good enough to frame were hanging on the walls, but they were the only personal marks she'd made on the apartment. She'd furnished it in one afternoon by choosing entire room arrangements from the store, and the walls were still the same nondescript beige they'd been when she moved in.

Her surroundings when she was at home here in San Diego weren't that important to her. The apartment was a base, a comfortable spot to store her belongings and replenish her energy between jobs, but each new assignment was another adventure, an opportunity to experience life in a whole new way.

Andrew Martin, the lawyer with whom she'd broken up after a six-month affair, had accused her of being an adrenaline junkie.

"You drop me and go running each time a new assignment comes along, no matter what plans we might have made," he'd raged at her. "Your work comes first, and that's just not good enough for me."

She'd countered, "*You* drop everything when a major trial comes along. What's so different between that and my job?"

He'd blustered through an explanation that had chauvinistic undertones, and that had been the end of that. The one trait Linda couldn't abide in a man was a sexist attitude, and this wasn't the first time her job had caused an upset in her love life.

She shouldered her pack, checked the apartment one last time to be sure everything was turned off. Her eyes went to the smiling faces of her parents in a family photo, and she fought a sinking, sad feeling in her gut.

After thirty-five years of marriage, her parents had separated a year ago, explaining to their astounded family that Linda's mother, Beverly, wanted to go back to university and study medicine, while her father, David, wanted to travel. So they were going their separate ways to do what they wanted. They had opposing life views, Beverly explained. So now, after years of being smug about her close-knit family, Linda had to get used to the idea that she came from a broken home.

As she locked the door behind her, she thought about her parents. She still hadn't stopped hoping that they'd get back together again.

The elderly couple from the third floor—Louise and Ronald?—were on the elevator, and they smiled at her backpack and wished her a good trip.

They looked alike, both scrawny and a little stooped, tanned mahogany from their most recent trip to Florida, and for a moment Linda felt a crippling pang of envy and longing. Why couldn't her parents compromise and head into old age like these two?

And what was it that made her want to see the world paired off, like some gigantic Noah's Ark? *She* was alone, and she was happy most of the time. Maybe her mom and dad needed to be free. Why this fixation on couples?

She thought about it as she waited for Jacob to pull up in front of the building in the station's van. Watching his relationships and her own crash and burn made her wonder if she, too, would eventually be forced to choose once and for all between her career and her someday dream of a happy marriage and a bunch of kids. The scary thing was that if that happened, Linda had no idea which choice was right for her.

But she'd deal with that little problem when and if a guy came along who made the effort worthwhile. So far, nada. It was a desert out there.

When Jacob arrived, she hurried out to the van,

and within minutes they were on their way. She had a job to do, and she assured herself that her job excited her more than any man ever had.

SEAN O'SHEA figured he was doing the job he was born to do. He'd lived in Courage Bay all his life, and he often marveled at his luck in being able to live and work close to his family.

A senior member of the city's fire department, he was also the foreman among the small, elite group of smoke jumpers based in and around Courage Bay. They all had day jobs. One man was a high school teacher, one worked at the hospital on the Emergency Response team and two were ranchers, although the majority were full-time firefighters, like Sean.

Sean's father, Caleb, often said that fighting fire was in the O'Shea blood. Caleb had retired as fire chief six years ago, and Sean's younger sister, Shannon, had completed her rookie year eighteen months ago. She was going off shift today just as Sean came on.

"I hear there's a TV crew around," she told him. "They're going to do a documentary on the fire department, especially the smoke jumpers."

"Gossip or fact?" In Courage Bay, stories could grow out of proportion and veer miles from the truth as they passed from one mouth to the next.

"Fact. I called Patrick a while ago—he confirmed it." Their brother Patrick was mayor of Courage Bay, and when the info came from him, Sean knew it was the straight goods.

He was less than thrilled by the news. "How long will they be around?"

Shannon shrugged. "Not sure. A week or two would be my guess."

He groaned. "Too bad I can't book off vacation time and head for the hills." Because of the heat wave, he was on twenty-four-hour alert with his smoke jumping team.

Shannon laughed. "Don't be like that. This might be your only chance to become a celebrity."

"Now, there's a fate worse than death." He had a deep-seated shy streak that made him cringe at the idea of interviews.

"You might just change your mind, boyo. Virgil says the photographer's one hot lady. He saw her having lunch today at the B and G." The Courage Bay Bar and Grill was a favorite hangout for the city's emergency service personnel.

"Courage Bay's full of hot ladies," he teased. "They start fires and phone in alarms all the time."

"Yeah, because maybe they're trying to get your attention, you big dumb hunk." Shannon's eyes softened, and the hand she put on his arm was gentle. "Kaitlin's been gone three years, Sean. Maybe it's time you got back on the horse again, big brother."

Sean smiled to hide his irritation. At times like this

he realized there were definite drawbacks to having his family intimately involved in his life. He wasn't about to tell Shannon that there *had* been women since Kaitlin. They just weren't the type he'd bring home for Sunday dinner.

"I'll get around to it." *Not*. It was hard to explain that although the pain had faded, the guilt was as strong as ever.

"Yeah, well, I only hope I live long enough to see it." Shannon gave him a less than gentle punch on the arm and headed for her car.

In the office, Sean started the day's journal and did entries on the computer. An hour later, he was hosing out one of the bays when Dan Egan, the fire chief, came up behind him.

"Some folks here I want you to meet, O'Shea."

Sean turned off the water. There were two strangers flanking Dan. He glanced at the man, but it was the woman who held his gaze.

Tall, lean and undeniably lovely, she didn't smile at him. Instead, she met his eyes with a self-assured, appraising look from behind glasses that didn't obscure arresting silver-gray eyes. *So Virgil was right for once*.

"Jacob Gibson and Linda Tate, meet Sean O'Shea, senior man here and foreman of the smoke jumping team."

Sean nodded and deliberately looked at Gibson instead of the woman. "How do you do?"

"Pleasure to meet you." Jacob stepped forward and offered his hand. Sean shook it, and then Linda Tate offered hers.

"Hello, Sean. You don't mind if I call you Sean?"

"Not at all." She had a throaty, husky voice, and when he touched her hand, Sean was taken aback by an instantaneous jolt of physical awareness. Caught off guard, he cut the handshake short, dropping her strong, long fingers after barely making contact. The way her silver eyes widened behind her glasses, he figured she'd felt it, too.

Thank heaven Dan hadn't noticed. Firemen were anything but subtle, and they loved catching one another in vulnerable situations.

Sean tore his gaze away from Linda and paid attention to what Dan was saying to him.

"Jacob and Linda are doing a documentary on our firefighting team, but they're particularly interested in smoke jumping. I told them you were the expert in that regard, O'Shea, and I assured them you'd give them anything they needed in the way of info and assistance."

Sean knew that affable Dan was telling him in no uncertain terms to cooperate, and although it rankled—Dan knew he wasn't comfortable in the spotlight—Sean figured he also knew exactly why this was important to the chief. Recent budget cuts had caused a lot of concern for the department. Dan was undoubtedly hoping that positive publicity from the documentary might help loosen federal purse strings.

"I'll be glad to help if I can." Despite his earlier ambivalence, it was almost true. Against his will, he felt drawn to this woman. He wanted to get to know her, to find out what this crazy, powerful first reaction meant. It was a shock to realize that he'd checked out her ring finger immediately. Nothing there, but that didn't mean much these days.

"Sean's family have lived in Courage Bay for generations," Dan volunteered, as if Sean wasn't standing right there. "His father was chief here at Jefferson Avenue before he retired, his sister's on Engine One and his brother's mayor." He was all but rubbing his hands together when he added, "So you'll be able to give our visitors some colorful background on this little city of ours, right, O'Shea?"

But Sean was looking at Jacob again, trying to intuit whether he and Linda were a couple. The thought brought an unsettled feeling to his gut, a ridiculous reaction when he'd only known the woman five minutes. What the hell was wrong with him?

He cleared his throat and looked at her again, because he couldn't stop himself. She had the most provocative mouth, full and sensuous. *Stop staring, O'Shea.*

"Can you give me some idea what you're looking for here?" he blurted out.

Before she could respond, Jacob said, "We'd like to follow you around, just get a feeling for what an ordinary day is like in a firehouse. Linda will be doing the photography."

That came as another shock. Sean had assumed she'd be in front of the camera, not behind it.

Jacob was still talking. "I'd like to ask a lot of pesky questions along the lines of what got you interested in firefighting in general and smoke jumping in particular."

Sean thought that over. "I'm not the most verbal guy around. You might want to talk to some of the other guys."

"You'll do for starters." Linda smiled at him. She had a crooked smile that made her look vulnerable. "I'll want to get shots of you and the rest of the firehouse crew during your ordinary workday."

"We'd also like to come along on one of your practice jumps," Jacob added. "We've both taken basic training at the smoke jumper's school in Redding, so we're well prepared. And of course we'll provide the usual legal disclaimers that absolve the smoke jumpers of any responsibility for our safety."

Sean frowned. "You both want to come along on a jump?" He felt himself tense, and he opened his mouth to say no way, impossible, sorry, totally out of the question.

At the last instant, he caught the warning glance and slight negative head shake Dan shot his way.

The chief knew how Sean felt about taking a woman on any smoke jumping mission. There was a greater possibility of hell freezing over, but Sean got the message loud and clear that right now wasn't the best time to say so. He settled for a reluctant and non-committal, "We'll have to wait and see how that goes."

He was all too aware that Linda was watching him closely. "Is it okay if we turn up tomorrow and follow you through a shift?" she asked.

"Sure." What else could he say? "I'm on nights. I get to work about four."

It was an incredible relief when Dan herded them off to meet the rest of the guys and Sean could turn on the water again, but washing out bays left way too much time to try to figure out what the hell had just happened to him.

Where were the four alarms when a guy needed them, anyhow?

CHAPTER FOUR

LORDIEMAY, THE MAN WAS HOT.

As the fire chief continued the tour, Linda tried to tell herself that the *ka-boom* she'd felt when she looked at Sean O'Shea and shook his hand was just a reaction to how well he'd come across on film. It was simply because he'd be irresistible to every single female viewer out there, right?

Who are you kidding, Tate? There was something intensely personal in her reaction.

Sure, the photographer in her appreciated his physical beauty, noted the various aspects of his body and face in wonder and delight. Part of the appeal was his sheer size and the natural presence it afforded him, because Sean O'Shea was larger than life, a good five inches taller than her five-eleven. He was broad-shouldered, narrow-hipped. The glutes and pecs were definitely evident. His white short-sleeved T-shirt delineated the muscles in his long, strong arms and upper body, his thick neck, his powerful chest. She'd even checked out his butt, and it was on a par with the rest of him.

He wasn't classically handsome, which in her opinion added to his appeal. His nose had been broken, maybe more than once, and his buzzed haircut didn't leave enough black curls to cover several white scars on his skull. He had a raised ridge of healed flesh near one eyebrow, and lines around his mouth and his eyes. There were hard miles on him, more than he should have for the thirty and a couple years she'd guess as his chronological age.

But oh my, those eyes. They were at odds with his tough guy looks, long-lashed, sexy, thoughtful. And the color, a unique and arresting shade of deep, clear blue. *Paul Newman eyes.* There was sensuality there, and kindness and humor and maybe more than a little wariness.

Shaken, she tried for control with a silent lecture. *You're being ridiculous here, Tate. So the guy has killer eyes, so his body makes you sweat behind your ears—other guys' bods have done that. It's spelled S-E-X. And you know all too well that nothing good ever comes of mixing business with sex.*

It didn't help. The physical attraction was overwhelming and visceral and shocking, and she wondered whether or not he felt it the same way she did. He'd certainly dropped her hand as if it was burning him. And when their eyes met, he seemed to have as much trouble as she did tearing his gaze away.

But when Jacob mentioned coming along on a jump, those blue eyes had narrowed, grown cold and wary. It was pretty obvious that O'Shea wasn't exactly thrilled about the idea. In fact, she'd sensed he was about to say no way. She'd seen the slight warning head shake Dan had given him.

What the heck was that about?

Heaven knew all too well that jumping out of planes wasn't her favorite thing, but Linda also knew the documentary wouldn't be complete without footage of an actual jump. And something told her that Sean O'Shea could be stubborn if he got something in his gorgeous black head. That jaw was the giveaway.

Oh, well. Not to worry, she assured herself. *I can be stubborn, too. Difficult I can do immediately—impossible takes just a little longer.*

The tour of the building was over, and Dan led the way outside again.

Sean was standing with a group of the men, going through some kind of drill. Linda wondered if it was her imagination working overtime or whether Sean's intense blue gaze was actually following her every step as she walked back to the van. It took great fortitude not to glance back and check.

Jacob gave her a knowing look once they were in the van, heading back to the hotel.

"I think our Mr. O'Shea likes you, Lindy Lou."

She tried for breezy. "I sure hope so, because we have to live in his pocket for the next while, and it would be a tiny problem if he took a dislike to me." But she couldn't meet Jacob's eyes. He knew her way too well, and she was certain he'd read her flushed face and bright eyes like a script.

"Did you notice his hands?" Linda was doing her utmost to get Jacob off the track. "All those calluses, and as solid as bricks."

"I saw what happened when he touched you. The vibes between the two of you were strong enough that even a guy dying of a broken heart felt the heat. Just don't you get burned, okay? One of us bleeding from the heart at a time is more than enough."

"I'm not about to volunteer for martyrdom, so relax."

She spent the remainder of the day with her camera, getting general shots of Courage Bay while Jacob visited the library and ferreted out interesting details about the city's history. But for Linda, superimposed on each frame of the picturesque coastal city was an image of a black-haired, blue-eyed boy whistling his way along these streets, fishing from this dock, riding a skateboard along this concrete path.

And that evening, while she and Jacob ate excellent fish and chips in a little seafood diner near the ocean, Linda couldn't concentrate on Jacob's monologue about sending Olivia a singing telegram and two dozen helium balloons.

She nodded and murmured and smiled, but she was still thinking of Sean O'Shea, wondering what he was doing during his shift at the firehouse, where he lived, what music he listened to, what his dreams and hobbies and passions were.

And she had no way of knowing whether he was single or married, involved in a relationship or as free of emotional ties as she was.

She was looking forward to the next afternoon, because she was sure as the dickens going to find out.

IT WAS AN HOUR AND A HALF into his shift, and Sean still had no idea what the connection was between Linda and this annoying pretty boy who'd been asking him a steady stream of questions. Jacob had said this would be easy, but Sean was finding it harder and harder to relax.

"How long have you been fighting fires, Sean?"

"Fourteen years now. I was eighteen, just out of high school, when I applied to the fire department." He was painfully aware of Linda and the video camera she was aiming at them.

It wasn't Gibson and his endless questions that put Sean on edge. It was Linda. Having her anywhere near him was like being in an electrical field, and although she didn't talk much—Gibson did enough for both of them—she seemed to be wasting more tape on him than Sean thought reasonable. He'd pointed out a little irritably that firefighting was team-work, and he'd done his best to deflect questions to the others on his shift, but so far, it wasn't working.

"You work here at the firehouse four days on, four off."

Sean nodded.

"What effect does that have on your family life? Do you find it disruptive?"

"I live alone. I've never been married. Hey, Marcello." Sean waved one of the other men over. "Marcello Salva here has a wife and five kids. He'd know better than I do about the effect on family life."

Dan had been clear about cooperating with the film crew. Sean was doing his best, but the barrage of questions and the camera—especially the person behind the damned camera—were making it more and more difficult to perform his duties in his usual relaxed and easygoing manner. His fellow workers weren't helping matters, either.

"Be sure you get Shreck's best side, now," they told Linda.

Sean had once remarked that he'd liked that movie, and ever since, he'd had the nickname. Everyone had a nickname at the firehouse. There was Buckethead and Spike and Donkey and Lefty. Sean figured he'd gotten off pretty light with his.

"Too bad about the nose," Lefty jibed. "Getting whopped in the kisser with that shovel didn't do much for Shreck's looks."

"We don't want a TV audience thinking we're pansies here, so flex those biceps, Shreck. And smile. Let's showcase the dimples." Besides the good-natured jiving, Sean noticed there was no shortage of admiring glances aimed Linda's way from his male crew members.

Not that she'd gone out of her way to look sexy—quite the opposite, he figured. She was wearing little or no makeup, low-slung loose khaki pants with a million pockets and a short sleeveless yellow T-shirt over a black sports bra. But there was no disguising the sensual lines of her well-toned, long-limbed body. She was sexy, no argument there.

He knew she was making an effort at being unobtrusive, but he couldn't for a moment forget that the eye of her camera was aimed his way about twice as often as it was centered on his co-workers.

Right now, however, Jacob was still talking to Marcello, and Sean made up his mind to escape. Since he was junior man, it was Marcello's job to go out and buy the groceries. Sean volunteered to do it so Marcello could go on talking.

But his plan backfired.

"Let's take a break, Gibson." Linda slung the camera around her neck. "Mind if I tag along to the store, Sean? I could use a walk and I need ice cream."

So she walked beside him out of the firehouse and along the street, snapping shots of the sun-drenched bay and the houses they passed, asking questions about different buildings, smiling and saying hello to people, once or twice asking politely if she could photograph them. He was impressed by the way she put them at ease, shooting away while she was talking to them.

Inside the store, she followed Sean up and down the aisles and, for the first time in hours, Sean began to relax a little, despite the curious glances aimed their way by the staff and patrons of the Sunshine Market.

Courage Bay was not large enough for anonymity, especially when his family had lived here forever and his brother was the mayor. Sean knew that by now, news of the film crew at the firehouse would have spread throughout the neighborhood, and the professional-looking camera around Linda's neck was a dead giveaway.

She seemed oblivious to the attention they were attracting, watching instead as he chose the groceries he needed.

"How do you decide who has to cook?"

"We take it in rotation."

"And it's your turn?"

"Yeah." It wasn't. He'd volunteered, hoping Jacob wouldn't find cooking interesting enough to talk about.

"So what're you going to make?"

"Snapper casserole." He picked up four bags of fresh spinach and a bunch of fresh parsley, tossing them into the cart. "One of the local fishermen dropped off fresh snapper this morning at the firehouse. And salad and buns, with zucchini cake for dessert."

She whistled long and low. "Some menu. Makes me hungry just to hear about it. And you're cooking for what, a dozen guys?"

"And you and Jacob." He pulled a wry face. "So let's just hope my mom's recipe turns out the way it's supposed to." But he wasn't concerned about that. He was a confident, careful cook; his meals always turned out.

"Anything made from scratch impresses the heck out of me." Her answering smile was reflected in her eyes. "You're talking to a woman whose idea of haute cuisine is ordering in from the nearest restaurant."

"You don't cook?" He carefully chose a pound and a half of button mushrooms and noted from the corner of his eye the way her shirt and pants parted as she bent over the cooler, leaving a couple inches of bare, tanned skin.

"Want one of these?"

He had to clear his throat. "Nope, you go ahead."

Linda opened the ice-cream bar she'd chosen. "No aptitude whatsoever in the kitchen, that's me." She took a bite and said, "Mmm. Goodness knows, my poor mom tried. She's a great cook. She had to be, what with my dad and my three older brothers and me. We all have appetites like loggers." She held out the bar. "Want some?"

He put his mouth where hers had been, but not because he wanted ice cream.

CHAPTER FIVE

"I MISSED OUT on the culinary gene," Linda said. "My brother Bradley, now, he can turn out a meal at the drop of a spatula." She licked at the melting ice cream on her fingers.

Three older brothers. Sort of like his family, although Shannon only had him and Patrick to complain about. "So where'd you grow up, Linda?"

"San Diego. But my mom lives in Seattle now. She went back to school last year. She's a nurse and now she wants to be a doctor." She hesitated and then added, "They separated a year ago. My dad was a history prof—he retired a year ago and he's been travelling ever since."

He could sense from her voice that it was a painful subject. "That must be tough, having your folks split."

"Yeah, it sort of came right out of the blue. I don't understand it, I'm not sure they do themselves."

"How about your three brothers? Are you close to them?"

Her crooked smile came and went. He watched her mouth a moment too long as she finished the bar. "Wow, you really pay attention, O'Shea. And yeah, I am close to them. Duncan's the oldest—he's a surgeon in Seattle. Bradley's next. He and his partner, Robert, have a pub in San Francisco."

So Bradley was gay. Sean had a cousin who'd just announced he was gay. It had caused a major upheaval in his cousin's immediate family, and a lot of heated conversation in the entire O'Shea clan. He wondered how Linda's family had dealt with the news, but now wasn't the time to bring it up.

"William's closest in age to me, just three years older," she was saying. "He's a free spirit. Last I heard, he was crewing on a yacht in the West Indies."

"You were the only girl?" He had to know things about her. He needed to know when she lost her first tooth, when she went on her first date, when she'd first fallen in love. And who she was dating now. He *really* wanted to know that.

Careful, O'Shea. She's no bimbo.

"The only girl and the youngest child," she said with a captivating grin. "Which should have qualified me for some amount of spoiling. Instead, the minute I could walk, I had to learn to hold my own in games of touch football, basketball and grass hockey. Fortunately I learned early that brains could ᴮ ᵉd to outsmart brawn."

He smiled back at her. "I'm not gonna touch that one. I have a tough-minded mother and a younger sister of my own. Sounds like you come from an athletic family."

"Oh, yeah. Mom was a college track star, dad was a linebacker for the football team. We were all expected to excel at some sport or other."

"Which one was your favorite? Not parent, sport." Sean headed for the dairy case and picked up a pound of butter and a carton of cream for the sauce.

"Running. Cross-country. I liked being alone. Three six-foot-whatever brothers sort of filled the house to overflowing."

"So how did you get into photography?" He took his time poking through the spices. He was doing his best to spin this shopping trip out as long as he could.

"My aunt gave me a camera for my twelfth birthday. By the time I'd used my first three rolls of film, I was hooked. And speaking of cameras, I oughta get back to work here." She shoved her glasses up her nose and aimed her camera at him as he loaded his groceries on the checkout counter. Everyone in line craned their necks to see what was going on, and Sean felt his ears redden with embarrassment.

He paid the simpering cashier, adding in the ice-cream bar. Then he shouldered three bags and handed Linda one, figuring that would at least keep her hands busy and the camera at bay until they were back at the station.

When they got outside, she said, "Thanks for the ice cream. You seeing anyone, Sean?"

"Nope. I'm very single. Haven't even been out on a date for a long time now." *Three years, to be exact, for a real getting-to-know-someone date.* "How about you?" *Don't react here, O'Shea. Because she's way too pretty to be single.*

He couldn't believe it when she shook her head. "Nope. Same as you, no significant other. Never been married. No kids, no pets, no prospects."

In spite of the load he carried, he felt suddenly buoyant. "So you live alone in San Diego. House, apartment, condo?"

"Apartment, just on the outskirts of La Jolla. I'm only two blocks from the beach. Not that I'm there enough to really enjoy it. I spend a lot of time traveling because of my job."

He opened his mouth to ask her what that was like, but she beat him to it.

"Tell me about your family, Sean." She was matching her stride to his long legged one, climbing the slight hill back to the station with no evident sign of effort in spite of the bag she carried. "Pretty impressive—mayor for a brother, firefighter sister, father a retired chief."

Without turning his head, he could see the long

muscles in her thighs flexing under the thin fabric of her pants. He really liked that.

"Sean? Your family?"

He yanked his attention back to what she'd asked. "Family, yeah. I come from Irish and native Indian heritage, big extended group. I've got cousins and aunts and uncles scattered all over this area. My mom and dad live not far from here. My paternal grandfather lives with them—gram died eight years ago. Mom comes from a huge family. Her parents are dead now, but there's lots of aunts and uncles and cousins from her side all up and down the coast. No lack of relatives."

"You live at home?"

"Nope. I bought a little house down on the beach six years ago. All three of us O'Shea kids are still single, much to my mom's displeasure. She lusts after grandkids."

"Your sister works with you, but she's not on the smoke jumping team?"

He knew she was looking at him. He kept his eyes on the sidewalk.

"Nope. No women on the smoke jumping team. Shannon's on the opposite shift to mine. You'll meet her." He tensed, wondering if she'd pick up the gauntlet now or leave it be.

She left it. "How long have your family lived here?"

He relaxed again. "Since 1848. An Irish ancestor

of ours, Michael O'Shea, was the navigator on an American sloop of war called the *Ranger*." It was an old story, one he enjoyed telling. He slowed his steps to give them time before they reached the fire station.

"The *Ranger* cruised the coast of Mexico during the Mexican War, and in January of '48, the ship got caught in a fierce storm at sea. The crew battled for two days, trying to keep it afloat. It was blown way off course, ending up out there." He freed one hand and gestured toward the deceptively calm, sunlit waters off the California coast.

"There was a bad electrical storm, and the native Indian tribe that lived here, the Chumash, watched as lightning struck the ship and the wooden hull caught on fire. The crew jumped overboard to escape the flames, but they couldn't make headway swimming against the waves. The natives knew this coastline. They knew that they were risking their lives when they set out in their boats to rescue the drowning men. Amazingly, not one Indian lost his life that day. And the American sailors whose lives were saved named this place Courage Bay, because of the Chumash's bravery."

"Wow. That's a beautiful story."

"It's more than a story, it's a heritage. Those courageous native men and women left us a legacy to live up to."

"Jacob's gonna want to get you on tape saying that."

"Damn. I keep forgetting I'm talking to the media. I guess I should watch what I say."

She stopped so abruptly he bumped into her. She turned toward him and looked him straight in the eye, and there was no humor in her voice. "I'd never reveal a confidence, Sean. I want you to know that."

"That's good news." He grinned down at her. Her nose was getting sunburned. Her gold-tipped lashes were long enough to touch the lenses of her glasses. She had a few freckles on her cheeks. And that mouth—man, she had a kissable mouth. If he just leaned ahead the slightest bit—

You're getting addled from the sun, Sean boy. "My life is an open book, so we won't have to worry too much about it," he said in a breezy tone, and then he remembered that it wasn't. There was Kaitlin. He was shocked that he could have forgotten so completely.

"Except for that body you buried one midnight under the statue in the center of town, of course," Linda teased.

He mumbled, "Everyone has bodies buried, things they don't want the world to know."

"Of course. That's why I don't believe in embarrassing people." She began to walk again.

They were silent for the rest of the way.

Back at the station, Jacob chose to talk to several other crew members while Sean was cooking, which was probably why dinner was a huge success.

"This casserole is amazing," Linda said as they ate. "This entire dinner is amazing." She raised her water glass. "My compliments to the cook."

Sean held his own glass up. "To my mother, God bless her."

Everyone cheered, and then laughed when Brian, one of the senior men, told a story on himself about being a rookie and botching his first attempts at cooking for the crew.

"I had an old-fashioned mother, and she spoiled me," Brian explained. "I'd never boiled water for myself, much less cooked. I was totally clueless."

"He hasn't changed much," the others chorused. "We call him Brainless."

Brian ignored them. "I was scared to death when my turn came to make dinner. I'd settled on serving chicken and rice, and I was relying heavily on the other guys to guide me through, but of course they got called out before I could get a handle on what a saucepan was."

Sean watched the way Linda's face reacted to every nuance of the story.

"I put in a panic call to ask how much rice to cook," Brian said. "The guys were in the middle of a substantial fire, but they said half a cup for each person should do it. I'd never heard of a measuring cup and had no idea how you measured stuff. So I got out all the cups in the firehall and filled each one with half a cup of rice, but there were only twelve cups around and I needed fourteen."

She had a wonderful laugh, low and straight from her belly. Sean laughed with her.

"So I radioed out again and told them what the problem was," Brian continued. "Which was the mistake of my life. I got called Rice Man for the next ten years."

They were all still laughing when the alarm sounded.

FOLLOWING ORDERS wasn't her strong suit, but for the next two hours Linda did exactly what she was told, shooting from whatever vantage point she could find within the boundaries of where she and Jacob were allowed to stand.

Sean's confidence and quiet air of competence came across clearly as he took charge at the scene of the fire, and Linda saw a whole new side of him here.

The fire was in an apartment on the second floor of a wooden building that looked as though it was falling down, and the first thing the firemen did was make certain the building was evacuated. The residents were mostly elderly, and they gathered in a frightened little group well away from the burning building.

Jacob talked to them as Linda filmed.

"That's Juan's place, Juan Rodriguez," a thin, elderly man told Jacob in a wavering voice, pointing up at the window where smoke was pouring out. "He's getting forgetful. We try to watch out for him."

Jacob nodded, his voice gentle. "Does he have any family living here?"

Everyone shook their heads. "Wife died two years ago," the man said. "He had a son but he went bad, ended up in jail. Juan doesn't hear from him now."

In a very short while, it was clear that the fire wasn't serious. There had been some smoke damage when Juan had forgotten that he'd left a pan of soup boiling on the stove, locked the door and wandered off to the pharmacy. The pan boiled dry.

The super was nowhere to be found, so the firemen had broken the lock on the door. Juan came tottering home, and Linda watched and listened as Sean took him aside, sat him down and explained what had happened.

"I lose my place this time for sure," Juan said in a trembling voice, wringing his hands. "I leave the water on last month. It runs down through the roof. The super, he tell me any more trouble and I'm out."

The old man was nearly in tears. Linda overheard Sean promise to come by the following morning and repair the lock on the door. Sean said he'd also install smoke detectors, and Linda watched him as he went around to the other residents, asking if one of them would invite Juan to their apartment until his aired out. Several of them offered.

On the way back to the firehouse, the men were subdued, obviously sympathetic to the old man. Jacob asked how many of the calls involved elderly people.

"About a third," Sean said. "Folks get old, they get forgetful. With no family to care for them, they end up in dumps like that one. The owner's been warned over and over that the building doesn't measure up to safety standards, but he does nothing about it. We could close it down, but where would all those old people go?"

Back at the station, Linda and Jacob waited in the kitchen while the fire crew stowed equipment and Sean made a detailed report of the call-out. When the work was done, the men all wandered in for the dessert they'd missed, and over zucchini cake and coffee, Linda overheard Mike, one of the rookie members of the smoke jumping team, ask Sean if the parachuting exercise into the mountains was still scheduled for the following week.

"Daybreak Wednesday morning, weather permitting," Sean confirmed.

Linda felt herself tense.

"We'd like to tag along on that exercise, Sean," she said to him. "Like we said before, Jacob and I are both qualified. We need active shots of the smoke jumping team. This would make a good introduction, right, Jacob?"

"Absolutely."

"Sorry, that's out of the question," Sean said.

"May I ask why?" Linda tried to keep her tone neutral, but inside she was beginning to work up a head of steam. What exactly was the deal here?

He gave her a steely look. "I have a hard and fast rule—no women on my smoke jumping team, period. If Jacob wants to come, fine. But not you, Linda."

Linda couldn't believe what she was hearing. *Don't go ballistic,* she warned herself. *Try for sweet reason before you blow a gasket here.*

"I think I did mention that I'm qualified," she began. Her voice was strained.

"Doesn't matter. It's a hard and fast rule, not up for discussion." Sean's appealing, open face was suddenly closed as tight as a steel security door.

CHAPTER SIX

HIS WORDS AND HIS ATTITUDE put Linda over the edge.

"In my opinion, nothing is ever closed to discussion." She took a step closer toward him and nailed him with a challenging glare. "Excuse me, but I find your attitude insulting and demeaning. Your sister's a firefighter, and yet you discriminate against females on the smoke jumping team?"

"It's not discrimination, it's policy. *My* policy."

"May I ask why?"

"You can ask all you like. My answer stays the same."

Why should she feel betrayed as well as outraged? Trying to hold on to her temper, she said, "There is this legislation about equal opportunity, in case you hadn't heard. And I distinctly remember hearing your chief ask you to cooperate with us."

Sean's voice dripped icicles and his blue eyes were narrowed and hard. "At this fire station, I'll do everything I can to assist you. When it comes to the smoke jumping team, I'm the final authority.

And I said *no women*. Case closed." His ears were as fiery as Linda's skin felt. And man, when that jaw set, it would take more than vise grips to pry it apart.

Jacob had been listening. He caught Linda's eye and shook his head. "We'll work something out," he said in a conciliatory tone.

Linda knew that he was cautioning her to let the matter drop, come at it from a different direction, but now her temper was well and truly up. Her voice rose along with her anger. "That's it? Just no? Not a single explanation, not a single reason why? Because that's just not *acceptable*, Mr. O'Shea."

"It is to me." He gave her one long, challenging look and turned away.

Linda longed to smack him one.

For the remainder of the shoot, she fumed in silence and photographed by rote, and not once did Sean look her way, the coward.

When she and Jacob were driving back to the hotel, she exploded.

"I'm not going to fold up my tent or my camera and slink away just because that chauvinistic *bastard* says I can't go on his precious smoke jumping exercise. I'll find a way—you just see if I don't."

Jacob grinned. "Now why doesn't that surprise me?"

Linda's voice dropped to a dangerous level. "So you find this amusing, Gibson? You think it's funny that O'Shea is sabotaging what could be an award-winning news documentary?"

"What's funny, Lindy, is how you push each other's buttons. I like watching the sparks fly. O'Shea has no idea what he's up against when he locks horns with you. It's like the irresistible force and the immovable object. I get the feeling he's no pushover when it comes to a scrap, and I've seen you in action, so the stakes are high, which makes it fascinating to watch. And I happen to know that jumping out of planes isn't your favorite thing, which makes it all the more intriguing."

Linda's voice dripped venom. "Gosh, Gibson, thanks so much for your support. I'll remember this the next time you ask for advice about your love life."

The van pulled up in front of the hotel, and Linda wrenched open the door, clambered out and gave Jacob a scathing look. Then she slammed the door as hard as she could. The bastard was laughing like a brainless loon, which stiffened her resolve.

She'd go on that cursed smoke jumping exercise or sell her camera and get a job directing traffic. There had to be a chink in Sean's armor and, by Zeus, she'd find it.

Why was he being so bullheaded about this?

Maybe that was the key, finding out why. After all, knowledge was power. She'd learn absolutely everything she could about him, she resolved. *Strictly in the interests of the documentary, of course.* If she could find out why he was so dead set against women on his precious team, she'd be one step closer to finding a way around his stupid, antiquated, idiotic, sexist attitudes.

Another thought struck her. Who knew more about a guy than his sister?

And Sean's sister just happened to be a firefighter, which was a legitimate reason for Linda to seek her out. She'd contact her under the guise of getting a female perspective on a traditionally male job. So it wasn't entirely honest—this was clearly a case of the end justifying the means.

Oh, yeah. Ms. Shannon O'Shea might just be the key to unlocking Mr. Sean the Consummate Chauvinist. Linda would invite her to lunch. She'd take her to some quiet spot where two women could eat and talk.

The talk part sort of intimidated her. Linda had always been way more comfortable behind the camera than she was doing interviews.

But what the heck. She'd spent enough time around Giggling Gibson, who was the crown prince of schmooze. She'd watched him charm the most reticent people into talking about whatever he wanted to know. Let's see, she'd start out with flattery and admiration—she'd point out that being a female firefighter took guts and determination—and then ever so casually, she'd get Shannon to spill the goods on Sean. It wasn't dishonest, Linda assured herself. It was in the best interests of her job. It had nothing to do with the purely physical response she'd had to him.

Nothing, absolutely nothing. Nada. And anyway, all that prickly stuff you felt was due to hormones, Tate.

HORMONES OR NOT, Linda felt more than a little nervous as she walked into Greens and Gourmet at quarter past twelve the next day. She'd arrived fifteen minutes early. She wanted to be able to observe Shannon O'Shea for a couple of minutes before they met, so she'd asked for a table near the back when she phoned in the reservation.

Jacob had done his job well finding the place, she decided. It was small and quiet, lots of green plants, a laid-back, intimate atmoshere. She might just have to let him off the hook for laughing at her.

"Linda Tate?" A dramatic young woman with midnight dark hair pinned into a casual, classy lump at the back of her head sprang to her feet and came over, smiling widely, hand extended.

"Shannon O'Shea?" No mistaking her. She had Sean's startling blue eyes and the same long, curling lashes. And she'd gotten the best of Linda by arriving earlier.

"The guys at the firehouse told me you were gorgeous," Shannon remarked, blue eyes shining with good humor. "They're such bullshitters, but for once, they're right."

"Thank you." Nonplussed, Linda extended a hand to the beautiful woman who was almost exactly her height. It wasn't often she met another women nearly six feet tall, much less as physically fit as she was.

Shannon's very short, simple sleeveless blue dress revealed impressive biceps and long, shapely, muscular legs. The confident, graceful way she moved as she led them back to the table Linda had reserved hinted at perfect physical condition.

A plump blonde came immediately to present menus, and Shannon smiled up at her. Sean's sister had a lovely, ingenuous smile. "Hi, Jenny."

"Hey, Shannon. You on days off?"

"Yeah. How's your grandma?"

"Better. They're letting her come home on Monday. She'll be staying with us for a while before she goes back to her apartment. Thanks for what you did for her, taking care of her dog that way."

"Just doing my job. Tell her *Hi* from me."

Jenny left and Shannon caught Linda's curious glance.

"Being in the fire department means you meet a lot of people," she explained. "Jenny's grandma fell outside the supermarket and broke her hip. We were the first on the scene. She was worried about her little dog, so I took him to the station for a while until the family could make arrangements." She grinned. "Cute little guy, but he chewed up everybody's shoelaces. Seems he has a thing about laces."

"You like animals?" It was a good starting point. "Me, too."

"I love them. You got a dog?"

Linda shook her head. "I wish, but this job means I have to travel a lot. It wouldn't be fair to an animal, having to constantly be in a kennel. Someday, when I settle down, I'll have a dog. Maybe even two."

"Well, let me know when the time comes. I have a good friend who's a vet. She's responsible for finding me my two dogs—Cleo and Pepsi."

Jenny came back with two glasses of white wine. "On the house," she said. She took their orders and left again.

After taking a sip of her wine, Shannon nodded in approval, then said, "The documentary you're filming here, is it about smoke jumpers or firefighters in general?"

"Smoke jumpers, but a small portion will be on firefighters."

Shannon nodded. "And I guess you hit the wall when you asked Sean to let you come along on a jump, right? I figured that was why you wanted to talk to me."

Sheesh. Linda felt herself coloring, embarrassed to think of how she'd plotted to pick Shannon's brains about Sean.

"It wasn't just that," Linda lied, needing to redeem herself. "I wanted to meet you—find out what it's like, being a female in such a male-dominated job."

Shannon wasn't buying that, either. "I imagine you already know. You must have to prove yourself right up front, make certain the guys know you intend to do your job to the best of your ability, that you don't want to be treated any differently than any of them." Her grin was mischievous. "And let's face it, it isn't *that* tough to be as good as any guy."

A soul sister. "Did it make it any easier, having Sean already working at the firehouse?"

"He clued me in on a lot of stuff that I'd have had to learn the hard way. But I had to work twice as hard at earning the other guys' respect, because they thought of me as Sean's kid sister, and at first there was an unspoken thing about not letting me do anything really dangerous, which basically meant not letting me do the job I was trained for."

"How'd you overcome that?"

"I had a talk with the chief, and the next time a big fire came along, he sent me in. I was scared out of my skull, but doing it gave me confidence, and it showed the guys I could hold my own under pressure. After that, they stopped with the baby-sitting."

Their food arrived. Linda attacked her crab sandwich and fries with gusto, and it was great to see that Shannon, too, didn't make any pretense about dieting. Too often, Linda had eaten with twig-thin women who nibbled two mouthfuls of salad and then sipped mineral water while she devoured something substantial and then ordered dessert.

Shannon swallowed a huge mouthful of her burger and asked, "You like your job, Linda?"

Linda was enjoying herself. "Love it. There's things about it that aren't perfect, but I figure I'm blessed to be able to do something that excites me. How about you?"

"I always dreamed of being a firefighter. It seemed the most exciting and satisfying job a person could have. And I was lucky, because physically I was able to complete the tests that qualify candidates. Growing up with two big brothers meant I had to work at staying strong, and that stood me in good stead when I applied."

Linda nodded. "I have three brothers. Mine are older, too—I was the youngest, just like you." This similarity in their family situations made a bond between them. They'd both grown up trying to keep up with older male siblings.

Shannon finished the last bite of her fries. "They make a fantastic chocolate cheesecake here and the portions are huge. Want some with coffee?"

"Oh, yeah." They grinned at one another and Shannon waved Jenny over and gave her their order.

No doubt about it, Linda mused, she and Shannon

had a sound basis for friendship. And she was about to test the bounds, because she absolutely had to know. Her heartbeat accelerated as she came straight out and asked the question that had been plaguing her since the previous night.

"Shannon, is there some specific reason Sean won't let me come along on the smoke jumping exercise?" *Or is he just a chauvinistic male dinosaur?* Linda's frustration hadn't faded overnight.

Shannon waited to answer until Jenny had brought them coffee and immense slabs of cheesecake laden with fresh raspberries and cream.

There was a mutual pause as they both took bites of the delicious concoction.

"I knew you were going to ask me," Shannon began, "so I called Sean this morning to find out if he minded having me talk to you. He bristled at first, but he finally said to go ahead. He told me you'd promised him you wouldn't use anything personal he didn't want used in the documentary, and this would definitely be something he wouldn't want broadcast to the world at large. He said that he'd have told you his reasons himself, but there were guys around when it came up and it's very private. Everyone knows what happened, but Sean doesn't like to talk about it much."

Linda wondered where this was going and felt more curious than ever. She looked straight into Shannon's eyes and said, "I gave him my word about confidentiality. I stand by what I said. I would never betray a confidence."

Shannon nodded, satisfied. "Three years ago, Sean was engaged to be married. Her name was Kaitlin Lorenzo. She was a smoke jumper."

Linda wondered why the cheesecake no longer looked as appealing.

CHAPTER SEVEN

"SEAN MET HER when he was taking his smoke jumping training, and they fell in love," Shannon explained. "Kaitlin pulled some strings and eventually got posted here, on his squad. She was a great person. We all really liked her. They had so much in common and they got along really well. The wedding was only six weeks away when there was a massive forest fire north of here, and the team parachuted in. Kaitlin went first, and a sudden gust of wind swept her parachute out of control, right into the fire."

Linda pressed a hand over her mouth. "Oh, no. Oh, that's horrible."

Shannon nodded. "Yeah. It was a nightmare. Sean was next to jump. He did his best to reach her, but there wasn't a thing he could do but watch, horrified and helpless, as she burned to death. It wasn't anyone's fault. It was an unavoidable accident, but Sean blamed himself."

Linda nodded, overcome with shame at the way

she'd attacked him the previous day. "Yeah. I can see why he would."

"Kaitlin was as well trained and capable as any of the men, and Sean knew that. But watching her die and not being able to do a blessed thing to save her did something to him. He got it in his head that because she was the woman he loved, he ought to have protected her. He ought to have been the one to jump first. And he vowed then and there that there'd never be another woman on his team."

"I understand why." And she did. But understanding didn't make her agree with him. Accidents were just that, and it was clear that no one had been to blame.

Shannon, too, had pushed her cheesecake away. "So that's where he's coming from. I don't personally agree with him, and we've had pretty hot arguments over it. I think he's way off base, and it's crazy of him to turn it into a male-female thing. But then, it wasn't me who lost someone I loved."

"Yeah. I know what you mean."

"I love my brothers with all my heart," Shannon said. "But they're both inclined to be boneheads when they get stuck on something. I'm not the only one who's tried to reason with Sean about this. My dad's tried, and my brother Patrick, too—but it's like talking to a fence post."

Linda thought about Sean's closed expression, his

set jaw, and agreed with the analogy. "My brothers are the same way—impossibly stubborn about some things."

She'd been accused of being mulelike herself on many occasions, most recently by Jacob, which made her add, "Being the soul of reason myself, of course, I've concluded that stubbornness must be a male thing."

Shannon laughed, and the atmosphere lightened. "Absolutely. It's one of the trials we females have to endure."

They went on to talk about other things. Shannon asked if Linda had ever been married.

"I've had a couple close calls, but I've never gone the distance. In fact, I've never even lived with a guy," Linda confided.

"Me either," Shannon told her. "Most of my friends are on their second husbands by now. I really don't want to go that route. If and when I finally take that long walk down the aisle, I want to be as certain as possible that he'll still be there when I'm old and gray. I know there aren't any guarantees, but I think there must be a certain feeling."

"A keeper," Linda said with a grin. "He's got to be a keeper."

"You got it." They smiled at one another in perfect understanding.

Linda paid the bill, and as they walked together

out of the air-conditioned café, the heat struck them like a solid wall.

"This heat wave is turning California into a tinderbox," Shannon said in a worried tone. "It's only a matter of time before we have a major forest fire. If you're counting on changing Sean's mind about taking you along if and when the smoke jumpers are called out, you're going to have to work fast."

"I really hope I can find a way to persuade him." She'd already made up her mind on that score. She just hadn't figured out quite how to do it.

"So do I. This phobia of his about women on his crew is bound to backfire sooner or later, especially if a women's group gets hold of it. He needs to get over it, which is easy for me to say. How come it's so simple to see what somebody else should do about their stuff? When it comes to my own junk, I'm blind."

"I think we all are," Linda said thoughtfully.

"What are you doing Sunday afternoon?"

Linda shrugged. It was Thursday. She hadn't really thought that far ahead. "Nothing special. Wander around with my camera, hang around at the fire station." Jacob was going back to San Diego for the day. He had some harebrained scheme that involved serenading Olivia from the street beneath her bedroom window. The balloons and the telegram had apparently made her more angry than ever.

Maybe she ought to tell him that the serenading thing wasn't such a brilliant idea, either?

On the other hand, he'd laughed at her.

"How about coming home with me for the traditional O'Shea Sunday dinner? I know my folks would love to meet you."

Linda hesitated. "I'd love to, but I wonder how Sean would feel about me being there? See, I was just a *touch* opinionated and maybe even a *tiny* little bit obnoxious over the smoke jumping thing."

Shannon laughed, and Linda couldn't help joining in.

"So there's a fair chance he wouldn't appreciate having me turn up at your parents' place."

Shannon blew a raspberry. "He won't even be there—he's on shift this Sunday. And as for you standing up to him, he's used to opinionated women. He's got me for a sister—and just wait until you meet my mother. Talk about single-minded women. She's a pro. Besides, one nice thing about Sean...he never holds a grudge."

That *was* a nice thing. "Okay, then. If you're sure, I'd love to come."

"I'm sure. You're staying at the Courage Bay Inn, right? I'll come by and pick you up around four."

"Thanks, Shannon. Thanks for everything."

As Linda headed back to the hotel, she found herself humming a song under her breath. She didn't have many women friends; it wasn't easy to form close bonds when you moved around as much as she did. Although her reasons for making contact with Shannon had been self-serving, talking to Sean's sister had felt like reconnecting with a dear friend. And it *had* helped her understand him.

She shuddered, imagining how it must have felt for him, watching the woman he loved burn to death. He'd suffered horrible loss and had his heart broken. Had it mended or was the damage permanent? She'd met men who clung to the memory of a past love, afraid to let themselves feel that deeply again. *Please, don't let Sean be like that,* she prayed, not exactly sure why it was so important to her.

Meeting his relatives would be one more step in getting to really know him. If Sean and Shannon were representative of the O'Sheas, she couldn't wait for Sunday to arrive so she could meet the entire clan.

EVEN THOUGH she'd been eager, Linda was more than a little nervous by the time Sunday afternoon arrived and Shannon led the way across the neat lawn and in the front door of the rambling old frame house where she'd grown up.

They were barely through the door when an imposing woman, as tall as Shannon but a good hundred pounds or more heavier, came sailing down the hall to meet them, arms outstretched.

"Here's my girl," she crowed, wrapping her arms around Shannon and still managing to give Linda a huge, welcoming smile over Shannon's shoulder. "So this is our famous visitor," she added. "Welcome to our home."

"Linda, meet my mother, Mary," Shannon said, and Mary drew Linda close for a hug, as well. She smelled of cinnamon.

"It's a pleasure to have you here, love," Mary intoned in her light, musical voice.

"Thank you." Linda handed over the roses and wine she'd brought, and as Mary exclaimed over them, Linda studied her.

She looked about sixty or sixty-five. On her large-boned, well-proportioned frame, the extra pounds made her voluptuous rather than fat. Her features were regular, handsome rather than pretty, and her hair was thick, snowy white and very long. It floated around her head and shoulders like the halo of an angel, curling wildly every which way. But Sean and his sister hadn't acquired those amazing blue eyes from their mother. Mary's were hazel, although similarly thick lashed and filled with humor.

"Come on through and meet the men," Mary said, taking Linda's hand in hers and leading her down the hallway and into a huge living room. There was an assortment of comfortable couches and easy chairs, and a magnificent grand piano sat off in one corner.

Large as it was, the room seemed filled to over-flowing with imposing male bodies. The men were all standing up and arguing heatedly over something. The noise level was considerable.

"Quiet down, you lot." Mary barely raised her voice, but the room instantly fell silent and every male turned towards Mary and Linda.

"This is Shannon's guest, Linda Tate," Mary said. "She does the camera work for that television show they're filming at the firehouse. Linda, this is my husband, Caleb."

"Good to meet you." Caleb, like his wife, was tall and heavy, probably nearing three hundred pounds, although on his six-foot-five-inch frame, the weight wasn't excessive. He was handsome and totally bald. Linda guessed that he'd made no effort to disguise his hair loss, turning it instead into a dramatic advantage by shaving away what little might have remained. And here were those arresting blue eyes that Sean and Shannon had inherited. He held out a massive, work-worn hand and shook Linda's, smiling at her, seeming to assess her and approve of what he saw.

"I have to finish the gravy, so you do the rest of the introductions, Caleb," Mary commanded, and Caleb turned to the man on his right as Mary left the room.

"This is my brother, Donald."

Another set of O'Shea blue eyes twinkled at her, and Linda's hand was once again engulfed. She thought the two men had to be twins, they looked so much alike.

"And this is our father, Brian."

Brian O'Shea wasn't quite as tall or as heavy as his adult sons, although he, too, was well over six feet and had also lost most of his hair. What remained was snowy white and fringed his head like a monk's tonsure. He looked to be in his early eighties, healthy and vibrant. Although the hand he proffered was veined and a little shaky, the smile he gave Linda was Sean's, wide and mischievous.

Sean also had his grandfather's well-shaped mouth. In fact, Linda could see that, apart from size, Sean strongly resembled Brian, more than his uncle or his father.

"Pleased to make your acquaintance, Ms. Tate," he said in a formal manner, turning to the last of the men in the room and taking over the introductions from his son. "This is my grandson Patrick. He's the mayor of Courage Bay, y'know, but it's only a technicality. Boy learned everything from me." Brian's voice brimmed with humor and pride, and Patrick O'Shea shook his head and reached out for Linda's hand.

Patrick winked at Linda. "Gramps has delusions—you'll have to excuse him. Pleasure to meet you, Linda. I've already heard great things about you from Sean and Shannon."

Linda wondered about the Sean part. "Let's

hope I can live up to my reputation, then." She smiled up into intense blue eyes just a few shades lighter than Sean's. Patrick was maybe an inch shorter, with the same dramatic coal-black hair. His was longer, curling around his well-shaped skull. No one would doubt that he and Sean were brothers, but Patrick resembled his mother more than his grandfather. He had a rich baritone voice and the wonderful grin.

Whew. The testosterone in the room was overwhelming, and the men's very size made Linda feel tiny, a rare occurrence for her. In her mind's eye, she envisioned Sean here and felt a pang of regret. She understood a little better now that his air of quiet competence and his ability to lead men into and safely out of danger undoubtedly originated here, with this remarkable family.

"I didn't realize it until Sean and I did some research, but we've all seen many of your news documentaries, Linda," Patrick said. "The average person doesn't pay much attention to the person doing the filming. You must have had to put yourself into some interesting situations to get some of the action shots you've filmed. You're obviously very talented at what you do." The other men chorused agreement.

Linda felt herself flush with pleasure, because the praise was so genuine and ingenuous, but also because Sean had taken the trouble to research what she did.

"Do you use just one camera, or a variety?" Patrick wanted to know.

"And how do you put the story together after you get it on film?" Caleb asked. "Do you do that, or is there a whole team?"

She answered their queries until Shannon appeared. "Dinner's ready. Come in and sit down."

Brian offered Linda his arm. The dining room was beautiful. Lined with tall windows that looked out on a back garden rampant with flowers, the long, narrow room was sun-drenched in the late afternoon. A butter-yellow linen cloth draped a table laden with a colorful and delicious-smelling feast. The overflowing platters indicated that this was a family who liked to eat.

"Linda, you sit over here on Caleb's right," Mary commanded. Everyone else settled into what was obviously a prearranged seating pattern. Brian opened the wine Linda had brought, and she noticed that Mary had carefully arranged the roses in a lovely gold-embossed vase for the center of the table.

When everyone was seated, they all joined hands and bowed their heads.

"Thank you for this food and for bringing Linda to share it with us," Mary said. "Bless her work and bring her joy. Watch over each of us as we go about our daily business, and protect those of us who may be in danger. Give us courage and strength and, most of all, kindness in our hearts. Amen."

The blessing brought tears to Linda's eyes and warmth to her heart.

CHAPTER EIGHT

AFTER THE SUMPTUOUS MEAL, everyone helped clear the dishes away and stack the dishwasher. Patrick and Shannon teased one another, and at one point Patrick flicked the tea towel at Shannon's butt. She retaliated by splashing him with dishwater.

Linda laughed. It was hard to think of Patrick as the mayor and Shannon as a responsible firefighter. It also made her homesick, because she and her brothers acted just this way when they were together.

"Behave, you two." Mary was laying out a wooden tray with coffee cups and chocolate chip cookies, and she winked at Linda. "There'll be blood flowing while I discipline these two heathens. Why don't you take this in the other room for me, so you don't get spattered, love? I'll be in as soon as I settle them down."

"What she means is that Grandpa is practically salivating, waiting to get you in his clutches," Shannon teased. "He loves telling stories and showing off his albums." She deepened her voice. "'Lots of history here in Courage Bay,'" she mimicked. "'Sit down right here beside me, Ms. Tate.'"

"Shannon, I'm warning you, now. Don't be disrespectful." But there was laughter in Mary's voice.

In the living room, Linda set the tray down. Mary arrived with the coffeepot, and she and Patrick served.

"Sit over here by me, Linda," Brian said, patting the sofa. There was a stack of photo albums on the table beside him. "Lots of history here in Courage Bay, if you're interested."

Linda caught the wink Shannon sent her way. "I love family photos," she assured Brian, sitting down beside him.

The albums intrigued her, particularly the photos that recorded major events in Sean's life. Linda's heart melted at black-and-white shots of him as a chubby toddler, a Boy Scout, a teenager trying to look cool as he leaned on the hood of his first car. There were pictures of him graduating from high school, and a heart-stopping formal photo of him resplendent in his dress uniform, fresh from the firefighting academy. In that photograph, Sean's raw male beauty took her breath away.

The albums revealed the diverse members of the widespread O'Shea family, and as one gave way to the next, Brian added intriguing tales about his relatives and also his ancestors.

"Sean told me about a boat that foundered off the coast," Linda said. "He mentioned a man named Michael O'Shea."

Brian told her the same story Sean had, but he added fascinating details.

"The Chumash people knew the coastline," he said. "They knew, as well, that even if they managed to get out to where the shipwrecked men were, their chances of returning were slim to nonexistent. The story goes that their shaman asked them to look into their hearts. If what they saw was the need for praise and personal glory, they should stay on shore because they would surely drown. But if what they felt was a real concern for those in need, then they should take their boats and go to the sailors' rescue, and they would come back safely."

"Not bad advice for the would-be altruists among us," Patrick murmured.

Brian ignored the aside and went on with the story.

"Michael had kept two of the ship's crew members afloat, but the boat that came to rescue them, called a tomal, could only carry four people. There was no room for Michael. His strength was giving out and he was exhausted after fighting the sea for the lives of his fellow seamen. As he was about to drown, he saw another boat heading toward him, and he managed to hang on until it got close. In it was a Chumash maiden, a highborn young woman named

Kishlo'w. She pulled Michael into the boat more dead than alive."

"Good biceps," Shannon remarked, flexing hers.

Brian, caught up in his story, ignored her.

"Kishlo'w was a proud and determined young woman," he went on. "She'd refused several suitors because of one of the deepest traditions of that particular branch of the Chumash people. See, there's a legend among them that high in the mountains above Courage Bay there's a sacred pool, fed by pure water that flows out of the roots of a pine tree many centuries old. The tree is split into several enormous trunks, and the spring that feeds the pool seems to originate in those mammoth roots. Even on the hottest summer day, the water's always cold and delicious. The Chumash believed that if a maiden looked into this pool, she would see the face of the man she was destined to marry."

Linda was entranced by the story. "And this Kish—Kishlo'w…she believed she'd seen Michael O'Shea's face in the water?"

Brian nodded. "Indeed she had. The thing that puzzled her was that when she looked into the pool, the man she saw had blue eyes. The Chumash all had dark eyes. When Michael came to and she saw his blue eyes, she knew that he was the one she'd seen in the pool."

"So many of us get taken by those same blue

eyes," Mary teased, but the look she gave her husband was filled with affection. "It's nice to know I wasn't alone."

"And so Kishlo'w married him and they lived happily ever after?" Linda had devoured fairy tales when she was a little girl. This ranked right up there with the best of them.

"Not quite," Caleb interjected. "They both died before their time in a bloody skirmish with the Spaniards, but not before they'd produced several healthy sons, who survived and grew up and became our ancestors."

Linda loved the story and didn't want it to end. "Has anyone ever tried to find the sacred pool?" She'd asked the question facetiously, and she was surprised when the silence lengthened. She saw Shannon and Patrick exchange glances.

After a moment, Brian said, "Oh, the pool's there, all right. Or it was twelve years ago, when Shannon and I last hiked up there. It's a rough trek into the high mountains—you need horses to reach it. I took all the young ones up there. It was my gift to each of them when they turned sixteen."

Linda turned to Shannon. "So did you see the face of the person you're going to spend your life with?"

Shannon shrugged. "By the time you trek up that mountain with an eighty-pound pack on your back, you can't hardly walk and all you want to do is soak your feet in a pond, never mind look into it, right, Patrick?"

"Eighty pounds? Obviously, Gramps went easy on you because you're a girl," Patrick said. "My pack was more like a hundred. He made me carry his whiskey."

Everyone laughed, and more teasing ensued, but Linda noticed that neither Shannon nor Patrick had really answered her question.

The rest of the visit was spent singing along as Mary played old favorites on the piano. The O'Sheas were a musical group. Shannon, especially, had a wonderful voice with an amazing range.

"You could have had a singing career with a voice like that," Linda said when Shannon was driving her home.

"Thank you. It's a gift from my mom. She was singing in pubs and dance halls all up and down the coast when Dad met her, and she'd done quite a lot of acting, as well. But I get stage fright." Shannon shuddered. "Singing in public or being on the stage is about the last thing I'd ever want to do. Sean's the same. He can sing like an angel, but getting him to do it is another thing altogether."

She pulled up in front of the Courage Bay Inn and shut off the engine. "I remember one Christmas when we were little, he and I were supposed to sing at the church concert, and we hid in the basement instead.

We missed Santa and all the goodies, and we damned near froze our butts off, but neither of us gave a damn. It was worth it to get out of standing up there in front of everyone."

Linda laughed. "I don't know how to thank you for asking me home to meet your family. It was just so much fun. You're wonderful, all of you."

Shannon smiled at her and shook her head. "You only saw our best side—we were all trying terribly hard to impress you. Wait 'til you get to know us better. We've all got awful foibles and dark secrets and terrible tempers."

"All the more fascinating." Linda reached over and gave Shannon an impulsive hug. "I feel so fortunate, having met you. I'll see you soon."

As Linda was walking away, Shannon rolled her car window down and called, "My money's on you with the smoke jumping thing. Don't let me down, will you?"

She drove off before Linda could answer.

Back in her room, Linda was too hyped to settle down with a book or watch television. It was only nine-thirty. What time did firemen go to bed?

Before she could talk herself out of it, she had her camera looped over her shoulder and was out the door, but as she neared the fire station, she started having second thoughts.

The last time she'd seen Sean, they'd had a heated

argument. Would he even speak to her? Shannon had said he didn't hold grudges. Linda hoped she was right.

He was watching a rugby game with the rest of the crew. He greeted Linda in a cool but friendly way and led her into the kitchen.

"I'm sorry for the other day," she began. "I think I said some things I shouldn't have. I lost my temper."

"I wasn't too great at holding on to mine, either." He was pouring them mugs of coffee, and he smiled at her as he handed her one. "So you met my family."

Astonished that he'd let their quarrel go this easily, she gave him a grateful smile.

"I had the best time. You have a wonderful family, Sean."

"Thanks. Patrick called a few minutes ago. He said Gramps was in fine form, whipping out one album after the next."

Linda couldn't resist teasing him. "I particularly liked the shots of you nude on that sheepskin rug. Nice butt."

"Back at ya." And instead of Sean blushing, it was she who felt herself turning pink, and he laughed as he set out a plate of chocolate-covered doughnuts.

Every few minutes a roar of approval or groans of disgust sounded from behind the half-closed door to the common room.

"I'm keeping you from the game."

"It's a rerun. I've seen it twice before. Canada wins."

Linda took a breath, gathered her nerve, and said what she'd come to say.

"Brian told me the story of Michael O'Shea, the same one you told me, Sean. But he also talked about the sacred pool. He said he took you up there when you were sixteen. Have you been there since?"

Sean nodded. "Only once. We were fighting a fire not far from there four years ago, and I walked in to see if it was still the way I remembered."

"And was it?"

"Yeah. The trees had grown taller, that's all."

"I thought at first it was just a legend. I had no idea the pool actually existed until Brian said he'd taken you and Shannon there."

"It *is* a legend. I can't say for sure whether the place he took us was actually the same place the natives thought had supernatural powers. Personally, I doubt it." Sean stirred another spoon of sugar into his coffee. "Maybe you didn't notice, but Gramps is inclined to exaggerate a bit for the sake of dramatic impact. And he's a romantic, which is why he hauled each of us up that mountain when we turned sixteen. Remember the story said only the *women* saw who they were going to marry, but Gramps was an equal opportunity guy. He took Patrick and me up there as well as Shannon." Sean's smile was both teasing and tender.

"See, sixteen is a special age for my grandfather,"

he explained. "He met Gram when she was sixteen, and he'll tell you he loved her from the moment he laid eyes on her. He still puts a flower on her grave every single day."

That brought tears to Linda's eyes.

"I think he wanted each of us to have the happiness he'd found with her, and by taking us to that pool, he wanted to make us believe it was possible to find the right person, fall in love and stay that way for your entire life."

"Do you believe that?" Linda could feel her stomach tighten. This was important to her. "That there's only one right person for each of us?"

He didn't answer straightaway. He stirred his coffee, then gave her an enigmatic look from those spectacular eyes.

"I know falling in love that way is possible for some people. I've seen it with Gramps, and also with my mom and dad. They're still in love, even after all these years, and they haven't had an easy life. There've been really tough times. My brother Thomas died when he was only two, before I was born. Dad has bad lungs as the result of smoke inhalation from a fire he was fighting. Mom had breast cancer six years ago. They've never had a lot of money, and with so much extended family around, there's been a lot of discord at times. But they've always hung together."

Unlike her parents, Linda thought sadly.

"But do you think there's only one special person for each of us?" She was thinking of Kaitlin Lorenzo, who'd died such a horrible death—with Sean helplessly watching.

"I used to think that," he said slowly. "I don't anymore. If I did, there wouldn't be much for me to look forward to. I know Shannon told you about Kaitlin."

Linda heaved a huge sigh of relief and gratitude. It was good to talk about it, to have total honesty between them. "Yeah, she did. I'm so sorry, Sean."

He nodded. "Thanks. It was a bad time in my life, but I'm over it." He gave her a steady look. "I'm attracted to you, Linda. I think you know that already."

Something in her chest expanded, lightened. "Yeah. I feel the same about you."

The idea that had been forming took definite shape.

"Could you take me up to that sacred pool, Sean?" She figured her chances weren't good, what with his shifts here and the danger of forest fire, but she had to ask.

"I'd really like us to use the story in the documentary, the part about your ancestors and the history of Courage Bay. Photographing the pool would add depth and human interest and more than a touch of romance." She held her breath and waited. She knew he was starting his long break tomorrow.

She was also beginning to know him. She knew

he would take his time making any decision, and she was right.

"Just you, or Jacob, as well?"

She knew what he was asking, and she made up her mind fast.

"Just me. Just us, you and I."

For several long moments, she watched and waited as he thought it over.

"You know that because of the heat and the fire danger I'm on twenty-four-hour emergency call-out. I'd have to ask Dan if he thinks it's advisable."

"But if he says it's okay, we'll go?"

He smiled at her enthusiasm and nodded. "Yeah. If Dan gives me the okay, we'll go."

"Hooray!" She leaped to her feet and without thinking threw her arms around his neck. "Thank you, Sean."

For one startled instant, her face was against his, her arms locked around his strong neck. Her glasses bumped his nose. Sometimes she wished contacts didn't irritate her eyes so much, so she could wear them more often. She could smell him, soapy clean and decidedly male. Her cheek grazed against his rough one, and his short, bristly haircut tickled her skin.

He made a sound in his throat, a low growl of surprise and approval, and before Linda could draw back, his arms came around her.

CHAPTER NINE

A SUDDEN ROAR came from the other room and Sean swore under his breath and then let her go.

She moved back, but her entire body felt hot. She shoved her glasses up her nose and drew in a shaky breath. "Sorry. I didn't mean—I just got sort of carried away there."

He was grinning, enjoying her discomfort, and his blue eyes held arousal and pleasure. "Could you maybe do that again when there aren't so many guys around?"

She swallowed hard. "You know, I think it's time I headed back to the hotel. You'll let me know about the trip?"

"I'll talk to Dan in the morning. If he has no objections, I'll line up a couple horses. One of the guys here has a ranch with good stock. I'll take a radio so Dan can reach me if he has to, and we'll need supplies for two days—it's too far to go and come back in one. Are you up for that?"

She had no doubts about his question or her an-

swer. They'd never be able to spend the night in separate sleeping bags.

"Yeah." She gulped and swallowed. "Overnight is
fine with me."

His smile was slow and sensual. It sent ripples up
her backbone.

"I have plenty of camping gear, but can you ride
a horse? This is a pretty arduous trip."

Linda bristled. "Of course I can ride. I did a show
on cowboys and the rodeo. They taught me everything there was to know about horses."

"Theory or hands-on?" His grin showed that he
was still enjoying himself.

"Butt on. I had bruises for months."

"Sounds as if you learned the hard way."

Linda tipped her chin up. "I learned really well. I
can stick like a burr on the back of almost anything."

"Really? I'll have to see that to believe it." He was
still grinning at her, obviously enjoying her discomfort. "If I can get it all arranged and find you a reli-
able old nag, we'll head out tomorrow, around noon.
But be prepared, this isn't a joyride for tourists. It's
straight up most of the way and it's rough going. We
have to go on foot the last couple miles. It's too rocky
and steep even for the horses."

She tipped her chin up and gave him a look. "Anything you can do, I can do just as well, O'Shea. You
won't hear me complaining." She felt like sticking

her tongue out at him. She'd show him what she was made of.

"We'll have to see about that." His low growl was filled with sexual innuendo.

Linda walked back to the hotel, and the thought of sharing a sleeping bag with Sean kept her awake half the night, which meant that she was still asleep when he called just after eight the following morning to say that his fire chief had said to go ahead with the trip. They'd leave at noon.

She'd barely hung up when the phone rang again.

It was Jacob. "I just got back. Can you join me for breakfast?"

"I'll be right down. I have something to tell you."

"That makes two of us."

Linda practically danced into the café, but when she saw Jacob she stopped short.

"Wow. How'd you get the black eye?"

"Sit down. I ordered you coffee. Here's the menu." He shoved it at her and slumped even further down into the booth. "Olivia and I are toast," he moaned.

"That's not exactly news. You pretty much told me that before. Is she the one who socked you?"

"No. Although she ripped me up pretty bad with her tongue." He gave Linda a pathetic look. "You were the one who said think outside the box, do something unusual, so I did. I thought for sure if I tried hard enough, she'd forgive me. I hired this guy with an accordion, and we were going to serenade her under her bedroom window. I planned to sing 'Five Hundred Miles,'—you know that song by the Proclaimers?" In a wavering voice he sang, "But I would walk five hundred miles and I would walk five hundred more, just to be the man who walked a thousand miles to fall down at your door."

"Yeah, I know that one." It was hard to picture Jacob singing it in front of an apartment building to an accordion accompaniment. Linda wanted to laugh, but he looked so dejected she held back. "What happened?"

"I had to wait for her to get home, and when she finally showed up at two in the morning, she was with this guy. She'd been out on a *date*. Then he kissed her. I lost it and socked him, the accordion player hit the taxi driver and somebody called the cops. We got arrested for disturbing the peace. I had to call the station's lawyer to get me out of jail."

"Wow. What did Olivia do?"

"Screamed at me and threw those diamond earrings at me, the ones I bought her for her birthday."

Linda was trying hard not to giggle. "Well, Olivia's generous," she added. "How many other women have handed back expensive gifts?"

"I don't want the fu—the bloody earrings." His voice rose. *"I want Olivia."*

Other patrons turned to stare.

"What else can I do, Lindy? I'm begging you here. Suicide has crossed my mind."

She was about to tell him it was hopeless, but the pitiful look on his face stopped her. She racked her brain, but nothing came to mind. Finally, just to give him something to get him through the day, she said, "Did you ever propose to her?"

He frowned and shook his head. "You were the one who pointed out how stupid that would be—three strikes and you're out, remember?"

"Well, you might give it a try. Desperate times, desperate measures. Now listen to this." She told him the story of the sacred pool, and the trip she and Sean were taking, and he brightened.

"Great, when do we leave? I really need some action to get my mind off this whole mess."

"You're—um, don't you have to stay here and interview the other smoke jumpers?" Linda improvised. "This is a story that's best told off camera. I'll get the shots, while you stay here and do more—um, more research. It's a rough trip up that mountain, and you don't like horses, remember?"

Jacob gave her a pained look and then understanding dawned. "You just want to be alone with O'Shea on an overnight jaunt," he accused. "You're planning to jump his bones, aren't you, Tate?"

"Don't be vulgar." She only hoped she remembered how. It had been a while.

"Okay, you're on your own. Just don't get in over your head, Lindy Lou."

"Never happen." She slathered jam on her toast and figured she probably was already.

IT TOOK SOME SCRAMBLING, but thanks to Shannon, Linda managed to be ready when Sean arrived at the hotel at ten minutes after twelve. One panicked call and her new friend brought over riding boots, a sturdy denim jacket and a wide-brimmed Stetson.

"Good luck with the pool thing," she said. "But whether that works for you or not, it's really romantic up there. And you're gonna nail him, right?" She saw the look on Linda's face. "Sorry, sorry. I've been around guys too long. I really wish you would, though. You two would be great together. We all think so. But Sean just might need a little encouraging. He's got everybody worried sick."

"Everybody?" For a horrible moment, Linda had visions of the entire fire house cheering her on as she crawled naked into Sean's sleeping bag. And what was the worried sick thing about? Was he—lordie, he couldn't be *impotent.*

"The family. Mom, Patrick, me. Gramps, Uncle Donald. He hasn't dated anybody since Kaitlin. Anybody *decent*, I mean. He's a guy, so there's been—" She stopped and blew out a breath. "Shoot, me and my big mouth. Let's just say we're all praying hard that he takes you out for dinner. After he takes you up to the pool. And, Linda?"

"Yeah. I'm in shock, but I'm listening."

"One thing about my brother. You can trust him to get you up that mountain and back *safe*. You know that desert island thing that women obsess about?"

"The one where you try and figure out which guy you'd choose to be shipwrecked with?" Linda had always thought it was a ridiculous premise, because there wouldn't be a choice anyway, and she just knew she'd get stuck with some wimp who couldn't dress himself without a laptop and an Internet connection.

"Yeah. Well, if he wasn't my brother, Sean would be the one I'd choose."

LINDA THOUGHT about that as she and Sean began the arduous climb up the winding trail that led deep into the forest and up the mountain. She snapped shots of Sean's broad back and the horse's rump. Then she concentrated on Sean's rump, which was far more interesting.

She watched the competent way he handled the frisky stallion as he rode up the trail ahead of her, and for the first time she really understood the fantasy. No matter how capable, and Linda was self-sufficient in almost every way, there still was a tiny part of any woman—okay, a tiny part of her—that wanted to be cared for, that longed for a man strong enough, intelligent enough, funny enough, wise enough, intriguing enough to trust implicitly.

To trust with her heart?

Sure, Tate, she scoffed at herself, turning her camera on the trees and undergrowth. *If you enjoy pain and really want to experience it in depth, go ahead and fall in love with this gorgeous hunk of burnin' love.*

But remember, Sean O'Shea has big fat issues with trust and control. Witness his refusal to let you or any woman do the smoke jumping bit. There's a message there. He got hurt once, and he isn't about to leave himself open to get hurt again, whether he's attracted to you or not. No women—on his crew or in his heart. And besides that little problem, there's no way you could fully love anybody who divides things into males can and females can't. And then there's the fact that your next assignment could take you God knows where, and his entire life is centered in and around Courage Bay.

So enjoy the ride, honey. Enjoy the night, but don't get any notions about the L word.

But even enjoying the ride became more and more challenging as the hours passed. *Anything you can do,* she'd taunted him the night before. So Linda doggedly kept up a cheerful patter about nonsensical stuff like the meaning of life and what Sean thought about God as they headed higher and higher up the mountain.

Why didn't the man get hungry? How come he didn't need a bathroom break?

There wasn't a trace of breeze, and sweat trickled in a steady stream from under her hatbrim and down her neck, under her armpits, her breasts, down her thighs. Mosquitoes and gnats gathered in thick clouds around her face, her water bottle was almost empty and, God, she really had to pee.

"You okay, Linda?" Sean turned and smiled at her. The trail wasn't clearly defined anymore, and although the trees still grew thick around them, the grass underfoot had given way to loose shale and the going was rough. The horses were picking their way carefully and her behind was one huge aching bruise.

"Absolutely fine," she lied, focusing her camera on his face, which was shaded by his Western hat. His skin was tanned, and there were lines around his eyes, just enough to be interesting. His dimples showed when he smiled this way. *Be still, my heart.*

She'd die of thirst and heat exhaustion and a burst bladder before she'd admit to him that this trip was turning into a killer. She filmed a bit and lowered the camera, doing her best to sound nonchalant. "Any idea how much farther we have to go?"

"About another hour and a half, maybe two. We'll have to stake the horses and walk for the last mile or so, remember."

An hour and a half, and then walk? Give me strength, Great Mother.

He grinned at her and added, "But I think there's

a plateau up ahead where we can stop and have something to eat, if you like."

Like? She felt like bawling with relief.

"That sounds okay." It sounded like Nirvana. She prayed there would also be some secluded tree she could perch on and use as a bathroom.

When they reached the plateau, she did her best to slide nonchalantly off the horse, but her knees buckled and her hat fell off. Her glasses slid to the end of her sweaty nose, and she ended up slumping to the ground in an undignified heap.

"Easy does it." Sean was beside her in an instant, helping her up. "Your camera okay?"

Damn the camera. "It's fine. I'm fine. I must have tripped on a root," she insisted, praying that her legs would carry her off into the woods. "I need to—" She waved vaguely towards the bush, and he nodded, but she could tell he was trying not to laugh.

"Just holler if you need any help. The bush is full of those pesky roots."

She gave him a killer glare and staggered off.

By the time she got back, she'd regained control of her legs, but she figured she was about to die from starvation.

"Hungry?"

"A little." Linda had never felt so grateful. He'd unwrapped sandwiches and set them out on a fallen log, and from somewhere he'd unearthed two huge plastic bottles of lemonade.

"This is so good," she sighed, trying not to finish off a fat cheese and avocado sandwich in two bites. She gave up the effort and reached for another. "When did you find time to make a lunch? Oh, wow, just look at that."

He was holding out a bag of what looked like fat, homemade chocolate-oatmeal-raisin cookies, and there were apples and oranges and peaches.

"I put in an SOS to Mom. There's no way we can light a fire or cook anything, so she packed enough to last us."

"I'm going to send her perfume and Godiva chocolates when we get back."

"She'd like that. She's a sucker for perfume and chocolate."

"Every woman I know is." Linda licked melted chocolate from her fingers and reached for just one more cookie. "I've always wondered what does it for men."

"A cold beer and the remote. We're simple souls, not as complicated as you females."

Linda hooted. "I wish. I admit you're wired different, but simple? Guys are more complicated than the *New York Times* crossword. Women spend untold hours trying to figure you out and we never seem to get it."

"Whereas men have just given up trying. We know we don't have a chance when it comes to second-guessing women."

"So what'd'ya think the solution is?"

He gave her a teasing look and a slow, lazy smile that looked sinfully lustful. "Sex. It's the great meeting place for all of us. It's the place where we both have a chance to get it right."

CHAPTER TEN

THE HEAT THAT SPILLED through her had nothing to do with the sun. She peeled an orange and tried for casual. "You're talking about love, not just sex."

"See? There you go, complicating something simple."

So being attracted to her was purely physical for him. Well, what had she expected? She'd known that all the time; there was no reason to feel disappointed.

They climbed back on the horses and before long they rode out of the trees and far below them was a breathtaking panoramic view of Courage Bay, tiny as a doll's village, sitting on the edge of the ocean far below. Heat lightning flashed over faraway hills.

"I don't like that much," Sean remarked, using binoculars to scan the scene. "There's a real danger of fire starting from lightning. This whole mountain range is as dry as tinder."

"Do you think the spring might have dried up in the heat?"

"I doubt it." Sean shook his head. "But we'll know

soon. We should be coming to the runoff stream. That's where we'll stake the horses."

It took another fifteen minutes, but at last Linda heard the sound of water, trickling down the steep side of the mountain, and when they reached the stream, they dismounted.

The water ran down in a trickle, not deep or wide enough for the horses to get a satisfactory drink, and Sean dug a portable shovel from his saddlebags and spent some time hollowing out a depression. The thirsty horses bent their heads to drink.

Linda waited until they were done and then took her hat off, dipped her hands in and scooped up muddy water, splashing it on her flushed face. In spite of sunblock and the hat's wide brim, she could feel that she was burned.

They loaded food and water into their backpacks and began clambering up the granite cliff. It was rough going and it took all Linda's stamina to keep up. Sean reached a hand back often and helped her over the most difficult parts, but she was breathless and almost exhausted when the ground leveled out into pine trees and underbrush.

Sean pushed through one last stand of heavy brush.

"Here we are," he said.

"Oooooh." Linda let out an amazed breath in an exclamation of admiration and wonder. The tiny glen held an aura of mystery and deep peace. Just as Brian had described, a gnarled and ancient pine tree seemed to be the source of the pure, cold water that sprang from its exposed roots. In this glen, there was no sign of drought, no indication that California's vegetation was parched by the lack of rain and the searing heat.

Here, all was quiet and lush and harmonious. Birds sang and the water bubbling up from the tree's roots made a faint, beautiful music.

Usually, Linda's first reaction to the unexpected was to immediately take photos.

Instead, she moved slowly over to the pool, mesmerized by it. She knelt down and dipped her hands in, cupping the cool water in her palms so she could drink.

Sean knelt beside her, and he, too, scooped up water and drank deeply.

"I don't know about you, but I'm gonna soak my feet in here," he said, pulling off his boots and rolling up his pantlegs.

It was such a practical, mundane thing to do in this divine spot that Linda laughed and tugged at her own boots. When they wouldn't come off easily, Sean pulled them off for her. Two sets of sweaty socks went flying, and together they plopped their feet into the pool. Linda squealed as the icy water covered her ankles.

"Oh, glorious," she moaned. She was sitting close

beside Sean, and he looped an arm around her shoulders, giving her a hug and then lingering. His big hand caressed her upper arm through her shirt.

"I'm glad we came here," he said in a quiet voice. "I was scared maybe the pool wouldn't be here anymore, and I really wanted you to see it."

Linda felt her heart slam against her ribs. She could feel the heat of his body, smell his clean sweat, and she experienced an overwhelming hunger, mixed with a deep awareness, as if something very special, very unique was taking place in her life.

She wanted to preserve this moment, not on tape, the way she usually did, but in her memory, in her heart. She wanted to preserve each tiny detail, the way the sun shone through the leaves, the sound of the birds, the sensation of the icy, clear water on her toes, the feel of him, breathing quietly beside her, his fingers gently stroking her arm.

It was ridiculous, but she felt as if she'd been waiting for this moment her entire life, just to sit here beside this man and dangle her hot, aching feet in cool water, in this strange and wonderful place.

"It's so quiet. Thank you for bringing me here, Sean." She turned her head and grazed an impulsive kiss across his cheek.

She felt his breath catch, and then he lifted his big, rough hand and tipped her face towards him, placing his mouth gently on hers, tender and eager, learning her response, asking silent, urgent questions about where she wanted this to go as fire and passion sparked between them.

She knew where they were headed. She'd known it on some level since the moment she'd first met his eyes. And at this moment she felt desire all the way from the roots of her hair to the tip of her numbed toes, but she didn't want to rush the trip. Time seemed suspended in this grove, and although she wanted him, they didn't have to hurry. She didn't want to hurry. She wanted to savor, to linger. She wanted slow motion. Maybe this was all they'd ever have. She drew back.

He put his hand against her cheek. "I've wanted to kiss you from the first instant I laid eyes on you."

"Me, too," she murmured, covering his hand with her own and then lifting her feet out of the water. "And I want more kisses, but I don't want to rush. This is too special to hurry." That sounded silly. Would he understand?

"You're right, it is special." He used the tail of his shirt to tenderly dry her feet, cradling them in his lap, and her heart contracted. She thought it was the most romantic thing anyone had ever done for her.

"You hungry, Linda?"

She smiled at him. "Yup," she drawled. "For all sorts of things."

Heat kindled in his amazing eyes. "So we'll do the food part later, right?"

"Nope. Food first." She was flirting, teasing him, making him wait, and it gave her a sense of incredible power. "I have this appetite, remember."

"Me, too. But it isn't for food at the moment," he said with a dramatic sigh, opening the packs and finding the sandwiches. He unwrapped them and found a flat spot on the ground, spreading paper towel carefully as a tablecloth. He took his time, and Linda smiled, watching him. He took such care with everything. She sensed that he'd take the same care making love with her.

There was something she needed to do, however, and she didn't want him to see. She felt silly, but she knew she had to try. When his back was towards her, she leaned over the pool, looking for the reflection that legend said would be there, the reflection of the one she was destined to love and with whom she'd spend her life.

Tiny ripples obscured her view. Her heartbeat increased and she held her breath, leaning forward even further, gazing down into the green depths—and suddenly, there was Sean's face, his amazing blue eyes, shining up at her.

Startled, she leaned back on her haunches—and banged into his shins.

"You—you rat." She scrambled to her feet. "You were standing above me all the time." She doubled her fist and took a swipe at him.

He ducked. He was laughing, mischief written all over his face.

"You—you bloody tease." Feeling ridiculous and taken advantage of, but laughing, as well, she drew back her arm. When she tried to smack him, he grabbed her, pulling her tight against his chest and pinioning her arms to her sides.

Linda struggled, but he was incredibly strong, and it dawned on her after a moment that he was also magnificently aroused.

She suddenly grew still, and they both stopped laughing. He blew out a breath, whistling between his teeth as he let her arms go and wrapped her instead in a close embrace. She tipped her head back, asking, daring him to kiss her, and in an instant, passion took the place of playfulness.

His mouth closed on hers, not gentle this time. He leaned forward, enveloping her in his arms, pulling her shirt out of her jeans and then sliding his hands under it, up the flesh of her back, making her shudder at the delicious feel of rough hands on her bare skin.

His voice was unsteady, husky. "You make me crazy, Linda Tate."

Hers was only a whisper. "You make me hungry, Sean O'Shea."

"We can fix that." He drew her away from the pool, over to a grassy spot. He took off his shirt, arranging it carefully on the ground. They knelt, facing each other.

Linda looked deep into his eyes, registering heat and need, but also gentleness. He unbuttoned her shirt, slid it down and off her arms. He unfastened her bra and she slowly slid it off.

"You are so beautiful."

She'd heard the words before, but she'd never believed them until now.

Together, taking time, they removed jeans and then underwear.

Linda felt the sun on her breasts and belly and thighs. She noticed how Sean looked at her, the sounds of admiration he made as he gazed at her body. He reached out to touch each breast, first with his fingers, then with his thumb, and then at last, his mouth. Hot. Wet. Hungry. Tender.

His naked body was all she'd imagined, taut and toned, lean and delineated with lines of muscle.

Then there was the softness of his shirt beneath her back, and the hardness of the earth. Swirling blue sky overhead and, much closer, Sean's incredible blue eyes focused intently on hers. There was golden light, dappled through leaves, and the dark heat of need rising in her belly as he touched and kissed and explored.

The sweet scent of pine needles mingled with the sharp and arousing tang of sweat as hard and wet, hot and urgent, they joined.

And then the world narrowed to desperate desire,

a sense that having him inside her was both ancient and new but, most of all, right in a way it never had been before. She'd been waiting her entire life for this place, this moment, this man.

He didn't close his eyes or look away from her as the dance between them heightened, grew frantic. Instead, he held her gaze, and the intimacy was almost more than she could bear.

Heat lightning flashed across the sky, and the ecstatic sounds she made and he echoed were muffled by a roll of distant thunder.

Spent, they lay entwined, gasping for breath, waiting for their hearts to slow.

"Am I crushing you?" He made a move to roll away and she held him, legs and arms weak and shaky but determined.

"Be still. Please. I need to memorize how this feels."

He didn't argue, but even though his body still lay in her embrace, she felt him pull away from her. He was resting some of his weight on his elbows. He even kissed her, gently, with none of the ferocity they'd just shared. But he didn't look into her eyes again.

So, she rationalized, men felt different after sex than women did, vulnerable, maybe a little embarrassed. But what the hell was *she* feeling? Sure, orgasm released endorphins; it was easy to get misled by that. But she'd never confused that pleasure with love. Was love what she was feeling now?

Lightning zigzagged in a crooked arc across the sky. She turned her head, tracking its course, and from somewhere on the edge of her vision she thought she saw the faintest plume of smoke trailing into the blue.

CHAPTER ELEVEN

"SEAN." LINDA POINTED at the sky and he rolled away and stared upwards.

"Shit." He grabbed his pants and tugged them on, then reached for the binoculars in his pack. "I'm going up the incline a ways to see exactly where that smoke's coming from. Grab something to eat, because we may have to pack up and leave in a hurry."

He strode off and she was alone in the grove. She washed in the cold spring water, less inclined now to gaze down into it. She was afraid of what it wouldn't tell her.

She pulled her clothing on, but instead of food she reached for her camera, automatically gauging light as she filmed, praying that she was capturing at least a tiny bit of the spirit of this wondrous place.

By the time Sean came hurrying back, she'd refilled their water canteens and had the packs ready to go. One glimpse of his face told her that the smoke she'd spotted was serious.

"The lightning's started several brush fires in a

draw just north of here," he explained quickly, "and the bush is like a tinderbox. The flames are spreading by the second. I have to radio the location to the captain, and then we need to hightail it out of here." He took a precious moment to come over to her and hold her close. "This isn't the perfect ending I'd planned. I wanted to spend the night here with you. I'm sorry, honey."

"It's not your fault." But as Sean used the two-way radio, she admitted to herself that she felt cheated all the same. She'd wanted conversation, laughter, hours of darkness and the intimacy they brought. She wanted an acknowledgement of something more between them than just an impetuous afternoon roll in the grass. She wanted to hear him say that what had happened was special for him, which had to be juvenile and, at best, unreasonable on her part.

She'd understood the ground rules going in.

But knowing that didn't make her want the words any less.

She shouldered her pack and said a sad and silent goodbye to the enchanted little grove as thunder rolled ominously and the sky turned suddenly dark and bruised.

"Come on, Linda. We have to get out of here fast. We could get trapped if the wind came up."

She nodded and followed him, but she felt as if she was leaving a part of herself behind.

MOVING QUICKLY, Sean led the way down the steep incline.

He should never have brought her here. Worse, he shouldn't have made love to her. From the moment he met her, he'd sensed what it might be like between them, and for the first time since Kaitlin died, he'd ignored his own rules.

If you're attracted to her in any other way than strictly sexual—run.

If she's the type to take home for Sunday dinner— bolt.

If talking with her is almost as much fun as having sex—flee.

Since Kaitlin, he'd been careful. Once time had dulled the pain and the shock of her death, his healthy libido had resurfaced. In the past several years, he'd had sex with a couple of women—but that's all it had been. Sex. A profound itch that needed scratching, a normal and healthy release with those who viewed it the same way he did. No strings.

He'd chosen his partners carefully, gauging which ones were as emotionally detached as he was, making sure they understood the rules—no repercussions, no embarrassing scenes involving love and commitment and a future and caring. He couldn't do that again.

He knew he was setting a killer pace. He had to, because of his smoke jumping crew waiting back in

Courage Bay. But there was more to it than the pressure of his work. Sure, he wanted to get them off this mountain as fast as possible. There was an ominous feeling in the air and in his gut—nothing he could put into words, but it disturbed him.

And there was the memory of looking down into her eyes and recognizing something in them that terrified him. He didn't want her love. He couldn't be responsible for that, because he couldn't give it back. He didn't have it to give.

"You okay, Linda?"

"I'm great. Don't hold back for me. I can keep up."

He shook his head, knowing she was nearly at her limit. He could hear her puffing hard, but she refused to complain.

On the trip up he'd felt like a louse, because by the time it dawned on him that she needed to stop, she was desperate for both food and a bathroom break. But she hadn't said a word, just kept up with him, talking and laughing all the way, pretending it was easy for her.

He really liked her spirit. He really liked Linda Tate.

Liar, O'Shea. Like was what you felt for casual acquaintances, for pizza, for your friends. Whatever this feeling was inside of him for Linda, this feeling he was struggling against, it wasn't *like*, unless you could use the word to compare the flame of a match with a four-alarm fire.

Thunder sounded again, closer than before, and

from far below Sean heard the horses whinny. Breaks in the trees revealed smoke, more than there had been before.

His nerve endings tingled. Something was coming, something big. He could sense it in every fiber of his being.

Sheet lightning flashed from the top of one peak to the next. The air was parched, hot, and it burned his lungs with each indrawn breath. He was sweating so much it was hard to see, and it seemed to take hours to reach the spot where the horses were tethered. But at last, at a half jog, they rounded a final curve and there they were.

He could see at a glance that the animals were agitated. Blaze had half uprooted the small tree to which Sean had tethered him. His ears were laid back flat, and Jingles's eyes were white.

Thunder rolled again, and the mare skittered and danced while Blaze reared and pawed the air.

"Easy," Sean soothed, moving towards Jingles in an effort to grab her bridle and settle her, but before he could, thunder cracked almost directly overhead, and with it a peculiar tickling sensation went through every one of Sean's nerve endings, as if he was being attacked by bees. A heavy stink of ozone filled his nostrils, and his throat stung.

"*Sean.*" Linda's voice was panicked, muffled by a deafening roll of thunder, which seemed to go on and on. When he turned towards her, alarm bells rang. Her hat was off, and her short shiny hair was standing on end, glimmering blue. All around her body the same eerie blue light flickered. The surrounding trees, the rocks, the horses were enveloped in the unreal glow, and suddenly white zigzags of electricity snaked their way across the small clearing.

The horses' manes, too, were standing on end, rimmed with blue, and now the animals went berserk, rearing and screaming, tearing at the ropes that held them.

He knew by her wide-open mouth that Linda was screaming, too, but the sound was buried in the reverberation surrounding them. Sean flung himself at her and, at that instant, lightning hit a tall pine tree only yards away. The force of the electricity threw both of them to the ground.

Sean rolled on top of her, trying to shield her in case the pine tree burst into flames. It seemed an eternity before the noise subsided and the hot air became breathable again. He could feel her body shuddering beneath him, and he knew he was shaking just as much.

When he dared look up, he saw that by some miracle the tree hadn't burst into flames. But it was split neatly down the trunk, as if a giant's axe had taken a single mighty swing and sliced it in half.

With a sinking heart, Sean saw that the horses

had broken free. He could faintly hear their shod hooves as they disappeared down the trail at a reckless gallop.

"You hurt, honey?" He slowly sat up. It took incredible effort to move. He felt boneless and weak, and he had trouble controlling his voice, the aftereffects of a powerful electrical shock. They'd come close to having the lightning directly strike them.

She tried to speak and couldn't, just shook her head no, but it was obvious she was trying not to cry. He pulled her on his knee and cradled her. She wrapped her arms around him and buried her face in his neck, half sobbing, and they sat that way until the trembling eased and Sean's strength slowly ebbed back.

"That was way too close for comfort," he said, getting control of his voice and brushing her hair back with his hand. "I've had electrical shocks, but never like that. We're lucky. We were right in line for a direct hit and it missed us."

"Did—did your skin prickle? Mine hurt…like bites, all over," she said, her voice still quavering.

"Mine, too."

"I could feel my hair standing straight up on end. The horses' manes were, too. And that weird blue light—" She raised her head and it hit her. "Oh, lord, Sean, the horses are gone."

"Yeah. They bolted. They'll be heading for their

home corral at full gallop. We haven't a hope in hell of catching them."

"So we're going to have to walk all the way down the mountain. Wow, and my legs are really shaky." Linda got to her feet, stumbling a little. He caught her and steadied her, aware that his own legs were none too stable. He held her close, trying to figure out how he could make things easier for her.

"Let's see if my two-way radio's still working. Maybe I can get a copter to come and pick us up." He tried the device repeatedly, but it was soon obvious that the lightning strike had totally disabled it.

"We'll eat something to give us energy, and then we're going to have to hurry," Sean warned her. "The wind's rising. Those fires in the next valley are spreading. They travel at an unbelievable speed once they get going. If we have to spend the night on the mountain, there's a very real chance of us getting trapped up here." There'd been a few light splatters of rain, and the sun was dropping towards the distant horizon, but it seemed as if the heat was even more intense. "We'll have to really push to get back to Courage Bay by nightfall. It's one hell of a walk. Think you can do it?"

He was tired himself. She had to be weary, emotionally and physically drained after the day they'd had, but Linda nodded, and her voice was confident. "I'm game. You just lead the way—I'll be right behind you."

"Good." She was so courageous. Something in his chest tightened, and he put an arm around her and gave her a fierce hug. The thought of the danger they'd been in brought a cold sweat of terror. What would he have done if the lightning had struck her?

What could he have done? A mental image of a parachute bursting into flames made him shudder, and he blanked everything from his mind except this moment.

They hurriedly ate sandwiches and cookies and fruit, drank water and then refilled their canteens from the tiny pool he'd created for the horses to drink. Sean made certain Linda's pack was as light as he could make it before they set off down the mountain.

At first, Linda talked and he answered, not about personal things, just lightning and fires and hiking, but soon the remorseless pace Sean set and the weight of their packs took its toll, and there was no energy for conversation.

It was long past dusk when they reached the outskirts of Courage Bay, and Sean was as tired as he ever wanted to get. He was amazed and impressed that Linda had doggedly kept up with him for the entire long walk. When the trail widened, he'd taken her hand in his, and he was still holding it, drawing comfort and strength from the feel of her skin, the way she squeezed his fingers now and then to wordlessly tell him she was okay.

Once they reached a main road, he hailed a passing cab and they climbed into the backseat.

"You've got guts, Tate," he complimented after he'd given the driver the name of the hotel.

"I also have visions of a hot bath and a soft bed," she said with a weary attempt at humor. She paused for a heartbeat and added in a teasing tone that didn't quite come off, "Bed and breakfast. Care to join me, O'Shea?"

God, how he wanted to. "There's nothing I'd like better," he admitted with a rueful sigh. "But duty calls. Those fires won't wait. Remember our 10:00 a.m. policy?"

She nodded. He'd explained that smoke jumpers always tried to control the fire by ten o'clock on the morning after it was discovered.

"Can I have a rain check, ma'am?" The memory of her naked in his arms, moving beneath him, brought a reaction that proved he wasn't as exhausted as he'd figured.

"It's yours anytime. When are you leaving with the smoke jumping team?"

"Dawn tomorrow. It'll take me most of the night to get things organized."

"Please, Sean, please take me with you." There was no teasing now in her voice. "You know that I'm capable and strong. You know I'm qualified. Please, Sean?"

It was tough to refuse her. He did it as gently as he knew how.

"I just can't let you come along."

"It's because of Kaitlin, isn't it?" Her tone wasn't accusatory. "You figure it was your fault that she died?" She made it sound like a simple, logical question, and he answered it the same way, as honestly as he knew how.

"Yeah, of course I do. Her death *was* my fault. And I won't ever put another woman I care about in jeopardy."

CHAPTER TWELVE

A WOMAN I CARE ABOUT. Damn his big mouth. The words had slipped out before Sean could monitor them. He waited for her to say something, but to his immense relief, she didn't seem to notice.

She didn't take her hand away, either. Instead she laced her fingers through his, palm to palm, and didn't say another word until the cab stopped in front of the hotel. Once he'd paid the driver and they'd gotten out, he pulled her roughly into his arms, wishing he didn't have a night's work ahead.

"I'm looking forward to cashing in that rain check, Linda." He bent his head and kissed her. "Enjoy your bath. Sleep well and long. I'll see you as soon as I get back."

YOU'LL SEE ME long before then, Mr. O'Shea.

Linda watched him walk away in the direction of the firehouse through eyes gritty with dust and a body aching with weariness.

A woman I care about, he'd said. And that woman

was now about to risk everything, because unless she did, she'd be sorry the rest of her life.

She wanted Sean O'Shea. She wanted him whole, she wanted him long-term, she wanted him as an equal partner, and there was only one way that would happen. He had to see, once and for all, that people had to make their own choices, that the consequences of those choices were no one's fault.

Unless she bulldozed her way past Sean's feelings about Kaitlin's death, there could never be even the hope of a future for the two of them.

She forgot her aching legs, the blisters on her heels, the pain in her shoulderblades from the pack, and fairly flew into the hotel and up to her room.

The bath she coveted was going to have to wait. A quick shower would do, but only after she'd talked with Jacob. She needed his help, and what she had planned was probably not exactly legal.

She figured that the end justified the means, because if this worked, the resulting story would make a lasting impact on viewers. With her footage of the smoke jumping and Jacob's commentary, the documentary would become a feature news item.

But there wasn't a moment to waste. It was already past midnight. She picked up the phone and dialed Jacob's room.

THE PHONE RANG five times, and then a languorous sounding woman's voice purred, "Hello?"

"Could I speak to—" Recognition suddenly struck. "Is that you, Olivia?"

"None other. Hi, Linda."

"How did Jacob—I mean, I thought—when—what are *you* doing *here*?"

Damn. She shouldn't be asking such personal questions.

But Olivia laughed and answered them.

"This maniac proposed to me on air today, just after the noon news. Can you believe that? Talk about reality TV. He spoke about honesty, and faithfulness, in front of millions of viewers. I wasn't watching, but the crew at the station called me in to watch the tape. I got the afternoon off, borrowed a friend's plane and flew here to accept in person."

For a moment, Linda was speechless. Then she punched the air with a fist.

"*Yesss!* I'm so thrilled for both of you. And I really want to see the tape of that proposal. Can he still talk, or is he stricken dumb with joy?"

When Jacob's ecstatically happy voice came on the line, Linda told him how delighted she was for him. And then, because there wasn't much time, she outlined what she needed to do.

If her plan worked, Olivia was going to be doing a lot of flying in the next few hours.

And so are you, Linda reminded herself as she hung up. Her stomach tensed at the very thought of what was ahead of her.

IT TOOK until 3:00 a.m. to get all the elements in place, which didn't leave Linda a lot of time to head out to the airstrip and stow away her camera and herself on the Fire Service's de Havilland.

Stowing away was a tricky maneuver. She had to wait until the supplies were loaded and the pilot had completed his thorough check of the airplane. He wandered away for a few scant moments to get a coffee and Linda scurried on board.

Curled on the floorboards at the very back of the cabin, she prayed that the lumpy piles of equipment that were nearly smothering her would keep her hidden until the plane was airborne. There was a very real danger that Sean and his jumpers might do a meticulous check and find her before the plane took off.

Her hiding place was suffocating, and the cumbersome gear she wore soon had her believing she'd drown in a puddle of her own sweat if she didn't asphyxiate first from a lack of oxygen. After what seemed like hours, she heard men's voices, Sean's distinctive baritone among them, and her heart hammered so hard she was certain they'd hear.

She hadn't had time until now to think much about what she was doing—every second had been filled with activity—but suddenly full awareness hit her. She knew exactly how angry and betrayed Sean was going to feel when he found out she was on board, and between that and the knowledge that she was once again going to have to hurl herself out of a plane into very thin air, she almost lost her nerve.

What if her plan backfired and Sean never forgave her?

What if her chute didn't open and her worst nightmare came true?

After what felt like an eternity, the engines started, and the plane began to taxi down the runway. Linda actually felt relief, because now at least it was too late for her to turn back, even if she wanted to.

She waited until they were well and truly airborne before she crawled stiffly out of her hiding place. The roar of the motors, as well as the special protective headgear the smoke jumpers wore, made ordinary conversation difficult, which Linda figured was a blessing when she saw the expression on Sean's face.

"What the *hell*—"

After the first instant of absolute amazement and disbelief, his blue eyes shot icy daggers at her. She tried not to let her hand tremble as she handed him the legal papers that exonerated him and his crew from any responsibility for her actions.

He glanced at the papers, rammed them into a pocket on his jumpsuit, and gave her a look that spoke eloquently of fury and betrayal. And after that he refused to look at her at all.

Linda's insides felt as if they were shriveling, even though she told herself she'd expected nothing less. She promised herself she'd find the right words to convince him why she had to do this. She tried not to let his attitude bother her, but she felt sick with anticipation.

However, there was work to be done. There were nine smoke jumpers on board besides Sean, and she hauled out her camera and began filming.

It seemed to take no time at all before the door on the side of the plane was opened and the equipment dropped. Then the first of the jumpers launched himself into the gray dawn. Feeling nauseous with fear, Linda caught it all on tape.

After that, the pilot circled, and in practiced sequence, the others jumped, as well, until there was only Sean and Linda left in the empty bowels of the plane.

Sean turned narrowed, icy blue eyes on Linda with a look that made her shudder. *"You stay here,"* he ordered, one forefinger stabbing at the plane's interior. His words were swallowed by the air roaring around them and the steady thrum of the motor, but Linda knew exactly what he was saying.

She shook her head and forced herself not to look away from the furious glare he leveled at her.

For a long moment, she defiantly held his gaze.

"That's it, then." He turned away, gripped the frame of the door and then launched himself out and away. Linda caught it on tape, and a moment later, heart hammering almost out of her rib cage in utter terror, she followed him.

Those first few moments of free fall were as agonizing as they'd been the first time, and she knew she was screaming with terror. The air rushing past deafened her, and the sense of falling into nothingness made her stomach lurch. Then, with a familiar jerk, her chute opened, and she dared to look down.

Smoke billowed up, and scarlet flames were clearly visible. The fires were burning only a few miles away. She clicked off shots as the earth spiraled up to meet her, but she quickly abandoned the camera as she tried her best to steer the chute into the wind and land close to where the others had landed.

Even at this considerable distance from the flames, there was a powerful updraft, and with a growing sense of panic, Linda understood exactly how a jumper could get sucked into the midst of the fire.

She came down hard, into the wind this time, but narrowly missing a huge dead tree, and the packed earth made it feel as if she was landing on cement. Stunned, she lay still, trying not to panic when she couldn't get air into her lungs.

At last she managed to breathe and then scrambled up. She'd gotten the chute halfway off before Sean reached her.

"Are you hurt?" His voice was brisk and businesslike.

"Nope, thanks, I'm fine," she said, although she still wasn't absolutely certain. Various parts of her hurt like fury. Her forearms and one knee were badly scraped, but she wasn't about to admit any of that to him. She struggled with the final straps on the harness, not looking at him as she folded the chute the way she'd been trained to do. She waited, expecting a tongue-lashing, but instead his voice was cold, remote and briskly professional.

"From here on, you do exactly what you're told, Tate. You stay with me, where I can see you every minute. The lives of all these men are my responsibility, and I don't have time to waste chasing after you. You follow orders instantly, stay out of the way and keep your mouth shut."

Under other circumstances, she would have snapped off a sarcastic salute and a mocking *Yes, sir.* Now, she just meekly nodded.

"Give me your word."

"Okay, Sean. I promise."

"You better mean it, lady," he gritted out between clenched teeth. "And cinch that pack on tight. We have to hike to where the fire is, and I'm not going to stop so you can adjust your gear."

She swallowed hard, wanting to lash out at him, but instead she silently did as he ordered.

The other jumpers joined them, and she filmed as Sean clearly and concisely outlined what he thought their plan of attack should be. In her head, Linda went over the things she'd heard Sean tell Jacob about the strategy of fighting forest fires.

The beauty of being a jumper is that we're all really in charge, he'd explained. *Sure, there's a formal structure, but everyone's involved in the decisions, because all of us are going out there to work ourselves to the bone and all of our lives are at stake.*

When he was done, Sean asked the men for their suggestions.

We try to attack a fire at its most inactive side, he'd explained. *Then we work our way around it with our control line.* That was the strategy he'd just suggested, and the other jumpers agreed.

"See that big rock outcrop?" He pointed at a spot high on the hillside. "That's where we head if this thing blows up. That's our safety zone." He pinned her with hard, cold eyes. "You got that, Tate?"

I establish a safety zone, and make certain all the guys know exactly where that is.

"Got it."

"Okay, let's head out." At a brisk half trot, Sean headed up the hillside. Linda kept up, doing her best to ignore her scrapes and bruises and the weight of the gear she wore. The smoke increased as they neared the fire site and the sky turned gray. The sun was a garish red ball punching through a dark sky, and the smell of burning seared her nostrils.

While Sean was busy setting up his crew, Linda, sweating and gasping for breath, taped images that she knew in her gut were both dramatic and terrifying. She was close enough to feel the searing heat. She filmed flames licking at trees and then devouring them. Chills shot up her spine as she watched the fire, skipping lightly among the pine needles in a macabre dance, and then, with a puff of wind, encompassing dozens of trees in the blink of an eye. She remembered how eloquently Sean had described fire.

It's like trying to figure out someone who's insane, brilliant and totally unpredictable. Each fire has its own personality, its own idiosyncrasies. There's never any pattern. It can be burning quietly, and for no reason you can fathom, it'll take off like a sprinter heading for the finish line. You have to remember every moment that it's your enemy, that if you don't pay close attention, it'll come for you. And it'll catch you.

She shuddered, remembering, because now, only a short distance from the inferno, she understood in her gut exactly what he'd meant.

"Tate." Sean waved her over. "This way."

He didn't explain, but because she'd paid close attention to Jacob's interview, she knew what he was about to do next.

As soon as the men are set up, I walk around the entire fire, or as much of it as I possibly can, and I gather information. I watch the fire and I try to feel what's happening, what kind of personality this particular blaze might have. Conditions change all the time. You can't let it catch you off guard. You have to know your enemy.

For the next hour, she scurried along behind him, pushing herself to the limit to keep up with his long, tireless strides, her camera always at hand. Twice he stopped to drink water from his pack, and she did the same. He kept in constant contact with the other jumpers by radio, but he never once met Linda's eyes. The only time he spoke was to brusquely answer the few questions she shot at him, technical queries about wind direction and the speed at which the fire was progressing.

His face and rugged features were soon streaked with sweat and dirt, and the smoke haze over the sun turned everything it touched to an incandescent orange, which lent a demoniacal air to his huge figure and stony expression.

You'll have to talk to me sooner or later, O'Shea, Linda told him silently, aiming her lens at him, capturing the incredible intentness with which he studied the fire, which was now burning with a ferocity that amazed her.

She couldn't help admiring his sheer physical presence, his assurance, his formidable strength. And his courage. She'd never met a more courageous man. No doubt about it, he'd inherited his ancestor Michael O'Shea's bravery.

But there was also his pigheaded stubbornness.

I won't let you get away with this silent act forever, she vowed. Any more than I let you get away with your nonsense about no women coming along on your team.

But the personal issues between them seemed more and more insignificant as she toiled up and around the mountainside, tracking the fire and keeping the promise she'd made him about never being out of his sight. She had a more difficult time with the one about keeping her mouth shut.

"Why does it suddenly feel so much *hotter* than it was a few minutes ago?"

They were partway down the side of a steep slope, and she was filming a tall pine that seemed to have combusted spontaneously. Although they were quite a distance from the flames, she knew the air temperature had *suddenly* shot up. She swigged water from her bottle, wiped oily sweat from her face. Her contact lenses felt glued to her eyes.

"It feels as if there's not a drop of moisture in the air."

He didn't answer, and Linda figured he was deliberately ignoring her. But then he pulled out his two-way radio, and she could hear the urgency in his voice as he spoke to one of the other men.

"Jerry, we're in the middle of an inversion here, this baby's gonna blow. Stop what you're doing, alert the other men, head immediately to the safe zone. Repeat, abandon efforts and head for the safe zone."

"What's an—"

"Run, Linda. We have to get out of here." His voice sent shivers up her back.

He grabbed her arm, half dragging her along. But suddenly, with an earsplitting *whoosh,* trees and undergrowth erupted into a sea of flames all around them.

CHAPTER THIRTEEN

CURSING, SEAN TURNED in another direction, but in the space of minutes, the fire had gone from a medium-sized blaze to an inferno. Flames shot up where there had been no sign of fire just minutes before. It blazed on three sides of them, and even as they staggered up the hillside, flames erupted above and below them.

Sean stopped and looked in every direction. His hand felt like a vise holding hers.

"Which way?" But with a sinking feeling, Linda knew the answer.

They were trapped. She was breathless from running. Her heart hammered against her ribs, and the sweat pouring from every pore turned her cold in spite of the unbearable heat of the sudden wind that scorched her face and made her eyes burn and water. She started to cough and couldn't get her breath.

"Get down." Sean dragged her to the ground, sheltering her with his body.

A burning ember landed on his arm, and Linda swatted at it, still coughing.

"Drink this." He shoved his water bottle at her, and she gulped down the tepid contents.

"I just drank all your water," she croaked after one last swallow.

With a groan, he pulled her into his arms and held her close.

"To hell with the water. I should have guessed what was going to happen...spotted the inversion sooner...gotten us to higher ground." He fumbled for his radio.

"This is O'Shea. We're surrounded—we need a copter, stat. We're on the western boundary on a ridgeline five hundred feet from the top of the canyon. There's a rock face to the south, but we can't get to it. We're cut off. I'm setting up fire shelters."

There was a muffled voice, a crackle of static, and then the radio went dead.

Linda swallowed hard. "Do you think—do you think maybe they heard you?"

"Yeah, they heard all right." There was absolute confidence in his tone. "There'll be a copter along in a couple of minutes, but right now, we're going to set these shelters up and crawl inside." He pulled a small metallic tent out of his pack and swiftly set it up.

"You first." He shoved her inside. "Jesus, Linda, why the hell didn't you listen to me and stay in town?"

Her throat was still raw, her voice hoarse. She stuck her head out to talk to him.

"I'm only gonna say this once, O'Shea." It dawned on her that with the fire advancing the way it was, she wouldn't get a second chance anyway, so she'd better make it good. "A man and woman have to be totally equal."

He was setting up his shelter in a sea of ash and sparks, and she thought how ironic it was to be spouting her philosophy of relationships at this time, in this place. Under any other circumstances, it might be funny.

She coughed and went doggedly on, talking as fast as she could. "If one person restricts the other, he takes on the responsibility for that person's happiness, and both people are gonna resent the lack of freedom that results. My job isn't usually as dangerous as yours, but I do it for the same reasons, because I need to push myself."

She took a searing breath. The smoke and heat made it harder and harder to breathe. "I need to be able to go after the life I want, make a difference in some way."

She drew in another breath and choked again. When she stopped coughing, she said, "I've done that, and I'm proud. The choices I've made have been *my* choices, Sean. Being here is what I wanted to do. So don't be arrogant and assume any of this is your fault, because it's not. You couldn't predict what was going to happen. You didn't start the bloody fire and you sure as hell didn't get us in this mess just to teach me a lesson."

She coughed again, and her eyes were streaming when she added dolefully, "Although I wouldn't put it past you, you stubborn idiot."

She was amazed when he actually laughed. "You've got a mouth on you, Tate." He finished with the tent, but before he crawled in, he kissed her, ferocious, wild, desperate. He tasted awful, like soot and brimstone. As kisses went, she figured it was a ten.

With his lips close to her ear, he growled, "That mouth is one of the reasons I fell in love with you, lady. I guess I should have told you that sooner, huh?"

"You're slow, O'Shea." Her throat burned from the smoke, every inch of her body was soaked with sweat, her eyes were streaming tears, and she was closer to death than she'd ever been in her life, but her heart still filled with incredible joy. "I feel the same way about you, God only knows why." She coughed and then managed to gasp, "I love you, Sean O'Shea, you stubborn, pigheaded, chauvinistic male idiot."

He groaned and held her tight. She looked up at the sky and let out a scream, because for an instant she thought a tree was falling on them.

"It's the copter." Sean yanked her out of the tent and onto her feet.

The noise of the fire had covered the sound of the

engine. Squinting up, Linda saw the news helicopter from KCTS. Jacob was half leaning out the open door, frantically waving at them.

The plan had been for Jacob to parachute down, once the jumpers were set up. Linda's idea had been that she'd get the pictures, and he'd arrive to do the on-scene interviews.

Sean was already racing towards the hovering craft, pulling her along with him.

"Grab on to the skids, they can't land here." He gripped her around the waist and hoisted her high. Linda made a frantic grab at the steel skid and missed, but on her second try, she was able to wrap her arms around it and hang on.

Sean leaped high and caught hold, locking Linda to him by wrapping his legs around her waist, supporting some of her weight.

And then her stomach seemed to rise into her throat as the copter rose straight up with the two of them clinging to its underside. She had no breath left to scream, but she knew for certain that this time, absolutely, she was going to die. This was a thousand, million times worse than jumping out of an aircraft.

The copter pitched from side to side, struggling against the updraft and the rising wind. Linda's arms felt as if they were being torn from their sockets. It was impossible to breathe. She couldn't have hung on if Sean hadn't been supporting her with his legs. They were locked around her waist like vise grips.

And then the copter was hovering over an open area, away from the fire, and again Linda's stomach reacted as the huge machine dropped towards the earth.

She shut her eyes tight. This was it, they were going to be killed when the copter crashed to the ground.

"Let go—let go *now*," Sean was screaming in her ear. But she couldn't see the earth or gauge how high they were, and she had no parachute. She was utterly terrified of falling. Her hands locked tighter around the steel bar.

With one free hand and sheer brute strength, Sean peeled them both away from the struts, and then she *was* falling, her screams lost in the deafening roar of the copter's blades.

CHAPTER FOURTEEN

LINDA DIDN'T REMEMBER hitting the ground. The world went dark and for a time there was nothing.

When at last consciousness returned, she was lying on her back, and the first thing she was aware of was the sun, fiery red and spinning around in an ominous, bruised purple sky. And she could hear Sean's frantic voice.

"Linda? Sweetheart, for God's sake, where does it hurt?"

The answer to that was everywhere, but she was too dizzy to talk, and she must have bitten her tongue hard, because she could taste blood. Her head hurt like fury, and something under her was jabbing her in the middle of the back. They'd laid her on a bed of rocks, for pity's sake.

She realized next that a medic was kneeling over her, pushing and prodding at various parts of her body and shoving a mask over her nose and mouth.

"Deep breaths," he instructed. "Oxygen. It'll help with the smoke inhalation."

She took one deep breath, and then another. She choked, gagged and shoved the mask away.

"Linda." Sean's voice again. He sounded frantic. "Can you breathe okay? Are you in pain, honey?"

Sweetheart. Honey. After forcing her to fall nearly to her death, he had the nerve to call her *pet names*?

"Yes. Yes, I'm in pain." She glared up at him and, with extreme difficulty, struggled to a sitting position. He was kneeling beside her. "I need water. There's rocks underneath me. I hit my head. I hurt all over." And she was lisping, for god's sake, because of her tongue. "What's wrong with your arm?"

He wasn't listening.

"Linda, does it hurt to take a deep breath? She could have a concussion." The medic was probing her ribs, searching for breaks. She jerked away.

"Nothing's broken. I don't have any concussion—stop pawing me," she said irritably. "Get me a drink before I die of dehydration here."

Someone put a bottle of water in her hand, and she lifted it and gulped over and over. The water was tepid and flat. Lordie, it was delicious.

"I'm just going to put some of these in—" the medic announced, firmly tipping Linda's chin back and dropping something into her eyes that made her yelp with pain.

"Ouch, damn you! Stop that. You've ruined my contact lenses." For a moment, it felt as if she was blinded, and it was all Sean's fault. She aimed her voice in his direction. "Why did you make me let go like that, you maniac? We were miles from the ground. I'll bet my camera got smashed, right?"

Jacob's voice now. "I think she's okay, Sean. She's mad and worried about her camera. That's always a good sign."

"We had to let go, Linda," Sean said in a reasonable tone. "Olivia couldn't land the copter with us hanging on the skids. Thank God she spotted those tents. We only fell about ten feet."

"*Ten feet?* People *die* from falling ten feet."

"Not often, Lindy," Jacob said with a callousness that infuriated her.

"Easy for you to say—you weren't the one tumbling out of the damned sky without a safety net," she accused. She could open her eyes again, although everything was blurry. She raised a hand to rub at them, but Sean restrained her with one hand. The other was strapped against his chest.

Lord, but his hand was filthy. And then she noticed that hers were, too. And his face—it was streaked and black with soot, and his blue eyes shone out like beacons. Blue and red beacons. His eyes were horribly bloodshot. But he was grinning at her, which was a really good sign. His teeth were the only part of him that was clean.

"Fortunately, you landed on Sean," Jacob said.

He was grinning, too, and Linda felt that was entirely out of place, given the circumstances. "You dislocated his shoulder—the medic just put it back. He might have a couple broken ribs. But your Nikon seems to have come through fine."

"If I fell on him, how come I hit my head so hard?" Gingerly, she fingered the bump at the back of her skull.

"Only your bottom end landed on Sean," Jacob explained cheerfully. "And your bottom end is definitely your heaviest area, Lindy. And then you managed to smack your head on the ground and knock yourself senseless."

He motioned to Olivia, who seemed to be doing a good job of filming. "Let's get this on tape while it's fresh."

Jacob, holding a mike, went into broadcast mode. "We're in the mountains east of Courage Bay, near the site of a forest fire that our brave smoke jumpers have been battling. They've just been joined by waterbombers, and the fire seems to be contained. Sean O'Shea, leader of the smoke jumping team, ordered his team to safety minutes before flames would have engulfed them, but then he found himself and our cameraperson, Linda Tate, trapped by the flames. Olivia Browne, piloting the network's helicopter, spotted the bright orange metallic tents O'Shea had set up and made a daring rescue attempt. It was only by clinging to the skids of our KBTS copter that Linda and Sean escaped with their lives."

Linda guessed that Olivia would be zooming in for a close-up about now.

"How did it feel to be surrounded by fire, Linda?"

Her instinctive reaction was to bat the mike away and give Jacob a tongue-lashing, but she remembered just in time exactly how much money KBTS paid her. And no matter how much she hated being in front of the camera instead of behind it, she had a new contract coming up next month. Plus, the professional in her recognized that this was, indeed, news. Jacob was right to get an interview in the can now, before the shock wore off. Before she had time to wash the soot off her face.

The heartless opportunist.

"Jacob, it was terrifying—I was as scared as I've ever been," she began, trying to get her addled brain to cooperate with her mouth. "We were surrounded by flames, and the smoke made it hard to breathe. We'd been some distance away from the fire, and then within seconds it burst out all around us. Sean said it was an inversion." She frowned at Sean. "What the heck *is* an inversion, anyway?"

Jacob smoothly turned his attention to Sean.

"An inversion happens when hot air gets trapped in the middle of the mountain's slope," he explained. "It jacks the heat way up and drives the humidity down, and the fire blows up. It happens really fast, and there's no way to predict it."

"But you *did* predict it," Linda insisted as Jacob swiftly moved the mike back and forth between them "You told all your guys to head to the safe zone."

"Yeah, and I let you get trapped," he growled.

"Bullshit." Linda was furious. She wasn't about to let him get away with a whole new guilt complex. Her voice rose. "Who the hell put you in charge of the world, Sean O'Shea? Or in charge of me, for that matter? I was *exactly* where I wanted to be. Where I *needed* to be in order to do my job. And in order to get there, I had to stow away on your plane, remember? Because you're *unreasonable*."

"You were on that plane in defiance of my orders." His jaw was jutting again. His voice was hoarse and loud. "I told you to stay in town."

"Yeah, well, I need to do my job. And you aren't my boss, or my baby-sitter, either." Her throat hurt, but she was hollering anyway.

"To hell with your job." He was shouting at her. "And you need a baby-sitter—you take too many stupid chances, Tate."

"You're a great one to talk, O'Shea."

Jacob smiled at the camera and said into the mike, "As you can see, sparks are still igniting here, and I think you've just witnessed an inversion, with the heat going up and the blaze exploding. This is

Jacob Gibson, reporting from the scene of the forest fire near Courage Bay."

OLIVIA FLEW THEM back to town. She and Jacob tried to keep up a cheerful patter, but once again, Sean wasn't speaking to Linda.

Well, the hell with him. She wasn't speaking to him, either.

Back at the hotel, one glance in the mirror was enough to make her take her contacts out so she couldn't see herself. The filthy, sunburned, soot-streaked woman in the mirror was no relation of hers. She had a bruise on her forehead, a bump the size of an asteroid on the back of her skull and a long, ugly scratch on one cheek. Her eyes were fiery red and her throat felt scraped raw.

It took a long, soapy shower and an even longer soak in the bathtub to reach some semblance of normal, and by that time, she was hurting badly all over. Whimpering and wondering if she had enough left in her to make it to the bed, she was toweling herself off when the knock came at the door.

Wrapping the hotel's white terry bathrobe around her and plopping her glasses on her nose, she hobbled over and opened the door.

"I have a rain check for bed and breakfast at this address." Sean was clean. That was about all that could be said for him. He was leaning on the doorjamb, and she guessed it wasn't just an effort at non-chalance. He was probably having trouble standing up, just as she was.

He had small burns and scratches all over his face and arms. His eyes were sunken, dark-rimmed with exhaustion and more bloodshot than hers, if that was possible.

Linda's heart did its usual polka at the sight of him, but she wasn't going to cave just like that. They could be setting precedents here.

"Oh? And what makes you think it's still valid?"

"Because this lady who called me a stubborn, pig-headed chauvinist male idiot also said she was in love with me."

In spite of everything, that was still true. But he'd said it first.

"If I let you stay, will you take me out to dinner?" She wasn't about to become one of his disposable bimbos.

"Now?" His voice was plaintive. "Jeez, Tate, couldn't we order in? *Please*?" He limped past her and collapsed on the bed. "I'm just too damned wiped to go anywhere right now."

"I guess tomorrow will do." She wasn't unrea-sonable. She could make concessions. There was probably a television station here in Courage Bay that would welcome an experienced cameraperson. She'd pretty much had it anyway with jumping out of planes and getting dragged by sled dogs. She adored his family. And who knew what a couple of blue-eyed grandbabies would do for her mom and dad and their opposing life views?

"I'll take you to dinner all the tomorrows for the rest of our lives, if that's what you want, honey. And if you're going to argue with me about it, come over here to do it, okay? Just lie down where I can touch you with my good arm."

She did. She didn't argue, and it was amazing, because she soon realized she wasn't all that wiped out after all.

And neither was he.

NO KNOWN CURE
Joanna Wayne

CHAPTER ONE

ALEC GIROUX pushed up the sleeve of his white lab coat and glanced at his watch again. Five-thirty. His ex-wife was probably already at his house with the kids, seething that he dare keep her waiting.

Stopping at the door of the examining room, Alec checked the patient chart. Male. Eighty-six years old. Lives alone. Son came by to check on him and found him listless and confused. Symptoms: Pulse low. Temperature 102.3. History of heart problems but no chest pains now. Raspy cough. Had an air conditioner but didn't have it on. That was the way with many of the elderly on fixed incomes. They didn't have the money to pay the high costs of cooling during the summer months and didn't want to ask for help.

"Weren't you supposed to clear out of here by five?" Mary Ellen, one of the E.R. nurses, asked, stopping at his elbow.

"Yeah, but I hate to leave you guys so swamped. I keep thinking I should see just one more patient."

"Oh, goody. That would leave us fifty more in the

waiting room. No, wait, I see a new one coming down the hall. Make that fifty-one." She took the chart from his hand. "Get out of here, Alec. You've been at this since five this morning. Besides, having your ex kill you won't help our situation."

"You've got a point." Mary Ellen usually did. Not only was she a very competent nurse, she tended to mother him and anyone else who needed it.

Fortunately, fifty patients was an exaggeration, and he was eager to see Stacy and Cameron. Cameron was seven and Stacy was five, healthy, noisy kids, that any normal overworked father should have been glad to get a break from.

And he had been—for the first couple of days they'd been with their mother. After that, the quiet, empty house had been a real downer, and he'd spent most of his time at the hospital, even sleeping there several nights. Not that he'd gotten much sleep. The City of Courage Bay was experiencing the most severe and prolonged heat wave on record and the hospital had been deluged with heat-related emergencies.

Mary Ellen put her hand to his shoulder and gave him a playful shove. "Move it, partner, you're blocking the door."

"Now you've done it," Alec teased. "You won't have me to push around anymore. I'm out of here."

Alec stopped at the admitting station to let them

know he was leaving, then headed toward to the exit.
If he didn't get caught in traffic, he could be home
in twenty minutes.

He was halfway down the hall when the door at the
other end opened and an elderly man staggered in. The
guy was pasty white and holding his chest. Alec has-
tened his pace, but before he could reach the old man,
the guy started coughing and fell against the wall.

"I've got you," Alec said, sliding the man's arm
over his shoulder. "Just hold on to me."

"Hurts when…I bre—" And then he collapsed in
Alec's arms.

"Is he dead, Daddy?"

Alec looked up to see Cameron and Stacy running
toward him, followed by their mother, prancing down
the hall in her high heels and short skirt. The desire
to strangle the woman with his bare hands had never
been stronger.

"He's not dead, son. But he's very sick. Go stand
by your mother until I can get him in a room."

Fortunately, one of the nurses noticed the com-
motion and rushed toward them with a wheelchair.
"Get him in an examining room and check the vitals,"
Alec said, easing the man into the wheelchair. "And
get the oxygen set up." He put a hand on the man's
shoulder to reassure him before the nurse wheeled
him away. "You hang in there. We're going to have
you breathing better before you know it."

When he turned around, Stacy was standing right beside him. "What's wrong with him, Daddy?"

"I won't know for sure until I examine him and run some tests."

"And give him a shot. That's what you do when I'm sick."

"Right." He stooped and took both of the kids in his arms, trying hard to keep his anger at Danielle in check for their sakes. He hugged them tightly, told them he'd missed them, then glared at his ex. "The emergency room is no place for children."

"Then you should have been home. You knew what time to expect us."

"We're overrun with emergencies. I couldn't just walk away. Take Stacy and Cameron to the coffee shop. I'll meet you there as soon as I check out the man who just came in and get him admitted into the hospital."

"I don't have time. Craig is waiting and we have plans."

His blood pressure shot up. "Make time, Danielle."

"You're not the only doctor capable of tending the sick, Alec, even though you like to think you're better than the rest."

Hard as it was to hold his tongue, Alec was not getting into a verbal sparring match with Danielle in front of the staff or their children. "Fine, Danielle. I'll handle the situation," he said, trying to decide how he was going to do that.

Danielle switched her tone, became sugary sweet as she told the kids how much she'd enjoyed having them with her and that she'd miss them until she saw them again at Christmas break. Then, without a word to Alec, she whirled in the direction of the main exit.

"You better go see if that man is dead, Daddy," Cameron said, his eyes still big as saucers. "I can watch Stacy."

"No," Stacy protested. "I want to stay with you, Daddy. I missed you."

Alec picked her up. She was petite, no more than a good armful. "We're going to have lots of time together. I just need a few minutes with the patient, and then we'll go home. Okay?"

"Okay."

She made the little pouty face that always got to him, and he put a finger to the tip of her nose. "I won't be long. I promise."

"He looked dead," Cameron said again. "Really yucky."

"I promise you he's not dead. And yucky is a treatable condition." Alec started back toward the emergency room area with Stacy in his arms and Cameron by his side.

One of the young nurses turned the corner, almost bumping into him. "Oh, excuse me, Dr. Giroux. I was coming to find you. Mary Ellen said you might need help with your children."

"Mary Ellen is right, as always."

"I'll take them to the staff lounge for you if you like."

"That would be terrific." He gave Stacy a kiss and Cameron a pat on the shoulder before hurrying back to the patient. Alec didn't know if the man's condition was weather-related or not, but there was a good chance it was. Prolonged heat waves were a killer for the elderly. There had been four deaths in Courage Bay so far. He didn't intend to let his newest patient make five.

THE EVENING with the children had gone well. Alec had cooked their favorite meal—hamburgers on the grill with ice-cream sundaes they'd concocted themselves for dessert. Then they'd played and swum in the backyard pool until it was time to bathe and get ready for stories and bed.

It was just the break he needed from the stress of twelve- to fourteen-hour workdays, and Alec had fallen asleep almost the second his head hit the pillow. But it was only 2:00 a.m. now, and he was wide-awake.

If the kids had still been with their mother, he would have gotten dressed, and gone back to the hospital, but that wasn't an option now. He tried to push thoughts of the emergency room from his mind, but that last patient claimed his attention.

Milton Muxworthy hadn't been dehydrated or shown other signs of heat exhaustion. At his age and with the presenting symptoms, chances were likely that he had a run-of-the-mill bacterial pneumonia, although the chest X ray and white blood cell differential hadn't been quite what Alec had expected.

Still, he'd started the patient on antibiotics and had him admitted to the hospital, about all he could do for now. The attending physician would have more to go on once he had the results of bladder and kidney cultures.

The man was likely breathing fine and resting now, but Alec wasn't, so he reached for the phone and punched in the number for the hospital. "Third floor nurses station," he required. A minute later he had one of the night nurses on the line.

"This is Alec Giroux."

"Good morning, Dr. Giroux. How can I help you?"

"I'd like to check the status of Milton Muxworthy. He was admitted just after six o'clock last night with a preliminary diagnosis of bacterial pneumonia. I'm not certain who the attending physician is."

"Hold on and I'll pull his chart."

Alec waited, then listened while the nurse filled him in as to the attending physician and the patient's temperature and blood pressure fluctuations. Not in the danger zone, but not what Alec had hoped for, either.

"Is he complaining of pain?"

"No complaints, but he seems disoriented. I'm not certain he knows where he is."

"But you did put him in a private room as I requested?"

"In the last one we had. It's a zoo up here. If this heat doesn't let up, we're going to have patients sleeping in the hall."

"Let's hope that doesn't happen." Alec thanked her for the information on Milton Muxworthy, then hung up the phone.

Wide-awake now, he crawled from the king-size bed and tiptoed down the hall to peek in on Stacy and Cameron. That was one of the things he'd missed most while they were away. Watching them sleeping peacefully had a calming effect on him, gave him the sense that no matter how many frustrating and sometimes downright heartbreaking things he'd dealt with in the emergency room that day, there was still a measure of goodness and right to the world.

Alec paused a few minutes at each bedroom, wishing he could hit the pillow and not open his eyes until morning, the way his children did, instead of prowling the house like a confused burglar. He walked to the back door, unlatched it and stepped outside.

Even in the wee hours of the morning, there was no relief from the heat. It was as if a thick, insulating blanket had been tossed over Courage Bay, virtually shutting out the cooling ocean breezes that usually made summers tolerable.

Alec walked to the edge of the pool, stepped out of his pajama bottoms and dove into the water. Swimming was his drug of choice for stress relief. Tonight he swam with even, rhythmic strokes, lap after lap until his body grew tired and his mind grew numb. Then he stepped out of the water and dried off on the beach towel that Cameron had left in one of the chairs.

He dropped onto a lounger and fell asleep, not waking until the first rays of morning sun beat down on his bare chest. It was the longest uninterrupted sleep he'd had in weeks.

"ANOTHER SCORCHER," Mary Ellen said. "Looks like the citizens of Courage Bay would have figured it wasn't wise to go jogging on their lunch break when we're in the middle of a heat wave."

"Is that the story behind the young woman who just arrived by ambulance?" Alec asked as he finished writing out a prescription for a patient.

Mary Ellen nodded. "Passed out on the jogging trail about a mile from where she worked. Dressed in one of those skimpy little running outfits."

"Which room?"

"Sorry, hotshot. Dr. Grayson took her. You get the sweaty, overweight taxi driver complaining of shortness of breath and dizziness. Room Ten."

"How can I ever thank you?" Alec pulled the admission chart from the door as he walked into the examining room. "Looks like you're not having the best of days, Mr. Cass."

"No. Not good at all. Butch… Call me Butch."

Pale. Voice a little shaky. Breathing labored. "And I'm Dr. Giroux. When did you start feeling like this?"

"Woke up with a cough and a sore throat yesterday. Didn't start feeling this bad until a couple of hours—" He broke into a raspy coughing spasm, then wiped a stream of sweat from his brow with the back of his sleeve. "I didn't start having trouble breathing until a couple of hours ago. It's this stinking heat. If it don't cool off, it's going to kill us all."

"How long has it been since you've had a flu shot?"

"Never had one. Figured those are for old people. I'm only forty-three—" He stopped again. "Can't get my breath. Just like that old man I brought in four days ago."

"You brought someone to the hospital?"

"The emergency room. I had to help him to the door. The guy was huffing and puffing so he could barely walk. Old guy, though."

Four days ago. The day Danielle had dumped the kids at the hospital. "Was that about five-thirty on Monday afternoon?"

"Pretty close. Right smack in the middle of rush hour."

Had to be Milton Muxworthy the cabbie had driven to the hospital. Possibly he'd caught whatever

Milton had. Alec took a look down the man's throat. Red, but not excessively so. "I need to get a chest X ray and some blood work."

"Will that take—" Butch was interrupted by another round of coughing. "I've got to get back to work."

Oh, yeah. Back in the taxi contaminating everyone who got into his cab. Just what Courage Bay needed. "It won't take long," Alec said, already writing the orders for the X ray and tests to determine white blood cell count.

Alec called the nurses station on the third floor while he waited for the results to come back. "This is Dr. Alec Giroux. I'd like to check the status of Milton Muxworthy."

"Mr. Muxworthy died a few minutes after 9:00 a.m. this morning of respiratory failure."

"You're sure?"

"Absolutely. I just reassigned that room. Dr. Ethridge said the lungs had totally whited out."

"What were the accompanying complications?"

"None noted. The infection didn't respond to treatment."

"What was the treatment?"

"An aggressive antibiotic and antiviral regimen, but the man's condition continued to deteriorate."

Dead in four days from a respiratory infection that didn't respond to treatment. That wasn't totally unusual in a man Milton's age, but it was reason for concern, especially considering that Alec had a man in the E.R. right now who may have contracted the disease from Milton during a cab ride to the hospital.

Dread crept into his mind as Cameron's words came back to him. *He looks dead, Daddy.*

Now he was. And both Stacy and Cameron had been practically in the man's face, breathing the same contaminated air.

CHAPTER TWO

JANICE REED sipped her afternoon coffee, trying to stay awake. The time change in returning to Atlanta after a couple of weeks of visiting her mother in Oregon always got to her.

"Hey, you're back," Martha Colfax said, sweeping into Janice's office with her usual flair, looking far more like a *Vogue* model than a specialist with the Center for Disease Control.

"Got back late last night," Janice answered.

"So did you miss us here at CDC?"

"You know, I did. Isn't that the pits?"

"Small-town life get to you?"

"Something like that. Slow me down, and I go nuts."

"You're an excitement junkie. I don't know how you ended up as a nurse."

"I did think of trying to get in the military as a fighter pilot."

"Which explains why you're still single."

"What? Men don't like fighter pilots?"

"No. Men are scared to death of women with more

spirit of adventure than they have. I mean, look what you drive to work."

"A freakin' fine Harley. What's wrong with that?"

"Can't take a passel of kids to school and soccer practice on the back of one of those things."

"I don't have a passel of kids." And never would, but that wasn't a point Janice wanted to dwell on.

"You should have kids. You'd be a great mother."

"Bad thing is they usually come with a husband," Janice wisecracked.

"And you know what I think about that."

"Yes, I do, so please spare me from hearing your erroneous theory again."

"You're afraid of love," Martha said, ignoring that last request. "Just plain scared to death some man is going to sweep you off your feet and you'll lose your independence."

"Not true. I'm just not in a rush to lose it." But Martha was partly right. Janice's one run at love had ended in disaster, and the only thing she'd felt when the marriage had been called off was relief. Truth was, she liked her life as it was.

"How was you mother?" Martha asked.

"Doing well, but still having trouble with her tennis elbow."

"So you two didn't even play tennis while you were there."

"No. Nor did we play racquetball. Or go rowing.

We played bridge with her cronies. Did I ever tell you how much I hate card games?"

"Every time you visit your mother. But whatever you did on the West Coast, it must have agreed with you. You look great."

"Thanks." Janice took the compliment the same way she took her margaritas—with a few grains of salt. She had a nice build, reasonable brown hair, cut short and practical, and she'd been told on more than one occasion that she had a nice smile. There was no way that added up to great. Attractive, maybe even cute—if you were generous—but not great.

"I've got to get back to work," Martha said, "but if you want to do something one night this week, let me know."

"Sure. How about some volleyball at that new sand court?"

"I was thinking more on the lines of going clubbing or catching a movie."

"There's a new George Clooney flick out," Janice said. "I could use a night with George."

"But would you give up your Harley for him?"

"For a night—or two—if I had to."

With a groan, Martha ducked out the door. Janice went back to compiling a computer graph on the number of measles cases reported in the Northeastern states during the past two weeks. Reports were the least favorite part of her job as an on-site CDC specialist, but they were a fair trade-off for getting to jump in the thick of things wherever a real emergency arose.

The intercom on her desk buzzed. "Call on line one."

She took the call. "Janice Reed, Center for Disease Control."

"This is Dr. Alec Giroux at Courage Bay Hospital in Courage Bay, California."

Dr. Alec Giroux. The name conjured up an instant image. Soap-opera gorgeous, with thick black hair, bedroom eyes and a smile that had done weird things to her equilibrium. And a kiss that should never have happened.

"How can I help you, Dr. Giroux?"

"I'd like to know if breakouts of an unusually infectious respiratory ailment have been reported anywhere on the West Coast."

"Not to my knowledge. Have you encountered cases in Courage Bay?"

She listened while Dr. Giroux filled her in on details of a patient who'd died of an upper respiratory condition and a new patient who may have contracted the ailment from the first man.

"How old is the patient?"

"The one who died was eighty-six. New patient is forty-three."

"What tests have you conducted so far?"

"Chest X ray. Complete blood work-up. Electrolyte panel. Took a sputum stain. All I have back so far is the X ray and white blood count on the new patient. WBC differential suggests this could be a viral infection, though results are not conclusive." He gave her the numbers and a brief description of the X ray. "The fever is low-grade and the lung tissue is not as inflamed as I would have expected."

"Are those results consistent with the findings of the patient who died?"

"Yes. According to his charts, his fever climbed dramatically during the last twenty-four hours of his life and fluid built up in his lungs until they completely whited out."

"Did you collect kidney and bladder cultures from the elderly man?"

"The attending physician did once he'd left the E.R. Findings were negative. This may be more hunch and physician instinct than anything else, but I'm afraid we're dealing with something a little different from the run-of-the-mill bacterial pneumonia or viruses we're used to seeing."

"I'll run a check on respiratory ailments and get back to you within the hour. In the meantime, I suggest you keep the new patient in isolation, just in case."

"I agree."

Janice began a computer search as soon as she broke the connection. The seriousness of Alec's request was foremost on her mind, but that didn't totally override the memories of their meeting two years ago in Seattle.

She'd been relatively new at the CDC, and the Conference on Emergency Medical Care had been the first major conference where she'd participated as a presenter. Alec had presented, as well, and his talk had been one of the highlights of the conference for her.

Actually, *he'd* been the highlight of the conference. She'd felt some kind of weird chemistry every time she'd seen him that week. Then, on the last night, the two of them, along with a half dozen other doctors, had talked into the wee hours of the morning, arguing the role CDC should play in emergencies. Alec had insisted the CDC should be strictly supportive, always secondary to the doctors in the field. She'd felt—and still did—that the CDC should take the lead in any situation where the danger of an epidemic existed.

But in spite of their differences of opinion, she'd been all but mesmerized by the guy and certain that the sparks that fired between them weren't one-sided. He'd walked her to the door of her hotel room.

And then he'd kissed her. Brief as it was, that kiss had knocked her for a loop. She grew warm even now, just thinking about it. Apparently it hadn't had the same effect on him. She'd hoped he would call. He hadn't—until now. And if he remembered her at all, he'd given no indication of it. So much for chemistry.

ALEC SAT STARING at the phone. What were the chances he'd make one call to the CDC and get Janice Reed on the telephone? She'd gotten to him pretty bad a couple of years ago in Seattle, but he'd attributed it to the fact that his ego had just taken a killer blow. That was the same weekend Danielle had called to tell him she was marrying a prestigious reconstructive surgeon as soon as the divorce was final.

He'd thought of Janice a lot after the Seattle meeting and had come close to calling her, but decided it would be a stupid mistake. It had been the right decision. His responsibilities at the hospital, along with two kids, took one hundred and ten percent of his time. Truth was, he'd hardly dated since the divorce.

Still, the moment he'd started talking to Janice, the memories of that week in Seattle had come hurtling back into his mind. She'd been intelligent, confident and a little hardheaded. She'd also been attractive and funny, and when she'd smiled at him, he'd felt virile and desirable—feelings Danielle had slowly sucked from him during their marriage and painful separation.

And none of this was anything Alec should be concentrating on now. Janice Reed was with the CDC, and that was the only connection he had time to concern himself with. He did his best to push her from his mind as he walked into the room of his next patient—a six-year-old girl who'd cut her hand on a bro-

ken toy and needed a few stitches and lots of reas-
surance.

Forty-five minutes later, Janice called with good
news. There were no outbreaks of serious respiratory
infections anywhere in the country. His relief was
short-lived. At four forty-five, tests in hand, he returned to the examining room of a new patient,
Di Di Grant, who presented symptoms very similar
to those of Butch Cass and Milton Muxworthy,
though her respiration was not as compromised.

"Have you been around anyone with a respiratory
ailment in the last few days?"

"I work in a drugstore, so I'm exposed to everything," Di Di said. "That's why I came in as soon as
I started running a temperature."

"Do you know an elderly gentleman named Milton Muxworthy?"

"I sure do. He's a customer of ours. A really nice
guy. Just moved here from the Sacramento area a few
months ago."

"Has he been in recently?"

"I sold him some over-the-counter cough syrup a
few days ago. He said flying always made his throat
dry and scratchy."

A trip. That was news. "Do you know where he'd
traveled?"

"Somewhere down in South America. He was a
retired missionary. Wanted one last trip before he

died. He said he wanted to see how his work was going and talk to old friends." Di Di started coughing again, then swayed a little.

"Are you feeling dizzy?"

"A little. I think it's the fever. All I need are some antibiotics and an afternoon at home to rest."

Antibiotics and rest. She'd get both, only not at home. "I'm going to admit you to the hospital, Di Di."

"For a cough?"

"I think it may be the beginning stages of something more severe."

"Like what?"

He explained as best he could, good practice for the explaining he'd have to do to the insurance company that held her policy, since her presenting symptoms wouldn't ordinarily suggest the need for hospitalization. But she was the second person who might have contracted the disease that had claimed Milton's life, and Alec wasn't going to risk letting this get out of hand before he even knew what he was dealing with.

If nothing else, the SARS epidemic had been a tough lesson in how fast a virus could spread if not caught in time. The good thing was that his brother Guy was the chief of emergency medicine at the hospital, and he'd be one hundred percent behind Alec with this. The hospital and emergency services were already stretched to their limits with just the heat wave to face. They definitely didn't need an outbreak of a mysterious, deadly virus.

Alec's mind flew back to Cameron and Stacy. They'd been around Milton for only a minute or two at most, but that was no guarantee they were out of danger. The taxi driver who'd been exposed the same day had come down with symptoms today, which would mean a three-day incubation period for him, four to five days for Di Di.

He'd have to watch both of his children very closely. Tonight, he'd start them on an antiviral medication, as well. It might not help, but it wouldn't hurt. He'd also have to alert the sitter and explain that he needed to know immediately if either of them developed a cough or started running a fever.

Not only that, but they would have to stay inside and away from other children until all danger of their coming down with the disease was past. The sitter would likely run out screaming when he told her the full story, but that was a chance he'd have to take.

And, of course, he'd also have to monitor himself.

THERE WAS A MESSAGE from Dr. Giroux waiting on Janice's answering machine when she arrived at her office just before eight the next morning. And he was on California time, which made it 5:00 a.m. for him.

She pulled the file she'd started yesterday and returned the call, listening attentively and asking questions as Dr. Giroux explained that their initial patient had just returned from unknown destinations in South America, and that two new patients had been admitted to the hospital isolation ward since he'd talked to her last, including one of the nurses who'd been on duty when Milton Muxworthy was treated.

None of the patients appeared to be responding to treatment.

"I checked the global situation for outbreaks yesterday," she explained. "There doesn't seem to be anything like you're dealing with, but that doesn't rule out the possibility that Mr. Muxworthy encountered the virus in an isolated village. Do you have any further information about the places he had visited?"

"No."

"I'll get someone on that," she said, jotting a note to herself.

"I just keep thinking about how quickly the SARS epidemic got out of hand," Alec said.

"I agree. In fact, I went to my supervisor with your concerns yesterday. He thinks we should treat this with extreme caution."

"So what is the CDC's recommendation for handling this?"

"Preventing the spread of infectious disease is our number one concern, so isolation of any new patients suspected of having the virus is of utmost importance."

"What about our duty to inform the public?"

"The concerns there are twofold—protection and avoiding unnecessary panic. I'd like to have the lab at CDC conduct expedited tests to try and isolate the virus we're dealing with," she said, making a quick decision.

"That should help."

"I'm flying out there today, Dr. Giroux. In the meantime, I suggest you alert all doctors on your staff and in the Courage Bay area to be on the lookout for these presenting symptoms."

"I'm not sure what good your being here will do."

"For one thing, it's my job as an on-site specialist to give direct assistance when a need is indicated. Hopefully, this will turn out to be only a mildly infectious virus, but better to err on the side of caution, especially when we're looking at an unidentified virus not responding to routine treatment."

"What kind of assistance would you give?"

"I'll help in devising strategies to keep the virus from spreading, but I'm also a registered nurse. I can help you gather cultures and blood from suspicious patients, both those going through your emergency room and those admitted by physicians through the regular channels, and we can utilize the CDC testing facilities to get overnight results on any cultures we send them."

"In that case, hop a plane, Ms. Reed. I'm sure my brother, who's head of emergency medicine, and our chief of staff, Callie Baker, will be thrilled to hear you're coming and will want to meet with you immediately."

The second she was off the phone, Janice notified the head of her department about her plans, then called the airline. She'd been impressed by Alec Giroux the first time she'd met him. Now, after talking to him on the phone and hearing how fast he'd jumped on this situation, she was downright in awe of the guy.

If all went well, she'd be teaming up with him in a matter of hours. Talk about the intimidation factor.

Then again, she thought to herself, *Alec Giroux was just a man. She'd do well to remember that. On the other hand, she was also just a woman, and therein might lie the problem.*

CHAPTER THREE

THE LAST THING Janice had expected was to be driving up Dr. Giroux's driveway that night, but here she was, parking the blue rental car in front of his garage. She'd hoped to arrive in time to see him at the hospital, but she hadn't been able to book a direct flight and had ended up with a long layover, made even longer by some kind of mechanical problem with the aircraft.

She'd made a quick change at the hotel, finally deciding on a white blouse, blue print skirt that fit loosely and fell below the knees and a pair of white sandals. Not the most professional of outfits, but the pale gray business suit she'd planned to wear to the hospital for the initial strategy and data-gathering session seemed too stuffy for an informal meeting at Dr. Giroux's house. Especially when the temperature was still hovering just under ninety and it was nearly eight o'clock.

She rang the bell and waited, then stared in shock when the door opened. The doctor was standing there, barefoot, shirtless, with a big glob of soapy foam glistening on his muscled chest. She took a deep breath and stepped back.

Alec looked down at his chest, then raked off the soap bubbles with his hand and blew them away. "Sorry about that. Stacy has to have the tub full of bubbles."

Way more information than Janice wanted to know. "I must have misunderstood the time we were supposed to meet. I can come back later."

"No, no. Come on in. I have all the reports laid out on the table in the kitchen. You can look them over while I get the kids to bed."

"So Stacy is your daughter?"

"Of course. Who did you think…" A broad grin spread across his face as he realized what she'd thought. "That explains the shocked look. I thought it was just the soap bubbles." He stood back for her to come in.

"We met two years ago," he said, "at a seminar in Seattle."

"I remember." So he hadn't forgotten the conference.

"I never expected to be meeting again like this."

She wasn't sure if he meant here with soap bubbles on his chest or in the middle of a heat wave with a possible epidemic to deal with. Either way, the two years hadn't changed him all that much. He was still devastatingly handsome, and still sent her pulse sky-rocketing. But they were facing a very serious situation, and that was all she needed to be thinking about right now.

"Daddy, I can't find my Nemo pajamas," someone called from upstairs.

"They're in the drier, Stacy. I'll bring them up."

"Why can't I get them myself?"

"Remember the rule. You have to stay upstairs as long as I have company."

"They won't bother me," Janice assured him. "I'd love to meet them."

"Might not be best tonight. They were…"

"Daddy, Cameron's hogging the toothpaste."

"I'll explain later. Right now I've got to root out a toothpaste hog. Just make yourself at home. There's fresh coffee in the pot and I put a cup out for you. If you want cream and sugar…"

"I take it black. And I'll be fine. Just point me to the kitchen."

"Straight down the hall. I'll be there as soon as I get Stacy and Cameron settled. Then you'll have my undivided attention. Count on that."

"We could do this tomorrow."

"Believe me, it may not seem so now, but it's much quieter and less distracting here. Besides, this infection we're dealing with really worries me. The sooner we get started on this, the better."

His tone and expression had changed from friendly to deadly serious as he spoke.

"You're right," she said. "Tomorrow could bring anything."

"Daddy, are you coming up to tell us a story?"

"Yes, so have your teeth brushed when I get there." Alec turned back to Janice. "I know this isn't the most professional of settings for what we're doing, but the kids need me as much as my patients—and I need them if I'm going to keep any kind of perspective though this."

"You don't have to apologize, Dr. Giroux. I seldom get to see the human side of the doctors I work with. It's kind of nice to know that when you're home at night, you're just like the rest of us. Well, except for the bubbles."

"My kinkier side."

And then he was gone, leaving Janice to find her way back to his kitchen. A soapy, muscled chest. A kiss dominating her memory. And files on what could potentially be an outbreak of a deadly virus. The mix couldn't get much more volatile—and it was only her first night in Courage Bay.

"YOU HAVE a phenomenal memory," Janice said as Alec rattled off a comparison of presenting symptoms among patients.

"I've been living with this for a couple of days."

Alec had pulled on a light blue T-shirt, but he was

still barefoot. Which made Janice really glad she hadn't opted for the gray business suit.

"How is the emergency room handling patients with suspicious symptoms?"

"Up until this afternoon, we hadn't had any specific plans in place. But the chief of staff and my brother Guy, who's head of emergency medicine, held an exigency meeting this afternoon. Patients presenting symptoms comparable to the still unidentified respiratory virus will be seen in a separate location operated as an emergency isolation examining unit."

"What about suspicious patients coming into the hospital via their regular primary physicians?"

"We haven't dealt with that yet."

"It has to be dealt with immediately. These patients cannot be allowed to sit in crowded waiting rooms. We'll have to notify all the doctors in the city at once and have these patients referred to the hospital's special unit."

"I'm not sure we have the staff to cover that."

"You'll have to find a way to make do or else we'll have to rely on hospitals in nearby locations. Who will be in charge of the new emergency room unit?"

"I will. There will be other doctors assisting as needed, but I'll make decisions on how the new unit is set up."

"That will make it a lot easier on me," she said.

"Some of my biggest nightmares have come from situations involving too many egos in the stew."

"This will be pretty much a one-ego stew," Alec said. "But then according to my ex-wife, that's more ego than most women can stand."

"I'm not worried."

"Somehow I didn't think you would be."

Janice wasn't sure if he'd meant that as a compliment, but all of a sudden the kitchen seemed at least ten degrees warmer than it had a few seconds ago. It was not the type of tingling heat she should be feeling in this situation.

They worked for another two hours, going over details and suggestions, and she forced herself to push her attraction for him to the back of her mind. It was the only way, given the circumstances. If he felt any similar attraction, it wasn't evident. He was too busy analyzing every suggestion she made and balking at a good many of them. Not that he wasn't just as concerned as she was about keeping the virus from spreading. But he had his own ideas and he didn't budge easily. But then, neither did she.

"The CDC has rules," she reminded him for at least the tenth time that night.

"So does the hospital—and limited resources. We're already stretched. I'm sure Callie Baker is going to make you well aware of that in tomorrow's meeting."

Early tomorrow morning. "I think I should go," she said. "It's past eleven."

"Already?" Alec glanced at his watch. "Seems like we just got started."

"What time should I be at the hospital in the morning?"

"I'll be there by six-thirty. That's the earliest the new sitter can get here. The last one came in at five, and that fit my schedule a lot better."

"When do you sleep?"

"Never. But don't let that out at the hospital. I try to keep them thinking I'm at least half-human."

"Your secret's safe with me. I'll be there by seven." She stretched her legs and tried to find the sandals she'd slipped out of hours ago. Instead, her toes brushed Alec's. Awareness hit again, an electrifying current that zinged along her nerve endings.

She took a deep breath, then faked a yawn, determined not to let him see how much the accidental touch had affected her. This was so unlike her as to be freaky. Sleep. She needed sleep and the sterile atmosphere of the hospital to reinstate her usually daunting CDC persona.

Alec stood and walked her to the door. "I don't suppose you had trouble finding a hotel room. According to the newspaper, there's a glut of them available. The heat wave is demolishing the city's tourist trade."

"I'm staying at one about a mile from the hospital."

Alec opened the door and she started to leave, then hesitated. "When you were getting the kids to bed, you said there was something you'd explain later."

He brushed a lock of hair from his forehead and leaned against the door frame, looking far too sexy for this time of the night.

"What were we discussing when I said that?"

"Why Stacy and Cameron had to stay upstairs while you had company."

His eyes darkened with worry.

"Stacy and Cameron were standing right next to me in the hall leading to the E.R. when Milton Mux-worthy collapsed in my arms. Their mother had dropped them off at the hospital—she was in too much of a hurry to wait for me at home."

"Oh, Alec. They've been exposed."

He nodded. "Just for a minute or two. They're not sick or anything. No fever or cough. But I'm keeping them away from everyone except the sitter until I'm sure the incubation period for the virus has passed. I leveled with the sitter about what we were up against, and she said she had no problems with staying on."

"Then she knows to watch them closely for symptoms of the virus?"

"Of course. Their health is my first priority."

The battle had become personal for Alec. That was supposedly the worst thing that could happen to a doctor—bad for him and bad for the patients he treated. But she didn't buy that theory this time. Alec might be worried for his children, but he was as much on top of things as any doctor she'd ever worked with.

She thought about that as she walked to the car. Thought about Alec the doctor, Alec the father and Alec the man. And she knew there was a good chance she'd learn more from this trip than from the extensive training the CDC had put her through, including the special classes at med school and stints of service in foreign countries.

She just hoped that when this was over, Stacy and Cameron would still be taking bubble baths and waiting for stories from their father.

ALEC STOOD in the doorway and watched Janice return to her car. She was exactly as he remembered her. Smart, determined, with a spark about her that crawled right under his skin. The last woman who'd turned him on like that had been Danielle, proof positive that sparks couldn't be trusted.

Still, for a few seconds there, when his bare foot had brushed hers, he'd felt a rush like he hadn't felt since that night in Seattle when he'd kissed her goodnight at the door and then stayed awake until morning thinking about it.

But he'd come a long way from the disillusioned, bewildered guy he'd been two years ago. Then, he'd been getting over the pain of watching his marriage go down the toilet and wondering how he'd manage two kids all by himself.

His edge had gotten harder since then. If love worked out someday, he'd take it, but he didn't need a woman to make his life complete. Especially a CDC number cruncher who lived halfway across the country.

JANICE SPENT the following morning in a four-hour strategy session with Alec, his brother Guy, who was the head of the E.R., and a committee of physicians and the hospital's chief of staff, Callie Baker. Callie was amazingly knowledgeable about every aspect of her hospital and Guy was equally on the ball. Working together, the team detailed exactly what symptoms should alert E.R. admitting personnel and doctors around the city to send a patient directly to the hospital's newly established E.R. isolation unit. They also established a protocol for at-risk patients who were admitted to the hospital's isolation ward.

Janice was amazed at how cooperative everyone had been, except for one physician. Dr. Mark Ethridge, a family practitioner, was convinced they were blowing the situation out of proportion as there had only been one death and the patient had been an elderly man who might have been in poor health when he contracted the virus.

Janice couldn't fault him for that. He made a good point, and before SARS, she would have agreed with him. But not now—especially since the other patients were not responding to aggressive treatment.

Once the meeting was over, Janice went to work helping collect culture samples to send to CDC along with chest X rays and data on all the patients who'd been identified and placed in isolation. The CDC lab in Atlanta had been put on alert and would be working constant shifts until the cultures and X rays were fully analyzed.

When she finished the last one, she pulled off the sterile gown, mask and gloves and deposited them in the appropriate container. When she turned around, Alec was striding toward her, looking drawn and tired—and worried.

"Butch Cass is now listed as critical. His temperature is rising in spite of efforts to keep it down, and the lungs are still collecting fluid."

"What about Di Di Grant?" Janice asked.

"Her condition is worsening, but she's not on the critical list yet."

"Not good, but we should have some answers soon. I have sputum stains and tissue cultures from all the patients ready to be flown to Atlanta."

"I guess the best news is that so far we've only had

cases contracted from the source carrier," Alec said, "but that can't last much longer.

"There's a bit of other good news, too."

"Hit me with it," Alec said. "I can use it."

"CDC employees have contacted the flight attendants and all the passengers who were on the plane back into L.A. with Muxworthy. No one has come down with anything that resembles a respiratory infection."

"That is good news. And all the patients we've taken in were around Milton after the disease had progressed to the point where they recognized he was ill."

"Which means it's extremely likely that he wasn't actually contagious until the symptoms appeared. Now we have to make certain that everyone who was exposed to our current patients after they exhibited symptoms isolates themselves and gets to the hospital at the very first sign that they're becoming ill."

"Of course, once they're here, I can't do a thing for them except pump them full of useless drugs, give them oxygen and make them as comfortable as possible."

"That's why we have to work fast, Alec. The more we know about the virus, the more likely we are to find something that will counteract its effects."

"Then it will have to be some kind of voodoo chant because I've tried the best antiviral drugs out there, and they're not working."

His cell phone rang, and he didn't try to hide his frustration when he answered it. She started to walk away, then heard the panic in his voice and stopped short, turning around to see his body stiffen and tiny blue lines pop out on his brow.

"Keep Cameron away from her, but don't frighten Stacy. I'm on my way home now."

Janice grabbed a few masks from the rack in the hall, then ran to catch up with Alec. "It's Stacy, isn't it? She's exhibiting symptoms."

"She said her throat hurts, and she's coughing. I'm bringing her in."

"I'm going with you, Alec."

"This isn't a CDC issue."

"I know." She didn't argue with him, but she didn't turn around, either. Forcing her help on him in a personal situation was definitely overstepping her authority. But he was running scared, and there was no way she could just walk away from him and leave him to handle this alone.

CHAPTER FOUR

JANICE OFFERED to drive and Alec let her, suddenly glad she was there. He felt as if he'd switched to some weird automatic mode where his body kept functioning even though his mind had gotten hung up and refused to budge from the one fact that hammered against his skull.

"Children develop sore throats and coughs all the time, Alec. This could be nothing."

He nodded, admitting she might be right, but consumed with a dread that was more real than the air he breathed. Air that Stacy could soon be struggling to pull into lungs devoured by a ravaging disease. "She won't understand isolation."

"She's only five, Alec. You won't have to go into a lot of details."

"She's a very smart five. She'll want to know why she's in the hospital, and the gowns and masks will frighten her."

"We'll make sure she's not frightened. We'll take

her favorite stuffed toys. And we can take turns sitting with her."

Alec was aware that Janice Reed was going way beyond the call of duty, allowing him this moment to fall apart emotionally. He let his mind wander as she drove.

Back to the first time Stacy had ridden her two-wheeler. She'd fallen a dozen times, but just gotten up and crawled back on. When she'd finally succeeded, she'd had the biggest smile he'd ever seen.

Back to the first night after her mother had moved out of the house, when she'd cried and held on to him and made him promise he'd never leave her. As if he would. As if he could ever let her go. So much hurt for a little girl. And now she had this to face.

"I think you should admit Cameron to the hospital, too, Alec."

"Don't worry. I plan to. I'd like to do the same with the sitter, though I doubt she'll go along with that."

"Then she should definitely quarantine herself."

"I agree."

"Will you start Cameron on the same antiviral drugs as Stacy?"

"I started them on those as soon as I realized what we were up against—for all the good it did."

"Hopefully it may lessen the severity. You take care of Stacy. I'll help Cameron pack."

"Thanks. Is handling doctors with personal emergencies part of the job for CDC specialists?"

"No, and you can tell me to butt out of your personal life if you want."

He seriously doubted that would deter her, but he didn't want to find out, not unless her duties as a CDC employee got in the way of his doing what he had to do to take care of his patients—to take care of Stacy.

"I'll let you know if you get too bossy."

"In that case, there is one other thing. Shouldn't you call Stacy's mother and tell her about this? I'm sure she'll want to be here."

Call Danielle and have her stalking the hospital corridors, blaming him for this, making demands, interfering, upsetting everyone and not doing one damn thing to make Stacy get better.

But she was Stacy's mother.

"It could just be a sore throat," he said, looking for an out. "If we find out differently, I'll call Danielle."

"Whatever you think's best."

But as they pulled up in the driveway and Cameron came running out the front door to meet them, Alec realized that he had no idea what was best for anyone right now, not even medically. That was a bitter pill for a doctor to swallow. It was pure poison for a father.

ALEC WAS AMAZED at the way Janice took over once they were inside the house. After he'd sent their sitter, Rhonda, home, with instructions for her own self-quarantine, he'd expected tears from Stacy and protests from Cameron. Instead, Janice had them bustling around, gathering a few of their favorite things as if they were going off on an exciting adventure instead of to the isolation ward at the hospital.

Janice wore her mask and had him, Stacy and Cameron wearing them as well, pretending it was a hospital game. It was not only protection, but the best way for Stacy to start adjusting for what was to come. Not that she'd have to wear a mask as a patient, but everyone else who came in her room would have one on.

"I don't think I'll take Amanda with me," Stacy said. "She's my very favorite doll and I don't want her to catch my sore throat."

"That's a good idea," Janice said. "And if you change your mind later, your dad or I can come back and get her for you."

"Are you going to stay with me at the hospital?" she asked.

"I'll be working there, but I can come to your room anytime you want me to."

"And read me stories?"

"All the stories you want. I can even go to the hospital library and get more books."

"I don't like shots. Can you say no shots?"

"That's the one thing I can't do. But I'll hold your hand if you have to get one, and we'll make funny faces at the person who's giving it."

"Yeah, even if it's Daddy." Stacy started to giggle, but the happy sound dissolved into a dry, hacking cough, and Alec felt as if he'd just fallen into a dark pit and was plunging to the bottom at breakneck speed.

He walked to the kitchen before Stacy picked up on his new dive into anxiety. Janice followed him. "You two go ahead to the hospital," she said. "I'll help Cameron finish packing and we'll come in a taxi. I think it will be better if he's not in the same car with Stacy, even with a mask on."

"I don't see how any of that is going to help at this point. Cameron was exposed at the same time Stacy was. If he's susceptible, it's just a matter of time before he starts coughing."

"It's just a precaution. And chances are he's not susceptible. You were exposed, and you haven't gotten sick. Only one of the nurses is down so far. So it's evident that some people's immune systems fight it off better than others."

"Or else some force out there is playing a lottery game with our lives."

"You know you don't believe that."

"Not most days. I'm not so sure about this one.

But you're right. You and Cameron should take a taxi and I'll see you when you get there."

She started to walk away, but he reached out and grabbed her hand. He only meant to thank her, but his emotions were too raw, and when she met his gaze, he opened his arms and she stepped inside them. He held on to her as if she were the rope that kept him from careening down a treacherous mountain slope, and right now, that was exactly how he felt.

He pulled away when he saw Stacy at the door, clinging to the stuffed bear she never went to sleep without. "I'm ready to go, Daddy."

He exhaled sharply as determination took over and pushed his fears and weaknesses aside. He had a job to do.

"I'll call the hospital on the way and make sure they have rooms ready for Stacy and Cameron," Janice said.

"I want the colorful print sheets from the pediatric ward on Stacy's bed instead of those hospital blue ones."

"You've got it, Doctor. Anything else?"

"Yeah. In case I forgot to tell you. Thanks."

BY NINE that evening, three more patients had been admitted to the hospital suspected of having the virus. Two had been passengers in Butch's taxi. One was Di Di's co-worker. All had been processed through the new emergency unit and admitted to the isolation ward.

Janice had collected samples from them, put them with the other cultures and X rays and sent them off to Atlanta. She'd also spent hours trying to contact family members of the affected patients in an effort to identify anyone who may have been in contact with them once they were contagious. It was pretty much an impossible task.

But as busy as Janice had been, Alec had been busier. He'd seemed to be everywhere at once. Meeting with family members of the patients to explain what little they knew of the disease, phoning doctors in other areas of the country, seeing if they'd found any combination of drugs more effective than others against hard-to-crack viruses, and conducting a meeting with the medical staff to discuss the potential epidemic and review what criteria they should use in determining which patients to send to the special unit for assessment.

And still, Alec found time to run back and forth from the E.R. to the isolation ward on the fourth floor in order to spend precious minutes with Stacy. So far she was feeling well. The coughing was getting steadily worse, but her temperature had barely nudged over a hundred.

Janice peeked in and said hello to Cameron, who looked up from the computer game he was playing and grinned. He'd had steady company all day, charming the nurses. At this point, he wasn't technically considered in isolation since he hadn't developed any symptoms, but neither was he allowed to leave his room.

Stacy had a lot less company, since Alec wanted all her energy channeled into fighting off the infection. Still, Janice couldn't pass her room without making certain she was okay. She donned a fresh robe, gloves and mask and peeked in.

Alec was sitting in a chair, holding Stacy and telling her a story, his voice muffled by the mask. Janice's chest constricted at the sight of the powerful, handsome doctor and the small, blond preschooler.

She lingered in the doorway, listening to the story and watching Stacy's rapt expression as she hung on Alec's every word.

"Tell me about the *Ranger*, Daddy, and the storm."

"Not that story again."

"Yes, please," she said, clapping her hands. "I love it."

"It was 1848," Alec said, "nearly a hundred and sixty years ago. Pierre Giroux was the French captain of the *Ranger*. It was an American ship and had been fighting in the Mexican War. Not far from Courage Bay, the ship ran into a fierce storm. Thunder rolled and lightning cracked, making zigzagged streaks across the black sky."

"Don't forget the waves," Stacy reminded him.

"We can't forget the waves. They were taller than grown men and crashing about the ship. Captain Pierre's crew had to struggle with all their might to keep the boat from tipping over."

"Next comes the lightning part."

"That's right," Alec said. "Lightning struck the ship and set it on fire. The crew had to make a choice. They could jump into the churning sea or burn to death on the sinking ship. So they jumped into the water, even though they knew they could never make it to land." Alec brushed wispy blond curls from Stacy's forehead. "But back on shore, some Indians had been watching the ship."

"Friendly Indians," Stacy said.

"That's right, sweetie. Not only friendly but brave. They knew the storm was very dangerous, but some of the bravest men climbed into their reed boats and went out into the storm to rescue the drowning sailors. And they did. All the Indians returned safely with the sailors they'd rescued."

"They were really brave," Stacy said.

"That's right. And that's how Courage Bay got its name."

"Firemen are brave," Stacy said. "And policemen."

"Little girls can be brave, too, Stacy. You're being brave right now."

Stacy reached up and put her arms around Alec's neck and gave him a big kiss on his cheek, and Janice was certain that there were tears glazing his eyes. She had a lump in her throat the size of a golf ball and felt an unfamiliar fluttering in her stomach. She wasn't sure about Pierre Giroux, but Dr. Alec Giroux was one very special man.

"Tell me the rest, Daddy. Tell me about Moon Mist."

"We could save it for tomorrow night."

"I don't want to save it."

"Then I guess we better talk about Moon Mist. Captain Pierre Giroux fell in love with the medicine man's daughter, but Moon Mist was very young and her father didn't think she knew what true love was. So he told her to go to the sacred pool and stare down into the water. If she saw Pierre's face reflected there, it would mean he was her true love and they could get married."

"But Pierre didn't trust the medicine man, did he, Daddy?"

"No way. He climbed right to the top of the big tree by the pool so that when Moon Mist looked in the water, she'd be certain to see his reflection. But when Moon Mist came, she just gasped and ran away. She told her father that when she looked in the water, she saw two faces. Pierre's and some nutty young man who'd climbed to the top of the tree and was about to tumble into the water."

"And did they get married?" Janice asked, stepping into the room.

Alec turned, saw her standing there and smiled. "You tell her the rest, Stacy."

"The medicine man said they could get married, but Pierre shouldn't climb any more trees."

"That's a beautiful story," Janice said. "I like that Pierre learned the power of love."

"Code Blue in Isolation Room 412. Code Blue in Isolation Room 412." That was Butch Cass's room.

Alec jumped to his feet and Janice took Stacy from his arms. Stacy held on to Janice, her arms wrapped tightly around her neck as her father bolted from the room.

"What's Code Blue?" Stacy asked.

"It means someone needs your daddy to help them."

"My daddy's brave, too, isn't he?"

"Very brave, sweetheart. And he loves you very much."

"I'm tired," Stacy said.

"You should probably go to sleep."

"I want to go home."

"You will soon." Janice brushed Stacy's hair back from her flushed face and her insides tightened. It was easy to say she'd go home soon, but unless they found something to control this virus, the little girl might die right here in this room. Janice swallowed hard, fighting a bout of mind-numbing dread.

There were lines CDC employees weren't supposed to cross. Invisible lines that separated them from the people they worked with. It had always been easy to stay behind those lines before, to be the person gathering data, examining test results and making recommendations to avoid the spread of contagious diseases.

Becoming emotionally involved with the doctor in charge and his children would blur those lines, compromise her authority and negatively affect her performance. She simply could not let that happen. Yet when she returned Stacy to her bed and the little girl wrapped her thin arms around Janice's neck, Janice felt the sting of tears.

Stacy fell into a restless sleep in minutes, but it was a half hour later before Alec appeared at the door and motioned for Janice to meet him in the hall. She didn't have to ask what had happened. The bad news was written all over his face.

"Are you hungry?" he asked.

"Not particularly."

"Me, neither, but there's a bar and grill a couple of blocks away and I have to get out of here for a few minutes."

He had to get out of there, and he wanted her to go with him. Yet if she did, she risked blurring those lines even further. Still, he looked exhausted and vulnerable and she couldn't bear to say no. "Can we walk to it?"

"If you can handle the heat."

And if she couldn't, she had a feeling she'd better catch the next plane back to Atlanta.

CHAPTER FIVE

COURAGE BAY BAR AND GRILL was housed in what must have been one of the first movie theaters in the area. The bar was U-shaped and many of the stools were occupied. Alec waved and spoke to a couple of guys, but it was clear he was in no mood to talk and they seemed to accept that.

He led her to one of the few tables in a dimly lit spot near the back of the bar.

"If you're really hungry, we can go into the restaurant," Alec said, "but we can get sandwiches and appetizers here."

"The bar's fine."

Janice knew Alec had needed a reprieve from the hospital, but he wouldn't stay away long. And he had his cell phone and his pager with him, so that even here, he wasn't actually cut off from what went on in the hospital.

Alec ordered black coffee and a burger. She ordered water and a small garden salad. Once the waitress left, Alec leaned back and stared blankly at the wall behind the bar until she returned with his coffee.

He took a sip, then toyed with the handle of the cup. "We lost Butch tonight. We did everything we could, and he died right there in room 412, just three doors down from Stacy."

"You did your best. So did the other doctors on the team."

"It wasn't enough, and we have seven more patients, including Stacy, infected with this virus. We can't just stand by and let this happen to them. I *won't* let it happen to Stacy."

Janice hurt for him, but there was nothing she could say other than meaningless reassurances.

"We need to know exactly how the virus attacks the lungs, what it does that causes them to deteriorate so rapidly," Alec said.

"Hopefully, the lab can supply you with answers."

"We needed them yesterday."

"That I can't provide, but we'll have some results by morning, and more complete data within forty-eight hours."

"Forty-eight hours is an eternity with this virus."

"I know, and I know how difficult this must be for you."

"Difficult? That's such an inadequate word for how I feel. Stacy and Cameron are my life…have been ever since the day they were born. I guess that sounds corny to someone as young as you."

"No. It sounds genuine and loving. And I'm not all that young, Alec. I'm thirty-three."

"Thirty-three. Only two years younger than me. But you seem eons younger."

"Comes from still being single, I guess."

"I'm sure that's not for lack of opportunity."

"I was engaged once. It didn't work out."

"Good that you discovered that before the wedding. Divorces are tough, especially on children."

"I can't have children. Actually, that's the reason we broke off the engagement. I had to have a hysterectomy due to a malignant tumor. The illness and the fact that I couldn't have children scared him so bad, he ran right into the arms of one of my friends."

"I'm sorry. I didn't mean to pry."

"You didn't. If I hadn't wanted to tell you that, I wouldn't have." In fact, she'd never told anyone she worked with, and she'd be hard pressed to figure out why she'd shared that part of her past with Alec. "I'm sure it worked out for the best," she said. "I absolutely love my job and I can't see how I'd ever work it into a marriage."

The waitress brought their food. Alec ate a few bites of his hamburger while she picked at her salad. "Marriage is strange," Alec said. "You think you know someone well enough to share your life with them, and then you find out you don't know them at all."

"Is that what happened between you and the children's mother?"

"That's probably an oversimplification of the problems we faced, but it boils down to that. Danielle blamed our problems on the fact that I wanted to be a lowly E.R. doctor instead of remaining in her father's very lucrative private practice. But it was more than my choice of medicine she rejected. It was me. She had social ambitions and loved going out all the time. I'm a boring workaholic."

"You may be a workaholic, but you're anything but boring. And you're a wonderful father. Still, you must have had to put up quite a fight to get custody of Cameron and Stacy."

"I was prepared to fight for them, but it never came to that. Danielle had never wanted a family."

"I can't imagine that you forced it on her."

Alec exhaled slowly, his lips drawn tight again. He leaned forward, propping his elbows on the table and staring into the black coffee in the bottom of his cup.

"In a way I guess I did. She got pregnant when I was in med school. She suggested an abortion. I insisted on marriage."

"But then you had Stacy."

"The second pregnancy wasn't Danielle's choice, either. She had to go off birth control pills for a while due to a medical problem, and the contraceptive method we were using failed. After Stacy's birth, Danielle had a tubal ligation—and hired a full-time nanny. But the marriage went downhill fast after that. Two years later she left me, and as soon as the divorce was final, she married an extremely prestigious and wealthy reconstructive surgeon in San Francisco."

Life played strange tricks. Janice had been devastated when she'd found out she could never have children. Danielle had them but didn't really want them. Surely she must love Cameron and Stacy in her own way. How could she not?

"You barely touched your salad," Alec said.

"I'm not hungry."

"Then let's get out of here."

"I'm sorry, Alec. You wanted to get away from problems and I just sat here and brought up a new set."

"They're with me whether you bring them up or not. I have to call Danielle and tell her about Stacy, even though I dread dealing with her at a time like this. But I really need her help with Cameron. I have so little time for him and I know this is hard on him, too."

The hot air slapped them in the face when they stepped from the air-conditioned bar back into the oppressive heat. But it was more than the temperature that seemed oppressive.

"I can get you a taxi," Alec said as they started

walking back to the hospital. "You may as well go back to the hotel and get some rest."

"I could stay in Cameron's room tonight. I mean, if you wanted me to."

"I couldn't ask you to do that."

"You didn't. I volunteered."

"Why? Why would you offer to do that when you could be sleeping in a nice comfortable hotel bed?"

She met his piercing gaze and felt a flush of heat wash through her. "It seems the least I can do."

Alec slid his hand to her shoulder and she felt his thumb on her neck, trailing a path from her earlobe to her shoulder and back up again. "You're a pretty phenomenal woman."

His touch surprised her, made her uneasy and excited at the same time. She took a deep breath and tried not to think of how much she'd like to slip into his arms. "I'm not phenomenal, Alec. I'm just here and doing what needs to be done."

"A typical CDC assignment?"

"No." She wouldn't lie. "Some things about this aren't so typical. I don't usually feel the kind of connection with doctors that I feel with you and your children. Maybe it's because we met in Seattle two years ago." Met. Kissed. Felt dejected when he hadn't called.

"I meant to call you after that."

"Don't worry about it. It wasn't that big a deal."

"I guess not. But for what it's worth, I'm really glad you're here now."

For a second she thought he might kiss her. Was afraid he would—even more afraid he wouldn't.

But he just stuffed his hands in his pockets and started walking towards the hospital. They were half a block away when his pager went off. "It's the E.R.," he said, grabbing his cell phone and punching in a number.

"What's up?" he asked, speaking into the phone.

She couldn't hear the answer but knew that whatever was up, it wouldn't be good. Hospitals never had good news at 10:00 p.m.

ALEC RUSHED toward the examining room where Darrell Kenton had just been admitted with a high fever, a persistent cough and chest pains.

A woman who was near hysteria almost flung herself at Alec as soon as he stepped through the door. "Why didn't they take us to the regular E.R.? And why are they making me wear a mask?"

"It's a routine procedure in this kind of case." He kept his voice calm, trying to assuage her fears. "How long has your husband been sick?"

"I don't know. I just got home tonight. The kids and I had gone to visit my mother in Portland. We walked in and found him like this, just sitting in his chair and struggling to get a breath. He didn't want to come in. I had to make him."

Alec put his stethoscope to the man's chest. He could hear the familiar rattle in the lungs. If it was the same virus that Milton and Butch had died with, it was already in the latter stages. Still, it could just be run-of-the-mill bacterial pneumonia.

Alec stood back as the patient fell into a coughing spasm, then had him try to take a few deep breaths. "Have you been getting regular checkups?"

Darrell Kenton nodded. "I try to stay well. I've got a family to support."

"What about the flu shot? The pneumonia vaccine?"

"He had both of those," his wife said, "but it was last fall."

"You're sure he got the pneumonia vaccine?"

"I'm sure. He's a taxi driver, exposed to everything. His doctor said he should get it."

"The doctor was right." Alec felt the man's neck for possible glandular swelling. "Do you know a taxi driver named Butch Cass?"

"I know him. Talked to him just the other day down at Maxie's Bar. Me and a friend was having a beer and he come in. Looked like crap and was coughing every breath. I probably caught this crud from him."

Alec experienced a stronger wave of apprehension. If Darrell Kenton had contracted this from

Butch, then the virus had moved beyond its initial carrier source.

Things would start to snowball fast. Men. Women. Children. Even babies would start pouring through the doors, all infected with a virus that destroyed the lungs in a matter of days. And the hospital didn't have one treatment that would stop it or slow it down.

He thought of Stacy. His own daughter's life was at risk. And Cameron, who so far was asymptomatic. Somehow the adrenaline kept pumping enough for Alec to complete the examination and get Darrell Kenton admitted to the isolation ward.

His wife settled down once she realized her husband was being admitted to the hospital. But then, she didn't know that the only weapon the doctors had to fight the killer was loaded with blanks.

Darrell Kenton died two hours later.

ALEC CLIMBED from the sofa in Stacy's room after two hours of restless sleep. He padded across the floor in his stocking feet to check on his daughter. She was sleeping soundly, her breathing steady. And the fever was still low-grade. So far, so good. He wouldn't let himself think beyond that, though the fear was still inside him, like a clamp tightened around his gut.

He slipped into his shoes, pulled on his shirt and stepped into the hall. The isolation ward seemed relatively quiet. A good sign. He walked the few yards to Cameron's room and tiptoed in, not wanting to wake either him or Janice.

Cameron was sleeping soundly, lying on his stomach, his arms and legs sprawled across the hospital bed. He'd been a trouper, not complaining at all and asking constantly about his little sister. Alec had tried to reassure him that Stacy would be fine, but he wasn't certain he'd been convincing. Cameron was a very savvy kid for seven.

Alec's gaze traveled to Janice. She was on her side, facing Cameron, her short brown hair falling into her face. He still had trouble believing she was thirty-three. Right now, she could pass for ten years younger.

He thought of the way her eyes had looked tonight when they'd stood on the sidewalk outside the restaurant. Misty and studying him as if she could see all the hurt and insecurities inside him and still thought he was great.

He'd ached to hold her close and kiss her the way he had back in Seattle. Strange that he remembered that kiss so well after two years. But it had reached inside him and heated places that had been left cold and numb in the face of Danielle's rejection.

Maybe, if things had been different...

Quietly he eased out of the room. The past was past, and the present was more than enough to deal with. He and the other doctors who formed the newly established V-Team had to work harder, had to find some combination of drugs and treatment that would stop the progress of the disease. He would *not* let Stacy die.

Alec headed for the nurses' station, where he poured himself a cup of strong, dark coffee. Since he couldn't sleep, he might as well go back to his research, combing through everything he could find on viral infections, drug research and past epidemics such as the recent SARS outbreak.

"I'll be in my office if you need me," he said to the young nurse who passed him in the hall.

"You can't go without sleep forever,"

"I don't have forever."

"You're right. I'll keep a close eye on Stacy. She's going to make it, Dr. Giroux. Some of the patients might not, but she will."

"I'm not giving up on any of them yet." But then he hadn't given up on Butch, either, or Darrell Kenton. That hadn't kept them from dying.

IT WAS MIDAFTERNOON when the FedEx package was delivered to Janice at the hospital. She started to tear it open, but couldn't bring herself to face the news by herself. Alec wasn't in the E.R. isolation ward, so she went looking for him.

He'd been the first doctor to realize they were dealing with a new and deadly virus, and his alert observations and quick action could be the factor that kept this from developing into a full-fledged epidemic. And now his own daughter was fighting the disease.

Good or bad, the news belonged to him first.

CHAPTER SIX

ALEC PROPPED his backside against the desk in his makeshift office just off the new isolation E.R. and scanned the first page of the report, praying for good news, finding about what he'd expected.

> A mutant, virulent form of microoganism that attacks the tissues of the lungs is causing a very contagious form of pneumonia. An illness similar to this has been reported in a couple of isolated jungle areas in South America, but the CDC has no actual data or test results from the alleged outbreaks. The virus is most likely airborne, and patients should be considered contagious from the time symptoms begin.
>
> There is no known cure.

"No known cure," he said, passing the full report to Janice without bothering to read the rest. "So what does the CDC suggest we do? Bring in a fiddler? Serve tea and cookies?"

She scanned the report. "They've provided some guidelines."

"Oh, great. More rules and guidelines. Won't that be helpful? So what do they have to say?"

"They haven't declared this an epidemic yet, but they emphasize the necessity of using the local media to alert the citizens of Courage Bay so that they can react quickly to the first sign of symptoms. And of course they recommend continued isolation of every patient who could possibly be infected with the disease."

"We can't handle many more patients than we have right now."

"If we don't have room for them here, we'll have to open a temporary facility or enlist neighboring hospitals. Hopefully it won't come to that. The scientists at CDC are working on this around the clock."

"Then they'll just have to work harder. There's only one thing I need from the CDC, and that's not a bunch of rules or guidelines or definitions of an epidemic. Have them find me a drug that works, Janice. Find me a miracle, and do it fast."

Alec's pager went off. He read the message then punched in a number on his cell phone. "Not another patient," he said into the phone when the admitting nurse for E.R. answered. "Please tell me this is not another coughing, fevered patient."

"No. It's a woman with an attitude who's demanding to see you. She says she's your ex-wife."

Exactly what he needed to drive him completely over the edge.

"What do I do with her?" the nurse asked.

"Wave a magic wand and see if she'll disappear. If that doesn't work, send her back here."

JANICE WATCHED as Alec dropped to the chair behind his desk. "Danielle has arrived at the hospital," he announced. "That, along with your report, just about makes my day."

"I'll get out and leave you two alone."

"I would if I were you. Actually, I'd do the same if I had a choice."

But Janice didn't get a chance to leave before Danielle stormed through the door.

"How could you have let this happen, Alec? How could you have let our children be exposed to some dreadful disease that no one even has a name for?"

"You know me. I'm just an irresponsible jerk."

"Well, you certainly can't call your actions in this situation responsible. I tried to see Stacy and they said I'd have to wear a mask, gloves and gown just to go into her room."

"You will, and I don't want her upset, so don't go in there carrying on like you are right now."

"I guess you'd like it better if I didn't see her at all."

"If I felt that way, I wouldn't have called you."

"Exactly how serious is this virus?"

"It's very serious, Danielle. We now have seven confirmed cases in the hospital, and none are responding to treatment."

"Well, you better find some treatment Stacy responds to, Alec." She put her hand over her mouth and started sniffing. "You better not let my baby die."

"I don't plan to."

"When this is over, we're going to have to talk about custody arrangements. If you can't take care of our children any better than this, I'll take them and hire someone who can."

"Do you want to see Stacy or not, Danielle? If you do, you'll wear the protective gear. If you don't, then get out of my office."

"You can't talk to me like that."

"I'm not going to stand here and argue with you about custody arrangements when our daughter is fighting for her life."

"Well, of course I want to see her."

"Then I'll go up to the isolation ward with you and make certain you don't upset her." He looked at Janice and rolled his eyes. "Stick around if you can. I'll be back in a few minutes, and I'll try to discuss the report more calmly."

"I'll wait."

Janice was more impressed than ever as Alec left his

office with his ex-wife. The woman had hurled accusations at him from the moment she'd stepped into the room and he had refrained from pointing out to her that she was the one who'd exposed Stacy and Cameron to the disease when she'd dropped them off at the emergency room instead of waiting for him at home.

A light tap sounded at the door and Janice turned. She walked over and opened it. She'd didn't recognize the woman standing there in the white doctor's coat, but something about her looked familiar.

"I'm looking for Alec," she said.

"He just stepped out for a minute."

"Then I'll wait. I don't believe we've met, but I'm Natalie Giroux, Alec's sister."

Natalie, the burn specialist and third Giroux on staff at Courage Bay Hospital. Janice had heard about her from both Guy and Alec but hadn't met her since she'd been out of town ever since Janice had arrived in Courage Bay.

"I'm Janice Reed, from the Center for Disease Control in Atlanta," she said, extending her hand.

"Alec's told me all about you." Natalie gave Janice's hand a warm squeeze instead of a shake. "He says you're a cross between Florence Nightingale and a superheroine."

Janice turned away, hoping to hide the blush that burned her cheeks. "I don't feel much like a superheroine around Alec. He works circles around me."

"He's a workaholic. It's a family trait. Is he with a patient now?"

"He's upstairs with Stacy and her mother."

"Really? Danielle actually showed up. That surprises me. I thought she'd stay as far away from the virus as she could. Was she raging or whining?"

"Both, but she does have quite a temper."

"It goes with her generally vile disposition. Do you have some coffee around? I came straight from the airport to the hospital, and I need a shot of caffeine to keep me going."

Janice excused herself to retrieve two cups of coffee from the pot in the makeshift conference room down the hall.

"Was it a long flight?" she asked when she returned, handing one cup to Natalie.

"London to L.A., then the drive into Courage Bay. I wanted to come back to the hospital as soon as I heard of the outbreak, but I was taking part in an important burn conference. Still, I came as soon as I heard Stacy had come down with it. I am so crazy about those kids."

"I can see why. It's hard to imagine that Danielle just walked away from them."

"They're probably better off that she's not in their lives too much, but they had a tough year adjusting to her being gone. It nearly killed Alec."

"He must have been very much in love with her."

"You'll have to ask him about that. What killed

him was seeing what his kids went though. Left the guy so gun-shy, he's hardly dated since then."

"Maybe he hasn't met the right woman."

"Not much chance of meeting the right woman if you never let one get close to you. But don't get me started on that. I'm sure you're not interested in the Giroux family saga."

Actually she was, Janice thought, but probably shouldn't be.

"Your work must be fascinating," Natalie said, "and probably every bit as time-consuming and demanding as mine."

"It is, but I love it."

"So what's the latest on this virus we're dealing with. Has it been given a name?"

"Nothing official. The CDC is referring to it as the Courage Bay Virus, but the doctors here just call it the virus."

Janice brought Natalie up to date about the progress of patients affected with the new virus and the findings of the CDC, but all the while they spoke, Janice couldn't shake Natalie's words about Alec from her mind.

He'd never let a woman get close to him, yet she'd felt close that night when they'd kissed. And even closer last night when they'd shared very personal info with each other, and later, when he'd taken her hands and looked into her eyes.

Not that it mattered. She had no room in her life for a relationship. So, what was it with her? Why did this one man get to her when no one else did? Maybe it was as simple as the fact that she knew she was safe with him. He lived too far away to become entangled in her life. Or maybe it was the challenge of a man who backed off faster than she did.

She was still considering all this when Alec strode through the door a few minutes later, looking as if he were ready to bang his head, or someone else's, against a wall. He brightened a little when he spotted Natalie.

"Welcome back to Courage Bay, the beautiful city by the sea," he said, giving her a warm hug. "Just don't breathe the air."

Janice left them alone. Alec needed some time with his sister, and there would be plenty of opportunity to discuss the report later that night.

She took the elevator to the fourth floor and passed Danielle, who was already striding away from her daughter's room. Afraid that Stacy might be upset, Janice put on a gown and mask to look in on the little girl.

Stacy smiled at her and started telling her about her mother's visit. But she looked tired, and her face seemed more flushed than it had the last time Janice had stopped in.

"How do you feel, little princess?"

"My stomach hurts and my throat..." The last word was cut off by a coughing spasm. But it was Janice who couldn't breathe. She took Stacy's temperature, then used the phone by the bed to call Alec.

"I think you should come to Stacy's room, Alec. And hurry."

ALEC DEALT with medical emergencies every day. He knew the fragility of life, the heartbreak of fighting to keep someone in this world only to lose them. But he had never felt so desperate as he did at this minute.

He'd held on to his composure in front of Stacy, but he was back in his office now and he couldn't keep up the charade. He wanted to scream, to punch his fist through the damned gray-green walls of this room, to lash out at Milton Muxworthy for bringing this fatal virus into Courage Bay—into his life.

He wanted to cry, just break down like he had when he was a kid and his dog Shep had been hit by a car and died right there in the street, his head cradled in Alec's lap.

But the tears wouldn't come. They were locked inside him, trapped by so much hurt and fear that he didn't see how he could possibly keep functioning. He paced the room, then collapsed into his chair and buried his face in his hands.

He heard the door open, but didn't look up, not until he heard Janice's voice.

"Are you okay?"

"No. I'm not anywhere near okay."

"Want to talk, or would you rather be alone?"

He didn't want to talk, but surprisingly, he didn't want to be alone, either. "Have you ever loved someone so much that you don't know how you can go on without them?"

"No."

"It happens when you have kids. You worry before they're born. You wonder if you'll connect with them the way people say you should. Then you hold them in your arms, and in a heartbeat they become the most important thing in your life."

"Stacy and Cameron are lucky to have a father who feels that way about them."

"I can't let her die, Janice."

"You're doing everything you can, Alec."

"I have to do more. I have to find a way to save her." His voice broke on the words, and the tears he'd searched for earlier burned at the back of his eyes.

Janice crossed the room, and without really thinking, he opened his arms and she stepped into them. He held on tight and buried his face in her hair as bitter tears squeezed past his closed lids. He didn't know how they'd gotten to this point, why, when he hurt more than he'd ever hurt in his life, he was standing here in the arms of a woman who was practically a stranger. All he knew was that it was the only thing in his life that felt remotely right.

But even as he held her, drowning in his fear and grief, he started putting together a new plan of action. When he pulled away, he saw that Janice's eyes were shiny with tears, and for the first time since she'd arrived, he heard desperation in her voice. "What do we do, Alec?"

"We pray—and we find a new drug to try."

"The V-Team has tried everything available."

"Everything available in the U.S.," Alec answered. "But I was reading an article this morning about a new drug that's been tried in Spain over the past twelve months. They've had remarkable success using it to fight stubborn viral respiratory infections. It hasn't been approved yet in the U.S., but it will be eventually."

"If it hasn't been approved, we can't get it."

"Not legally."

"You can't obtain and use black market drugs. They're dangerous. And you'll lose your license for bringing them into the country."

"Damn my license. I'm talking about Stacy's life, and if there's anything out there that has a chance of saving her, I'll find a way to get it."

"What's the name of the drug?"

"Cybalexvir. Call your co-workers back in Atlanta, Janice. See what they know about it."

"No matter what they know, they're not going to say it's safe to use if the FDA hasn't approved it."

"Just ask. And I'll make some more phone calls,

as well. I have physician friends in western Europe and I met a brilliant researcher at a medical conference in Madrid last winter."

"Can't you try another combination of antiviral drugs? What about acytlovir?"

"You're stalling, Janice. You know I'll keep working with what I have, but I need more. You said when you came here that you were prepared to offer the full backing of the CDC in getting this virus under control. Don't let me down now."

"I was talking anything short of illegal, Alec."

"I'm talking desperation. And I'm counting on you."

Alec started flipping through his Rolodex, searching for phone numbers. He found one for the researcher in Madrid.

Janice turned and walked away without speaking. He knew what he was asking of her. She'd lose her job if she helped him obtain illegal drugs for use in the hospital. But he'd also call in favors from the devil— sell his soul in a heartbeat—if it would save Stacy.

Only it wasn't the devil he needed. It was a miracle.

"ARE YOU ASLEEP?"

"No, Cameron. I'm right here." Janice jumped to her feet and scurried to the little boy's bedside, straining to see the hands on her watch in the dim glow of moonlight that filtered through the cotton curtains. Three-ten.

"Are you feeling all right?" she asked, her hand

shaking as she put it to his brow. But his forehead was cool.

"I feel okay, but I'm worried about Stacy."

"She's just down the hall, in her own room."

"Why can't I go see her?"

"She's sick and she doesn't feel like playing yet."

"I won't bother her."

"I know you wouldn't, Cameron, and she'd love to see you. Maybe in a day or two." It was all Janice could do to push the words out of her throat.

"When we get out of the hospital, will you still be our friend?"

The question was painfully direct, and one she'd tried not to think about since leaving Alec's office this afternoon. No matter what happened to Stacy, no matter what it took to get the virus under control, when Janice left here, she'd be leaving for good.

The things that bound her to Alec were tied to the situation. And even if the closeness they felt went much deeper, it wouldn't be enough to overcome the odds against them. Their jobs were in different parts of the country. He was a family man. She was nowhere near ready to settle down. She would never have children of her own and would have a devil of a time sharing Stacy and Cameron with a selfish, arrogant woman like Danielle.

Not that she could explain any of that to Cameron. "We can write each other and send e-mails."

"That's not the same. You have to be here."

"No. You're right. It's not the same at all."

"So why can't you stay in Courage Bay? It's a nice place."

"My job and my apartment are in Atlanta."'

"You can get a job at this hospital. My dad can get you one. And then you can come see us all the time. You can even come to my soccer games."

"That would be fun. Maybe I'll just fly out one day and show up at a soccer game and surprise you."

"That's cool!"

They talked a while more, about swimming and school and soccer. Finally, Cameron closed his eyes and fell asleep again.

But now Janice was wide awake. With cybalexvir on her mind. She'd called the lab in Atlanta to see what info was available. The drug had proved very effective in Spain and also in Italy, with limited side effects. The problem was there had been no conclusive studies as to its long-term effects.

It was going to be tested in the United States starting in September in a very controlled setting. Samples of the drug were stored in the Atlanta lab, but Janice did not have the authority to authorize its release to the Courage Bay Hospital.

It was possible to secure a release, but that involved going through so many different departments, and dealing with bureaucracy always took time. Time that Stacy might not have.

If Janice managed to get one of the research technicians to send her the drug without proper clearance and anyone ever found out, she'd lose her job and her reputation, and so would the technician. If the treatment produced any negative side effects, she could be prosecuted and sent to prison.

She'd do anything to help Alec save Stacy—anything short of this. He'd have to find another way.

THEY GAINED six more patients over the next two days and lost three to septic shock and total respiratory failure. News of the deaths was the lead-in for every local news broadcast and the headline story in the local paper. Coverage had also extended to the major network news shows.

Alec had relinquished his official duties so that he could spend all his time with his daughter, whose condition was deteriorating in spite of everything he and the rest of the V-Team could do to save her.

He'd been unable to get his hands on any cybalexvir, but Janice knew he was still searching for an illegal supply. He'd also called the highest authorities at CDC at least ten times already today, demanding to know why they hadn't granted permission to use the drug on an emergency basis in Courage Bay. They'd promised him and Janice an answer by the end of the week. But the end of the week could be too late for Stacy.

Janice put on her gown, mask and gloves and stopped by Stacy's room. It was four in the afternoon, and she was sleeping in Alec's arms. Her breathing was labored, her tiny chest rising and falling slowly. Blond tendrils clung damply to her flushed face.

Alec looked up and met Janice's gaze, and she felt his pain sear into her, squeezing her heart until she felt it might burst into jagged pieces.

"I'm going to lose her," Alec murmured, heartbreak shattering his voice. "I've done everything I can, and I'm going to lose her."

Janice walked across the room and put her hands on Alec's drooping shoulders. "You can't give up, Alec. You can't."

"Get me the drug, Janice. Please. Give Stacy a chance."

She swallowed hard, her heart feeling as if it were dissolving inside her. Before she'd come to Courage Bay, everything about her job had been black and white. Now it was all a dingy, bleak gray. Before, her job had been all-important. Now nothing seemed to matter more than a tiny girl and how much her father loved her.

She bent and kissed Stacy's cheek, then tiptoed to the door of the room, the decision she'd never dreamed she would make already a done deal in her mind. "I'll have some cybalexvir flown in by courier, Alec. It should be here in a matter of hours."

Alec tucked Stacy back in her bed, then crossed the room and took both of Janice's hands in his. "I don't know how I'll ever thank you."

"No problem there. I expect to see you in prison every visiting day."

CHAPTER SEVEN

THE CYBALEXVIR arrived at Courage Bay Hospital five hours later, and Alec started Stacy on the drug at once. There was little change in her condition for the first few hours after her initial injection, and the entire hospital staff, unaware of what Alec had done, seemed to be collectively holding their breath and praying for the little girl whose life was slipping away.

But by the next morning, the apprehension had begun to shift to cautious optimism.

So far, no one but Janice and Alec knew the reason for the dramatic improvement in Stacy's condition. All the staff knew was that Stacy was the first victim of the virus to sink that low and then show signs of improvement. Most attributed the reversal to Alec's dedicated search to find a combination of drugs that worked. Others just attributed it to answered prayer.

Janice knew it was both—and the cybalexvir.

She ducked into Alec's office in an attempt to get a grip on her emotions before she made a call to her supervisor at CDC to tell him what she'd done. It would likely mean her job and possibly prosecution, but she wouldn't lie about it. She couldn't, really, not when she needed to stress to them the importance of giving Courage Bay Hospital approval to use the life-saving drug on the other patients who were facing almost certain death without it.

A week ago, losing her job would have been the end of the world. A week from now, it might seem that way again. But right now, she was erupting with what had to be the purest form of joy she'd ever experienced.

She had the phone in her hand when Alec walked through the door. "She's going to make it, Janice. She's going to walk out of this hospital alive." His voice cracked on the last word. "I owe it all to you."

"I'm pretty terrific, huh?" she teased in an effort to keep the moment light enough that she wouldn't dissolve into tears again.

"You're *very* terrific."

He walked toward her, smiling, the same gorgeous, confident doctor who'd sent her pulse racing two years ago. It was racing again, only this time the feelings went deeper than a sizzling awareness. She'd seen him at his best and at his worst. And there hadn't been one part of him that hadn't touched her to the core.

He opened his arms and she stepped inside them.

"I know the risk you took in getting the cybalexvir," he said when he finally her go.

"It was worth it. Whatever it costs me, it was worth it."

"We're in this together, Janice. If you go down, I'll go down with you. Guess we can always pool our resources and go live in a shanty on a Mexican beach."

Funny, but that didn't sound half-bad.

"I was about to call my supervisor at the CDC and confess my sins."

"I need to talk to you about that."

"I can't be less than honest with them, Alec."

"I'd never suggest that. I just wanted to let you know that I also have to tell the hospital chief of staff what I've done, and that the drug was effective with Stacy. I'm hoping Callie can give your request added clout and that the FDA will allow the CDC to release the drug to us based on its foreign testing and the fact that it's now been proven effective on this particular strain of viral pneumonia."

Janice breathed a sigh of relief, knowing that Alec felt the same way about total honesty as she did.

"And one more thing…"

"What's that?"

"You're one hell of a CDC Specialist."

He leaned over and kissed her. The quick burst of passion caught her by complete surprise and left her hungry for more as he darted from the room. Off to save the world, one patient at a time.

"THEY'RE HERE," Cameron shouted, rushing from the window where he'd been keeping watch. He jumped onto the stool at the kitchen counter and stuck a finger into the peanut butter fudge frosting Janice was piling on the homemade chocolate cake.

She washed and dried her hands, then made a quick survey of the dining room table. All set with balloons, party favors and Stacy's favorite doll, ready for the welcome-home celebration.

It was one week since Stacy had been given her first dose of the drug that had saved her life and turned a deadly virus into a manageable illness. There had been two deaths since then, Di Di and the E.R. nurse. Their conditions had become critical before Courage Bay Hospital was given approval to administer the drug to patients testing positive for the virus.

Another twenty-four hours and Stacy would have reached that stage, too. Janice still got shaky when she thought of how close they'd come to losing her, and she was certain Alec felt the same, though you'd never know it. He was back on top of things, working full speed in spite of the heat wave that showed no signs of letting up.

Just like the heat wave building inside Janice. She no longer tried to deny that her feelings for Alec were more than just a passing attraction. She cared for him a lot, was probably falling in love with him if she wasn't already there, but that didn't change anything.

Even if he felt the same for her, the relationship would never work. It had too many strikes against it. Besides, except for the quick kiss in his office the other day, he'd shown no signs of falling for her.

But she wouldn't let that bring her down. Not tonight. This was Stacy's moment, and she deserved it to be perfect.

"Hey, look—presents," Stacy sang out as Alec carried her through the front door and into the dining room. Her big, blue eyes widened. "Is it somebody's birthday?"

"It's your welcome-home party," Alec said, letting her down to stand. "And that's way better than a birthday."

"You're never gonna guess what I got you," Cameron said. "But it's something you're gonna love. Janice and I picked it out."

Stacy ran to the chair with the balloons and picked up her doll. "I missed you, Amanda. I didn't like the hospital. Except for the ice cream. And Daddy said I was as brave as Captain Pierre Giroux."

"Even braver," Alec said. "Because he was a man when he faced his fierce storm, and you were just a little girl when you faced the fierce virus."

"What about me?" Cameron asked. "Was I brave for staying in the hospital, Daddy?"

"The bravest seven-year-old boy I've ever seen."

Alec put his arms around both of them, his face

beaming, and Janice blinked like crazy to hold back tears that she couldn't begin to explain.

"IT WAS THE PERFECT party," Alec said, once the children were settled for the night. "And that cake—wow."

"I bet you thought all CDC Specialists could cook was test-tube soup over a burner."

"Not me. I never underestimate you. So, what's the latest on the job situation?"

"I'm officially reinstated, though I'm on what amounts to probation. Break one more rule and I'm out the door for good."

"They should be praising you for saving lives."

"It doesn't matter. I'd do it all over again if it came to that."

"Yeah, so tell me, what's life like for a risk taker back in Atlanta? What do you do for fun?"

"Ride my Harley."

He groaned. "Don't tell me that. Do you know how many crash victims I see every year in Emergency?"

"Okay, I won't tell you. I also love rock climbing and scuba diving, though I don't do either of those in Atlanta. And I adore sailing and rowing and play a mean game of tennis."

"Sounds like you stay busy. When will you be going back?"

"Tomorrow afternoon."

"So soon?"

"I've been here almost two weeks."

"I just didn't think you'd be leaving that soon."

"Can you think of a reason I should stay?"

"I guess not." He closed the dishwasher, then leaned back against the counter, finally letting his gaze lock with hers. "I don't know how I can ever thank you for all you've done."

"Invite me to a soccer game sometime."

"Anytime at all." He looked as if he wanted to say more, but he just hooked his thumbs inside the corners of his front pockets and studied the tips of his shoes. "Let's go for a swim."

"Tonight?"

"Why not? It's early yet. The kids are both down for the count."

"I don't have a bathing suit."

"A risk taker like you shouldn't mind skinny-dipping."

"I could handle it, but I'm not sure about you."

"Didn't know you knew me that well. But Natalie usually leaves a suit or two over here. I'll look in the guest room and get one of hers for you."

So she'd be saying her final goodbyes with wet hair and clad in an ill-fitting bathing suit. She was certain Moon Mist had not snared Captain Pierre Giroux like that.

Now where had that thought come from? No way was she out to capture Dr. Alec Giroux.

ALEC CHANGED into his bathing suit upstairs, but he didn't wait for Janice. He just tossed her Natalie's swimsuit and headed to the pool, diving in and going straight into laps.

What was wrong with him? His life was perfect again. He should be feeling terrific, not agonizing as if someone were about to amputate his right arm.

Sure, he'd miss Janice, but he'd never expected her to be here forever. Her work was in Atlanta. Hell, he'd led the hospital and the State Emergency Medicine Association in an aggressive campaign to make certain she was reinstated.

The kids were already becoming far too attached to Janice. It was good that she was leaving. Better for all of them. He kept swimming, pushing himself to the limit, waiting for the numbness that total exhaustion brought to both mind and body.

It didn't happen. He finally swam to the edge of the pool and stood on the bottom in chest deep water while he caught his breath. But when he looked up, he lost it again.

Janice was standing there in the black bathing suit, looking so damn hot that his willpower turned to melted slush.

"You do nice things for a bathing suit," he said,

thinking even Cameron would have come up with something cooler to say.

"It doesn't quite fit." She tugged on the bottom, pulling it down so that the fabric covered the enticing curves of her smooth, firm buttocks.

Alec tried to concentrate as she climbed down the ladder. Tried to remember why it was good that she was leaving as she lowered her svelte body into the water. Worked to control the crazy hunger that was devouring him as he wrapped his arms around her and pulled her close.

But then her body pressed against his, and when she captured his lips with hers, all he could do was kiss her back and become totally lost in the thrill of it.

JANICE FELT as if she were swirling in a dream as Alec kissed her senseless, over and over again, his tongue inside her mouth, his hands tangling in her hair, then roaming her back and settling on her behind. He pulled her against him so that she felt the hard length of him, and suddenly the dream hit the fringes of reality.

When he fit his hands under the straps of the black suit and started to lower them over her shoulders, she caught his fingers with hers. "We can't do this, Alec. Not here. Suppose one of the children peers out their bedroom window."

"They're sound asleep."

"But what if they wake up?"

"Then come with me." He crawled out of the pool and grabbed the worn quilt that Cameron had used to turn the metal patio table into an enclosed fort. He threw the quilt over his shoulder and reached for her hand, tugging her along behind him to the grassy area behind the garage.

The only light was the glow of the stars and the moon. No refreshing pool water caressing her body. No cooling breeze. Just the stillness of a torrid summer night and a desire that ran so hot inside her she could barely breathe.

Alec spread the quilt, then peeled off his wet suit. She stood in silence, watching, mesmerized by the perfection of his hard, muscled body.

"We don't want to get the quilt wet," he said, fitting his fingers once again beneath the straps of her bathing suit. This time he tugged them down until her breasts were exposed. He brushed her erect nipples with the tips of his thumbs, then stooped and sucked each one, while she ran the flat of her hands over the smooth flesh of his back.

Impatient with the wet fabric between them, she took his hands and helped him slide the bathing suit over her hips and down her legs. Tossing it aside, Alec fell to the quilt and pulled her down beside him. He kissed her lips, her face, the curve of her neck, the swell of her breasts, slowly nibbling his way down to the silky curls at the apex of her thighs.

She was ready for him, wet with desire, hot with a wanton hunger that seemed to come from somewhere deep in her very soul. They didn't talk at all, not until he dipped his fingers inside her and released a rush of sensation that made her moan with pleasure.

"I want you, Alec. I want you more than I've ever wanted any man before."

"Janice, my sweet, sexy superheroine."

"I'm not a superheroine, Alec. I'm just a woman." And then she reached for him, felt the surge of desire coursing through his taut flesh and knew he wanted her the same way she wanted him.

He entered her on a wave of passion that didn't stop until they'd both climaxed. It was over too soon. She couldn't let go of him, not yet. So she clung to him in the moonlight, their bodies slick with their lovemaking, her heart still pounding wildly in her chest.

They stayed that way for what might have been minutes or hours, locked in each other's arms until Alec fell asleep. Janice eased herself from him and slipped back into the bathing suit. She'd change, check on the kids, then let herself out. But she stopped one last time before she rounded the garage.

She stood there for long minutes, staring at the gorgeous and dedicated Dr. Alec Giroux, naked, on a quilt under the stars. It was a memory that would live with her forever.

"YOU ARE absolutely nuts, Janice."

One thing you could count on with Martha was blunt honesty, Janice thought, holding the phone slightly away from her ear.

"No, I'm smart, Martha," she replied. "Too smart to read something into a single act of lovemaking."

"It's more than that and you know it. Alec Giroux has been every other word out of your mouth since you've been in Courage Bay."

"He's a very competent doctor."

"Like that's what turned you on last night?"

"It's part of it."

"So what's the rest of it?"

"It doesn't matter. The guy's scared of commitment. Even his sister said so. And he's certainly never asked me to stay around."

"So, give the guy a push."

"What about my job?"

"You're a nurse. They have a hospital in Courage Bay, and you already have an in there."

"It's not that simple."

"Nothing worthwhile is. If you want the guy, go for it. Take a risk with your heart for a change instead of pushing your body to the limit."

"And if he says *no thanks*?"

"Then what have you lost?"

"I knew I shouldn't have told you anything about this."

"Hello! You hardly needed to tell me, when he and his kids are all you talk about."

"That's the other thing. Suppose it does work out between us. How do I know I'll be a decent mother?"

"Why wouldn't you be? Sounds as if they're already crazy about you, and you're definitely crazy about them. Admit it, Janice. You're mad about the guy and his kids and it scares you to death. You are just one big coward."

"He thinks I'm a superheroine."

"Then go prove that you are. Take a chance on love."

"What if he doesn't want to take a chance?"

"Some men just need a push to take the plunge. You'll never know until you put him to the test."

"Nice girls don't push."

"So be naughty for once. You might like it."

"Gotta go, Martha. I have a plane to catch."

Janice hung up, then grabbed her luggage and headed for her rental car. Time to go back to Atlanta. Back to her own life.

But it had been some fierce heat wave she'd experienced over the past two weeks. And not just the weather.

CHAPTER EIGHT

ALEC HAD THE CAR'S air conditioner pumping full force as he made the drive from Courage Bay Hospital to his house. It had been another hectic day in the E.R. Lots of heat-related problems, a kid with a broken arm, one mild heart attack, a sprained neck from a fender bender and two new cases of the virus that had turned his world upside down and kicked it around like a football just days ago.

But only two cases was a good sign. Although the virus was highly contagious, so many people who had been exposed hadn't developed symptoms, including himself. It would take more testing to figure out exactly why that was, but apparently certain people had an acquired immunity to the virus.

Even with so much to keep him busy, Janice had haunted his mind from the time he'd gotten up this morning. He missed passing her in the halls of the hospital, missed having coffee with her, missed hearing her voice as she spoke with the nurses and patients. Missed the smell of her perfume and her terrific smile.

And now he'd go home and think of making love to her on the quilt in his backyard last night, and he'd miss the taste of her and the feel of her and the sound of her voice when she'd whispered his name in the heat of passion.

He'd have expected his body to grow hard at the thought, but all he felt was a hollow ache in his chest, as if it had swallowed up his heart and left nothing but a vacuum in its place.

But letting her go without saying how he felt was the right thing to do. Sure he'd miss her for a while, but he'd get over it in time. And missing her now was far better than letting Stacy and Cameron grow to love her. He couldn't risk putting them through the kind of heartbreak they'd experienced when their mother had walked out on them.

But when he turned the corner onto Summerside Drive and saw Janice's rental car parked in his driveway, his resolve took a serious nosedive.

The house was empty when he walked in, but he could hear laughter and squeals coming from the backyard. He stepped outside just in time to see Cameron toss a brightly colored ball through the floating hoop in the middle of the pool.

"Point for my team," he yelled as he splashed the water with the palms of his hands.

Alec looked past Cameron to Stacy, who was swimming toward the ball. And to Janice, who'd spotted him and was making her way to the side of the pool, staring up at him with only a hint of a smile on her lips.

Janice, in the same black bathing suit she'd worn last night. Looking seductive and innocent at the same time. He walked to the edge of the pool, nervous, confused, and for some reason having difficulty making his feet move.

"I thought you were leaving this afternoon."

"I changed my mind," she said quietly.

"Why is that?"

"I decided to give you a chance to take the plunge, Alec."

"I don't know what you mean."

"I know you're gun-shy of commitment. I know Danielle did a number on you and on the children. But look at me, Alec. I'm not Danielle. I'm Janice Reed, a woman who is crazy about you and your children. I'd like to stay around and see if we can make this work, but not unless you're ready to let go of the past and give us a chance."

"A chance to lose."

"Or a chance to win."

He stood there in the hot sun, feeling the rays burning his back through his shirt, listening to the laughter of his kids, thinking of all he had to lose. And of all he had to gain.

Janice. Who'd risked losing her job and facing a jail sentence to save his daughter. Who'd stood at his side without faltering through the worst hours of his life. Who smelled of springtime and kissed with passion.

"Your call, doc. Take the plunge, or tell me you're not going to and I'll walk away right now and catch the red-eye back to Atlanta."

Take the plunge or lose her forever.

So he did what any man with half a brain would do. He took the plunge—jumped right into the pool with her, clothes and all.

"Happy now?" he asked, taking her in his arms as both the kids raced over to them.

"Extremely, Dr. Alec Giroux."

And so was he. A man couldn't ask for more than that.

WARNING SIGNS
Kay David

CHAPTER ONE

BUTTER PICKED his own path toward the beach.

The buckskin gelding had made the trip so many times that he knew the way better than the man he carried. Nickering softly in the gathering dusk of the Friday evening, the horse quickly cleared the dunes and headed for the water, gaining speed as his footing became more secure. Sitting astride Butter, Robert Kellison tightened his knees without thinking, his response to the animal's canter automatic.

As usual, the beach crowd had thinned with the setting sun. During the day, when the area was packed, a full-time Courage Bay officer patrolled, but Kell and Butter had handled the evening and weekend shift for five years.

Kell was swamped, keeping up with his horse ranch and boarding stable, Whispering Dawn, but he'd never give up the beach patrol. The peace and calm of the shore was better than any kind of therapy. Almost everything in his life that was complicated and messy dissolved in the spray of the waves. The cool evening breezes blew away what remained, and once again, Kell would find himself a sane man. Courage Bay was the only place in the world that brought him that kind of serenity.

Unfortunately, everyone else loved Southern California, too. Spotting a couple ahead of him, tangled in the sand, Kell shook his head. He routinely found a pair of lovers, usually just teenagers, on the water's edge. He hated to run them off, but city council had recently laid down the law. No more public displays of affection on the beach. Courage Bay was a family place.

Butter trotted a few more paces, then Kell pulled the horse up short. Despite the council's decree, Kell's policy was one of subtlety; he generally came close enough for the kids to hear him, then he'd head down the beach in the other direction. By the time he came back, nine times out of ten they had dressed and departed.

Tonight would likely be no exception, yet Kell found himself hesitating. An apricot glow, tinged with lavender and scarlet, hovered over the sand and water, making it hard to see. Narrowing his eyes, he stared through the gloom. The profile of the bodies didn't look right, and for a single, fleeting second, Kell thought he saw something he couldn't possibly be seeing.

Something that didn't exist.

He nudged the horse forward one step, then tugged on the reins once more. Leaning over his saddle horn, Kell held his breath and peered.

Logic gave way to imagination and the form took on the shape he thought he'd seen.

A fin and flippers at one end. A woman's figure at the other. Lush breasts. Golden hair. Smooth shoulders.

Butter wasn't a skittish beast but as Kell tensed, the horse sidestepped nervously and began to tremble. Kell told himself the animal was simply reacting to Kell's own uneasiness. He needed to get a grip on himself and the horse would settle down.

On the other hand...

Kell patted Butter's neck and made a soothing sound. "It's okay, buddy. Take it easy."

The gelding threw his head up and down, then snorted softly, denying Kell's admonition. He wasn't encumbered with his master's reasoning and disagreed completely. It wasn't okay and he wasn't going to take it easy, either.

Butter knew a mermaid when he saw one.

Kell blinked, the impossible word echoing inside his head. Mermaids didn't exist, and he was staring at what had to be a woman and a man making love on the shore.

Mermaids did not exist.

Suddenly feeling foolish, Kell lifted Butter's reins and turned the horse to the right. He'd stick to his usual plan, and when he came back, *the people* would be gone. If they weren't, then he'd shoo them away and go about his regular business. Mounted patrol officers were supposed to be stable, law-fearing people, not wackos who saw imaginary sirens stretched out languidly on the beach.

Butter took off with seeming relief, his step quick. By the time they reached the halfway point—the city's covered pavilion—Kell's thoughts had coalesced into a logical explanation. He felt even more foolish as he realized the trick his mind had played on him.

He'd been thinking about Melody Harper for several days so seeing mermaids on the beach shouldn't have been a surprise: she'd always reminded him of the mystical sirens.

He had seen dead and dying fish on the shore and had read about the bay's problems in the local paper, but until Jackie, his sister, had mentioned seeing

Melody in town, Kell hadn't connected the "expert biologist" in the paper with Melody, his high school sweetheart.

He made a clicking sound and tightened the reins. With no further urging, Butter took them around the picnic area while Kell flashed his light into the corners. Everything looked quiet and he drew the horse to a stop, his thoughts taking over once more.

Courage Bay High had held its graduation ceremonies two evenings ago and, as always, the beach had been crazy. Every senior class held an unofficial celebration here after the formal functions were done. Sixteen years before, the night of Kell's own graduation, they'd partied on this very spot, and the year after that, Melody's class had done the same.

That year, the year she'd finished, Kell's grandfather, who'd raised Kell and his siblings, had passed away. Kell's parents had died years before, so when the old man had gone, Kell had inherited the ranch *and* total responsibility for his brother and sister. At nineteen, he hadn't been ready for the monumental task, and Melody's party had offered a chance—brief as it was—for him to be a kid again. The evening had gone wrong fast but by the end of the summer, Kell had come to think his whole life was over.

That hadn't been the case, of course, and after a

while, he'd managed to put the events into perspective. The scars were invisible now to anyone but him. Every summer, though, Kell found himself thinking of Melody.

He glanced to his left then back to his right, his decision coming quickly. Usually he made the full circuit down the sand—a trip that generally took about an hour—but tonight that wouldn't be the case. Kell tensed his legs and kneed the horse back the direction they'd come.

He'd be damned if he'd let old memories make him see things that didn't exist.

ALL MELODY HARPER had wanted was a simple walk along the shore.

Knowing the sight of the surf would calm her, she'd headed to the beach for some quiet time, but like everything else that had happened to her lately, her stroll turned out to be neither calm nor quiet.

Somehow, she wasn't surprised. Dr. Robert Martin, her boss, had called her into his office last week at the Scripps Institution of Oceanography and "rewarded" her with a trip to Courage Bay. Off-site investigations were considered to be recognition for work done well, and Dr. Martin had been delighted to be able to give it to her.

He had no idea that a return to the town where she had grown up was anything but a prize.

Melody had voiced her reservations as politely as she knew how, praising a colleague and generously recommending him for the perk instead.

"Nonsense," Dr. Martin had boomed from behind his desk. "Of all the biologists here, you're the most qualified to uncover what's happened in those bay waters. We've got to figure out why the fish are dying." He'd made a dismissive motion with his hand and pointed toward the door. "No one has worked harder than you since you've come to Scripps, Melody. You deserve a break. Make up for all those holidays you volunteered to work for everyone else. Enjoy the beautiful place you're lucky enough to call home."

Melody lifted her eyes. Dr. Martin had gotten one part right; Courage Bay was beautiful. Blanketing the cliffs that surrounded the beach, wind-slanted trees with twisted trunks gave the impression they were protecting the coastal city and everyone who lived in it. Tonight, the last rays of the sun shimmered over the mountains to the sapphire-blue waters, spiking the bay with peach tints. The community almost seemed too perfect to be real. But it *was* real.

And Melody hated every square inch of it.

An unexpected jingle pulled her head up and she squinted into the growing darkness where the outline of a horse and rider materialized. She jumped to her feet and began to yell. "Hey! You on the horse!" She waved her arms. "Over here! I need some help!"

She jogged toward the horse, holding up her hands to get the man's attention. "Do you have a cell phone?"

The rider cantered to where she stood, swinging himself over the saddle even before the horse had completely stopped, sand spraying from its hooves. The man was tall, she realized belatedly, with a powerful frame and wide shoulders. In the dusk, she couldn't see the details of his face beneath his hat but she immediately sensed sharp edges and well-defined features.

Suddenly it occurred to her she'd just flagged down a stranger on a very deserted, very dark beach. A very tall, very muscular stranger.

Her heart gave an extra beat, but she knew that even if she had given more consideration to her actions, she would have still taken the risk. She had to have help. She stepped closer to greet him and explain the problem. That's when she realized he wore the uniform of a mounted officer.

That was also when she realized who he was.

CHAPTER TWO

KELL STARED at the slender woman standing in the sand. Feeling as if he were in a dream, he shook his head and closed his eyes. When he opened them, she was still there. "Melody? My God, is that you? Jackie told me you were in town…."

Melody Harper's expression went from surprise to irritation. She was clearly as shocked to see him as he was to see her. "Yes, it's me and I *am* in town, but not through choice, that's for sure. My boss sent me."

Kell looked closer, the features he'd once thought he'd never forget slowly coming into focus with the prompting of her voice. Fine blond hair, cut shorter now, big blue eyes, more serious than before, a body still thin but toned by time and hard work. She wore a pair of shorts…and a bra. His glance dipped to her breasts then came back up.

"The bay's having environmental problems and I'm here to figure out what's going on. Do you have a cell phone?" She abruptly tilted her head to the sand behind her. "I need to call the rescue society."

She'd never been one for small talk, Kell remembered. Stepping past her, he looked in the direction she'd indicated then almost began to laugh. What he'd thought had been a mermaid had been a shirtless Melody...and a dolphin.

But Kell's amusement morphed quickly into concern. Floundering in the shallows, the animal was in obvious distress, blowing air and heaving on the sand. Looking closer, Kell saw the reason why. A large, ugly gash ran from his front fin to his tail.

"My phone's in my car." Melody interrupted Kell's amateur assessment. "But I couldn't leave him to call the rescue team. He might have drowned or dried out. His skin has to stay moist, but at the same time, I've got to keep him out of the deeper water." She put her hand on her chest, her expression turning sheepish as she seemed to remember her state of undress. "I had to use my shirt to wet him down."

The wind shifted and the scent of Melody's perfume came to Kell. The fragrance was the same one she'd worn in high school. Beautiful. He'd saved for two months to buy her a bottle.

Kell thrust the thought away. Kneeling beside the animal, he touched it gently and spoke, mainly to distract himself from thinking of the past. "Poor fellow. He really tangled with something, didn't he?"

When he looked up, Melody's expression had shifted into one of such pain that he found himself wincing.

"A boat propeller probably hit him." She dropped to sit beside him. "Their skin is incredibly delicate. Even a fingernail can damage it. He *has* to be kept cool and wet until the rescue guys can get here."

Without a word, Kell unsnapped the cell phone he kept on his belt and handed it to her. Dialing a number from memory, she spoke urgently, gripping the phone as she stated her name and location.

"We can't wait that long!" she said, after listening for a moment. "This animal needs help now. He has a severe slash reaching from his tail flukes to his—"

She stopped and listened, her expression turning angry. "Look, you don't understand…"

She continued to talk but Kell didn't listen. The moon had risen and a pale platinum light painted her with a silvery sheen, highlighting her hair and breasts. Every detail seemed perfect, every inch of her gorgeous. Unexpectedly Kell was nineteen again and with an intensity that was shocking, desire washed over him, hard and swift.

MELODY PUNCHED the end button and thrust the phone at Kell. "They're doing a rescue at Los Pecados. They might not be here for hours."

He seemed to give himself a mental shake. "Then we'll have to take care of him until they get here."

Kell's words surprised her. "Are you sure? It can get a little tricky."

"We can't leave him here to die." Kell stood up. "I've got a bucket in my horse trailer. We can use it to splash him."

He turned and mounted his horse, wheeling the animal back in the direction of the dunes. As soon as he was out of sight, Melody let her shoulders slump. "Damn it…"

She'd known sooner or later she'd run into Kell so she'd tried to prepare herself for the eventuality. All she'd done was waste time, she realized now. Ten thousand years wouldn't have been long enough to get her ready. Her heart would still be racing, her palms would still be wet, her mouth would still be cottony. When she was eighteen, Robert Kellison had had the ability to turn her world upside down, and apparently that hadn't changed.

Like the scientist she'd become, Melody rocked back on her heels in the sand and tried to evaluate the situation. Kell meant nothing to her at this point in her life and she had no good reason to respond to him this way. She was acting like one of those women who mooned over their first boyfriend twenty years after the fact. Get a grip, she told herself.

Before she could castigate herself further, Kell returned, a plastic feed bucket bouncing off the horn of his saddle, something pale draped over his shoulder. Dismounting, he came to where she waited and handed her a white T-shirt. "I keep clean ones in the truck," he explained. Turning away to give her some belated privacy, he went to the water and dipped the bucket into the waves.

Touched by his thoughtfulness, Melody pulled the soft cotton over her head, but her heart began to rock even harder. The fabric held Kell's scent, and wearing it made her feel as if his arms were around her.

He came back and she took the bucket from him, pouring the water over the dolphin, being careful to avoid its blowhole. Melody could almost see the animal's relief. She wished she had another pailful to pour over her own head. It might bring her to her senses.

Kell knelt beside her. "What else can we do?"

"I've made pits under his flippers. We need to keep those clear." She looked up. "Thank God the sun's gone down."

Kell palmed away a bit more sand from underneath the animal's flippers. "He'd get hot?"

"Yes, the heat would be bad, but having people around would be equally unsettling. Any kind of loud noises or light flashes will disturb him." She glanced toward the horse. "Actually you might want to tie him somewhere else. Injured dolphins don't like sudden movement, especially from something that large."

Promptly Kell rose and led the pale-colored animal down the beach, staking him out in the sand. When he came back, he handed Melody a bottle of water.

"I had this in my saddlebag. I don't know how long you've been here, but I thought you might want some."

She took the plastic container from his outstretched hand. Their fingers did not touch—they didn't even come close to touching—but that fact didn't seem to register with Melody.

Her response to the near encounter rippled its way up her arm, through her shoulder and into the rest of her body, where it terminated in a heated core. She felt as if she were trapped inside a furnace.

Sinking to the sand beside her, Kell opened his own bottle of water. As he drank, Melody watched his throat move for as long as she dared, finally forcing her eyes away at the last moment.

It was going to be a long night.

KELL TRIED not to stare at Melody as he drank, but it was impossible. She still wore the determined yet vulnerable air that had attracted him the first time he'd seen her. She hid it better now, but time hadn't changed her that much and his heart twisted. She seemed jittery.

He lowered his water bottle and pressed the cap to close it, looking over at her. "Tell me more about what you're doing here," he prompted gently. "Jackie said something about a red tide? I read about the problem in the newspaper but the article didn't give much detail…."

Relief filled Melody's eyes at his question—she could clearly handle anything as long as it wasn't personal.

"'Red Tide' is actually a misnomer. The situation has nothing to do with the tide and the water isn't always colored. 'HAB' is the term we prefer now."

"HAB?"

"'Harmful algae blooms.'"

"And that means?"

"Fish are dying in the bay and we suspect an influx of algae may be the cause."

"I've seen some of the dead fish, but I didn't know algae could do that."

"Certain kinds are very deadly, but I have a feeling this might be more than a simple outbreak. I've collected samples and done some preliminary work. Things appear a bit more complicated than we first thought."

Kell went still, inside and out. "Then your investigation might take a while?"

Her eyes glittered when she looked at him. "Not if I can help it."

For a second, they sat in silence, then Melody seemed to realize how abrupt her words had sounded.

"You haven't sold the ranch, have you?" She tilted her head toward his uniform. "Is this what you do now?"

"I only patrol on the weekends and at night," he explained. "They needed someone just for that and I offered. It gives me a chance to get away from the ranch, which, yes, I do still own."

"How do you have time for it all?"

"It's easy," he answered, "when all you do is work." He paused. "You know what I'm talking about, don't you? Something tells me you're the same."

"I take my share of time off," she said defensively. "I find time to date."

"That's good," he said. "Anyone special?"

She was silent for so long, he thought she wasn't going to reply. Finally, she spoke, her voice distant. "No."

A rumble of confusion pounded in the back of Kell's mind. Why had he asked her that? Why did he even care?

Melody pulled them back to safer ground. "Tell me about Whispering Dawn. Things still the same there?"

"Actually, they aren't. Over the years, I've expanded and added a lot of services."

"Like what?"

"Well, for one, we do more training."

"Horses or their owners?"

He smiled. "Both, although sometimes I wonder why. The horses are a helluva lot smarter and they learn ten times faster." He picked up a handful of sand and let it dribble through his fingers. "We still stable, too, but most of the owners now are weekenders. They're the only ones who can afford the fees. As it was, we had to spruce up the place to get it to L.A. standards."

She smiled and turned his joke around. "Horses have standards?"

"No, but the people who own them do. We built a dozen new extra-large stalls, heated and cooled, and put in a six-horse walker, too. Then we replaced the old arena with a big new one, one hundred by one hundred and fifty. There's twenty-four-hour security, as well as on-site cameras."

Her eyes widened. "Wow, your grandfather would have been proud. I bet he never expected his quiet little spread to turn into such a large-scale operation."

"You're probably right," Kell answered, "but I'm not so sure about the proud part. He was a stubborn old goat—I doubt he would have approved of spending the money, but we had to. It was that or go under."

"Your brother and sister help, don't they?"

"As much as they can, but they're busy with their own lives. Nate's a paramedic and Jackie works at Courage Bay Hospital as a trauma nurse. She's had a tough go of it, though. She lost her husband a while back."

"Oh, I'm sorry to hear that, I didn't know. I kept up with things a little better when Ida was still alive."

Their eyes met over the dolphin. One of the bonds that had originally brought them together was the fact that they'd both been raised by grandparents, Kell because his mother and father had died, Melody because her parents had divorced. They'd been the only kids in school without at least one parent around.

"Do you ever see your father?" Kell asked.

"I try not to. I think he's back in New York, but I

don't know for sure." She spoke quietly, staring at the waves rolling in and out before them. "Mother lives in London. I saw her last Christmas. She's doing well."

Melody's parents had split when she was a budding teenager. She'd always avoided Kell's questions about the situation, and after a while he'd come to realize why; she couldn't talk about what had happened because the breakup of her family had devastated her.

Once, before he'd come to that understanding he'd pressed her about it as they'd sat in the darkness not far from here. She'd given him the barest details.

Her parents had been married twenty-two years when her father, a banker in New York, had left her mother for a much younger woman. Six months later, Melody's father and his wife had a new baby, and no more time for Melody. Until then, the only home she'd known had been in Manhattan, where she'd attended private schools. Shortly after the baby was born, Melody's mother, a native of Courage Bay, had sold their home and dumped Melody off at Bay Villa, her own mother's home in Courage Bay, before heading for Europe. After that point, Melody's upbringing had been in the hands of her grandmother, a kind but somewhat bewildered elderly widow. The two of them had lived in her huge rambling home near the Point.

"My mother was a professional musician—a violinist—but my father wouldn't let her work after they got married," Melody had explained that night. "He said she didn't 'need' to anymore. He wanted her to stay home and be a mother and a wife, so she did. But in the end, he left her for a woman who worked at his bank. A career woman."

She'd turned to Kell. "It was so unfair! Why didn't she stand up and do what she wanted to? Why didn't my father see how he messed up everything?" In typical teenaged fashion, she'd seen the situation only through her own eyes. "Why did they have to ruin my life, too?"

Interrupting his memories, Melody grabbed the bucket and stood. Kell looked up at her, her angst still vivid to him after all these years. He never had been able to answer her question and he wasn't too sure he could now. Her parents had been foolish, selfish people who'd thought of no one but themselves, and Melody had suffered greatly because of them.

"We need more water," she said stiffly. "I'll be right back."

"I'LL COME WITH YOU."

Kell jumped up and took the container from Melody

without asking. Together they waded into the deeper surf, their steps in sync. Melody didn't want to be so aware of Kell but she couldn't stop the details from registering. He'd filled out from their days in high school, his body more solid and firm-looking than when he'd been a kid. The basketball coaches had begged him to join the team, but he hadn't had time for games.

Even before his grandfather died, Kell had worked hard at the ranch, but after his death, Kell had taken on full responsibility for his siblings.

She glanced at him sideways as they approached the water. There had always been more to Kell than just good looks; he'd been a sympathetic, responsible man, even as a teenager. But perhaps circumstance had made him that way. With his path set in stone, he'd had little choice but to follow it.

He bent to fill the pail and she noticed that his hands were scarred and rough-looking from working at the ranch. Did he carry some internal wounds as well? The question reminded her of what a hard life he'd had. And how much he'd cared.

In silence they walked back to the dolphin. Kell gently poured the water over the animal, dousing Melody's shirt, which was still stretched over him, avoiding his blowhole just as she had done earlier. Had he watched her, or did he know he could drown the dolphin that way?

When he finished, he set down the bucket and dusted his hands on his pants. "Let's walk down the beach a bit. He'll be okay for a while."

Alarm rose in her at the thought of being alone with Kell. "We can't leave him—"

"He'll be all right."

"But if the rescue team arrives—"

"We'll see their lights."

She couldn't come up with another excuse without being more obvious than she already was. "Okay," she conceded, "but we can't be gone long. He'll need more water."

"We'll just go a short way down the beach then come back."

As they walked, they fell into the rhythm of their earlier friendship. Kell carried the conversation easily, catching her up on the local gossip. Melody was grateful—she still hadn't mastered the art of making people comfortable, whereas Kell had always been great at it, even as a teenager. After a bit, she began to relax. Almost immediately, Kell slowed and put his hand on her arm.

Her heart stopped. When he spoke, it started again, but his words made it beat so fast, she thought she might pass out.

"It's been fifteen years since you left, Mel." She

looked up at him, her breath trapped inside her chest. In the moonlight, his eyes were grave, his expression serious. "I know that's been a while, but don't you think it's time we talk about what happened?"

CHAPTER THREE

MELODY STARED at Kell with what she knew was a shocked expression. She quickly rearranged her features into something she hoped was more neutral and shook her head. "As a matter of fact, I don't. What happened between us is over and done with. Why don't we leave things alone?"

"Is that what you've done all these years?"

She frowned in confusion. "What do mean?"

"Have you 'left it alone'? You seem nervous around me...."

She hid the surprise she felt at his words, then she remembered—Kell had always been able to read her emotions, sometimes better than she could.

"I'm not nervous. I'm just worried about the dolphin," she said in a dismissive voice. "And as for what happened back then...well, we were kids. I haven't thought of those days in years."

"You're lying." He reached up and touched her

cheek. "It's in your eyes, Mel. You never could fool me, you know."

She took a step back, giving herself—and her heart—more room. "We were teenagers, Kell, that's all. We had a summer fling. Then you went your way and I went mine. End of story. It happens all the time." With a sharp turn in the sand, she started walking back to the stranded dolphin.

He caught up with her in one stride. "Is that really how you think of it now?"

"Of course," she lied. "How else would anyone see it?"

"It was more than that to me…and I thought it was more than that to you. It was our first time, and that whole summer we were inseparable—"

She stopped. "Don't be a revisionist, Kell. It's not attractive."

Her words stung him—she could tell by the way he narrowed his eyes.

"I'm not revising anything, Melody. You're the one who rewrote the story, and I never even got the ending."

Her anger flared. "You don't know what you're talking about."

This time when he took her arm, he didn't let go. "C'mon, Mel. We might have been young, but I loved you, and you blew me off like I meant nothing to you. I must have called a thousand times the week before you left, and you talked to me *once*. And that was to tell me you were heading for college the next day. The *very* next day. I didn't even get a chance to kiss you good-bye. After all these years, I'd like to know why you ended it like that."

Surrounded by nothing but sea and sand and the stars above, Melody looked into Kell's dark eyes and held her breath. Then she lifted his fingers from her arm and dropped them. "I left because it was over, Kell. We had our summer together, then it finished, okay? What we shared didn't mean any more than that to me, and it shouldn't have to you." She took a shaky breath. "Let the past go, Kell, and forget about it. I certainly have."

KELL WANTED to grab Melody and shake her, but she was already ahead of him, walking toward the dolphin, her little speech delivered with a sincerity that would have fooled anyone but him. When was she going to realize that he could tell when she lied?

He caught up with her and they headed back toward the animal in silence. Images of the night they'd first come together flashed through his brain.

He'd been out of school a year when her class had

graduated, but Kell had had no trouble remembering who she was at the party on the beach. Melody had taken some advanced senior-level courses, and in Kell's final year they'd had two classes together. He'd been intimidated by her brains and bowled over by her looks. What had really done him in, though, was the uncertainty in her eyes. To realize that somebody like Melody Harper could feel that way had been a real shocker to Kell.

Rich and smart and beautiful Melody Harper.

He'd finished late at the ranch and had headed directly to the beach that night after work. The party had been going on for hours already and the drinking even longer. He'd been passing over the dunes, heading to the bonfire, when he'd heard her. The urgency in her voice had brought him to an immediate halt.

"No, Todd! Stop it!"

"Don't be such a tight ass. All I want is a little—"

"I don't care what you want, okay? Just stop it! And leave me alone."

Kell instantly recognized the boy's voice. Todd McKnight had been a wide receiver on the football team and he'd fit every cliché associated with jocks. Big, loud and obnoxious, he wasn't the kind of guy Melody would have ever dated.

"You don't want me to leave you alone…. I saw

that look you gave me before you started for the dunes. You wanted me to follow you, so don't play hard to get."

"I didn't give you any kind of look, Todd. Wh-what are you doing?"

The next thing Kell heard was the sound of fabric tearing. Melody gave a yip of surprise and then panic entered her voice. "Todd! Stop it—"

Kell didn't wait to hear more. He pushed aside the sea grasses and headed to his right. Plunging recklessly across the sand, he almost fell on top of them before he could stop.

Melody's expression filled with relief and then embarrassment as she grabbed her torn blouse. Todd stumbled to his feet.

"What the hell are you doing, Kellison? Get outta here."

"I think you're the one who needs to leave, Todd," Kell said quietly. "What do you think, Melody?"

She scrambled to her feet. "I think you're right." She was blinking hard and trying not to cry.

The football player mumbled a curse and took a swing at Kell. His movement was so awkward and slow Kell almost didn't respond. Then he thought of Melody and what might have happened if he hadn't heard her. His fist connected solidly with Todd's jaw and the other boy went down without a sound.

Kell grabbed Melody's arm and pulled her away. Five minutes later they were in his truck.

That's when the real trouble started.

THEY REACHED the dolphin in a matter of seconds. The animal looked comfortable but Melody picked up the bucket and handed it to Kell without a word. He took it from her outstretched fingers and went to fill it up, giving her the time and space she wanted.

None of the seeing-Kell-again scenarios she'd run through her mind before returning to Courage Bay had included him bringing up the subject of their past so quickly or so bluntly. She wondered why she hadn't considered the possibility. Kell had always faced things head-on; she'd been the one to dodge the truth if she could.

That was the problem, though, wasn't it? Something incredible had sparked between them and they'd made love the very night he'd rescued her. After that, nothing had been the same. They'd been inseparable the whole summer, never apart for more than an hour or two.

By the end of the season, she was a different person. Relationships changed things, she learned. There were no guarantees and each day brought surprises.

Only one fact had seemed certain to Melody: Kell's love made her feel satisfied and protected. And that had scared her to death.

She'd seen firsthand what happened when a woman depended on a man for too much. An eye-witness to the disaster of her mother's capitulation and her father's selfish ways, Melody had promised herself she would do things differently. Only foolish people looked to others for what they needed, and because of that, they were doomed to disappointment. It made much more sense for her to turn her life out-ward. She was going to do something worthwhile, she had vowed, something that mattered, and at the same time, she'd be independent and support herself as well.

To accomplish those goals, she knew she had to leave Courage Bay. She needed more choices. More diversity. More opportunity. More...everything than the small coastal city could offer.

Too young to explain and too terrified to try for fear Kell would make her change her mind, she'd left with barely a word. Later, when she'd come to a deeper understanding of the situation—and of her-self—she'd wondered if she'd made a mistake.

Plenty of women balanced love and work, family and marriage, duty and pleasure. And plenty of men were faithful, too. Her parents hadn't made the right choices, but that didn't mean that Melody was doomed to do the same.

By the time she came to this realization, though, it was too late. She'd achieved her professional goals. Moving back to Courage Bay wasn't an option.

Kell returned and handed her the bucket. Grateful to focus on the task at hand, Melody poured the water over the dolphin then softly patted him. "It's okay," she said in a soothing voice. "We're going to get you some help...."

Kell's steady gaze remained on her until she could no longer ignore it. He wasn't going to let the subject drop.

"A lot has happened to both of us since we were a couple," she said, looking up. "Can't we please just forget about it?"

"Answer one question for me," he said.

She sighed heavily. "What is it?"

"Why wouldn't you talk to me before you took off?"

She searched for a way to explain. "I was getting ready to leave," she said finally. "I'd been accepted for some accelerated classes and I had a lot to do. The university didn't give me much notice and—"

"It wouldn't have taken ten minutes."

"You don't understand—"

"Then explain it to me."

"I had other things on my mind." She leaned forward and began to dig at the sand beneath the dolphin's flippers. "I wanted to leave Courage Bay as soon as I could. I know everyone loves this place but I never have. I wanted to do more than I could have if I'd stayed here, and I was afraid that if I tried to tell you—" She stopped abruptly. "Look, I didn't handle it right, but I was just a kid."

For a minute she was silent, and when at last she spoke, her words came slowly. "I've worked like hell to get where I am at Scripps, Kell. People around here are too sheltered to understand this, but let me tell you something…it's hard out there in the real world. The person who wins is the one who works the longest and does the most. I had to be single-minded if I wanted to accomplish my goals."

He didn't move. "And have you?"

"Yes," she answered. "I have. I earned my degree and I got my job and I'm good at what I do."

"I'm sure you are," he said, surprising her. "But are you satisfied with your life?"

She was about to say yes, but he held up a hand and stopped her.

"Don't just pop out the 'right' answer. This is me you're talking to. Kell. Tell me the truth."

She glanced down at the dolphin then back up at him. "What I do is important and it matters. When I left here, that was the goal I had and I've reached it, so I believe my answer would still be 'yes.' I'm satisfied."

"You 'believe'?"

She made an impatient, dismissive motion with her hand. "A figure of speech, Kell. C'mon, I'm not going to play word games with you."

"You aren't going to answer my question, either, are you?"

"I did answer it," she said hotly. "You just don't understand—"

"You're right." His expression tightened and so did his voice, his frustration more than obvious. "I don't understand. And I never will. Because I look at things a lot differently than you do. Goals are great and careers are important, but they aren't what makes life worth living." He took a deep breath, then spoke again. "*People* give meaning to our lives, Melody. The people we live with. The people around us." He paused until she met his eyes. "The people we love…."

KELL AND MELODY continued to wait for the rescue team in tense silence. Kell knew he'd probably said more than he should have, but that was his way. He believed in telling the truth, whatever that truth might be. Melody had always kept her feelings to herself.

When the rescue team finally arrived, the moon had almost disappeared. Melody greeted the woman in charge of the group and explained what had happened as they huddled around the animal. In addition to monitoring the dolphin's pulse and breathing rate, the woman took its temperature and drew a blood sample. Over the sound of the surf, Kell caught only bits and pieces of the conversation but it became quickly apparent that refloating the animal wasn't an option, not with the wound on its side.

One of the team members ran back to the pickup truck they'd arrived in and returned a few minutes later with a cushioned air mattress. Kell stood by silently. He'd seen people moved with less attention to their injures, but he sensed that Melody and the others might not appreciate this observation. Two hours after they arrived, the team drove away, the dolphin suspended by stretchers over the bed of the truck, two men on either side gently attending to it.

Kell turned to Melody. She looked beautiful but exhausted in the breaking light, lavender shadows darkening beneath her eyes.

"Are you all right?" he asked, the animal forgotten. "I can drive you back to your hotel—"

"I'm not staying at a hotel." His question appeared to irk her for some reason. "I cleaned out a room at Ida's."

He raised his eyebrows in surprise. "Your grandmother never sold that big old place?"

"She left the house to me so I figured I'd stay there. There's no need to spend Scripps' money on a hotel room when Bay Villa is sitting empty."

"But it's so quiet…and lonely."

"I'm a big girl, Kell. I can handle it."

He looked at her steadily. "I'm sure you can handle anything, but that doesn't necessarily make it fun." He seemed to gather himself then he spoke again, his gaze burning into hers. "Would you at least come over to the ranch tomorrow night? I'd like to talk some more, but I also want to show you all the changes I've made. I can throw a couple of steaks on the grill and give you a tour."

As he waited for her answer, Kell listened to his heartbeat. The sound was so loud he could hear it over the roar of the surf, and a crazy urge to pull Melody closer rolled over him like one of the waves at their feet. She looked up at him and he felt himself falling into the deep blue depths of her gaze. Her eyes were the kind a man could get lost in, and never find his way out.

"I appreciate the offer." Her voice was low and smooth. "But I don't think that would be a very good idea, Kell. I'm not here to renew old friendships— I'm here to work, and as soon as I'm done, I'll be leaving again."

CHAPTER FOUR

"YOU TURNED HIM DOWN? Are you crazy? Has the smog down there in San Diego sucked the brains right out of your head?"

Melody raised her gaze from the clipboard she held and looked at the slight redhead who sat on the other side of her desk. The office and secretary had been arranged by Dr. Martin's assistant before Melody had even agreed to come. A small weather-beaten building on the road heading to the docks south of the city, her new "office" wasn't anything like her setup at Scripps. The two rooms did have a gorgeous view of the bay, though, and when she'd walked inside and found Bitsy Sandoval was her new assistant, Melody had been surprisingly happy to see her.

She and Bitsy and a third girl, Lisa Montgomery, had been the outcasts at Courage Bay High; Melody because she wasn't from Courage Bay, Bitsy because she'd been too outspoken and Lisa because her family had had no money. With no other choice, they'd hung out together and soon became close. Since Melody had lost touch with both women over the years, Bitsy had quickly brought her up to date: Lisa still had no money and Bitsy still spoke her mind.

"We don't have brain-sucking smog in San Diego," Melody answered her friend, "but even if we did and I *didn't* have a brain anymore, I would have turned Kell down. I'm not here for that."

"Well, you should be," Bitsy replied. "Practically every female in Courage Bay between nine and ninety would like to be here for 'that.' Since he and Louisa divorced, Kell's been our most eligible bachelor."

Melody felt her jaw drop. "Kell was married?"

"For two years," Bitsy told her. "To Louisa Blakely. She was a gorgeous brunette with curves you'd have to see to believe. She boarded her horses at the ranch for a while and they hooked up. It didn't last too long, though."

"Why not?" Melody asked.

"Apparently living at Whispering Dawn turned out to be different from visiting. She was from L.A. She went back. The end."

"No kids?"

"No." Bitsy raised an eyebrow. "But I thought you weren't interested...."

"I'm not." Melody returned to her list and checked off two calls she hadn't yet made. "I was just making conversation, that's all. Has the sample report come back yet?"

Bitsy rolled her eyes. "No, ma'am, not yet. But the mailman ought to come by anytime now. He's early on Mondays cause he has to take his daddy over to the hospital for physical therapy. He broke his hip last month and—"

Melody turned away in the middle of Bitsy's explanation. She wasn't going to be here long enough to get to know the mailman or his father. She hoped. "Just let me know when the report arrives," she said. "I'm anxious to read the results."

Stepping inside the second room, which served as her office, Melody shut the door behind her and went to her desk. She didn't sit down, though. Instead, she stared out the window and tried to see Kell as a married man.

The image came easily, especially after what he'd said on the beach about caring for friends and family. His implication had stung. Deep down Melody suspected he was right, but her life was already on its track and she'd made her choices, good and bad. She loved her job and the satisfaction it brought her; nowhere else but at Scripps could she have found that. If she'd had to make some sacrifices along the way, then so be it. At least they were *her* sacrifices. No one else had made the choices for her.

An hour after lunch, Bitsy knocked on the door then opened it without waiting for an answer. Standing beside her was a tall, thin blonde with a baby on one hip and a toddler at her side. It took Melody a second to realize the rough-looking woman was Lisa Montgomery. Dressed in jeans and a T-shirt, she'd obviously been working outside. Her hair was wind-blown and her face ruddy. "So you really are back," she said in wonder. "Bitsy told me you were coming but I thought she was pulling my leg. I had to come by and see for myself."

"I'm here all right." Melody greeted her old friend warmly, then admired the children. "I can't believe you're a mother! I knew you had kids, but wow...."

"That's Gerald," Lisa said, nodding toward the little boy, "and this is Lily." She untangled the baby's fist from a lock of her long hair. "It's a real challenge being a mommy," she said. "Especially since their daddy took off last year without so much as a good go to hell. You wanna hold the baby?"

She thrust the child forward and Melody took her. The baby smelled sweet and fresh. Motherhood was a foreign concept to Melody, but that didn't seem to bother Lily. She wrapped her arms around Melody's neck and hung on tightly.

"These kids are the best thing that ever happened to me and I love them to death. But sometimes…" Lisa glanced at Melody. "Sometimes I'd just like to look like you do today, all clean and neat and… young."

"Oh, c'mon. You look great yourself." Melody reluctantly handed the baby back as Lily held out her hands to her mother. "What are you talking about?"

Lisa took her little daughter, cradling her head and gently kissing the top of it. "Oh, heck, I don't really mean it," she said. "Nothing comes close to how my babies make me feel. All I want to do is keep these guys fed and happy." She shook her head and changed subjects with a smile. "But enough about me! We have to get together. Just the three of us, okay?" She looked at Bitsy then turned back to Melody. "I have a day off next week. Let's meet for lunch. I can leave the kids with Mama. I want to hear all about your glamorous life in San Diego."

"It's not glamorous—"

"Don't tell me that! We need our fantasies, right, Bits?"

The other woman nodded and smiled, then suddenly tapped her forehead with the heel of one hand.

"Melody, I forgot! That report you wanted came in. It's on my desk—" She turned, the toddler stumbling after her.

With a groan, Melody followed Bitsy, and Lisa trailed behind. "I wanted that as soon as it got here, Bitsy—"

"I know, I know…" The redhead waved off Melody's complaints. "You've got it now, so be happy. Let's plan our date instead of complaining. Where do you want to meet?"

"You guys pick." Melody took the brown folder Bitsy held out, her mind already focusing on what might be inside. "Whatever you want is fine with me. Just tell me when and where and I'll be there." Ripping the envelope open, she left the two women and returned to her office, shutting the door behind her.

MELODY'S REFUSAL of his dinner invitation had hurt Kell, but he didn't regret what he'd said. Working on his books the following week, he put down his pencil and rubbed his eyes, the numbers on the computer printout running together and blurring as he continued to think about their encounter.

Her sudden departure all those years ago had bothered him for a long time. They'd been very close and very in love. He'd even considered asking her to marry him. He'd only held back because he'd known he wouldn't be able to give her the kind of life she'd had before. Kell had seen how money troubles affected a person—his grandfather had been relatively young when he'd had his fatal heart attack. If Kell couldn't offer Mel more than a broken-down ranch, he wasn't going to offer her anything at all.

But he'd loved her so much.

Standing up, he walked over to the windows of his office. His view encompassed the arena and workout pen and he watched as one of the boarded horses trotted behind a trainer, the animal's gait brisk and high-spirited.

Although he stared at the horse, his mind stayed on Melody. She was searching for something, he decided, but what? He doubted she knew the answer herself. In fact, were he to ask her, she'd probably deny she was looking for anything. She'd always focused almost entirely on her professional goals, yet even all those years ago he'd known something was missing in her life, and from the sadness in her eyes, he was pretty sure it still was.

A soft knock sounded on his office door. "Come in," he said.

As if he'd conjured her, Melody stood on the threshold looking uncertain. "I saw your secretary in the hall-way and she told me to just come in. Are you busy?"

Too surprised to speak, Kell shook his head. She wore a long-sleeved blue blouse that made her eyes glow and a pair of khaki shorts that showed off her taut, tanned legs. She looked spectacular and he realized that he was holding his breath.

"My report on the bay came back and I need to talk to you about it."

"Of course," he managed to say. "I'd like to know what's going on. Please come in and sit down." He indicated a sitting area off to one side of his office. Owners looking for the perfect spot to board their expensive and much-loved horses wanted as much information as they could get about Whispering Dawn. Kell frequently spent hours explaining how the ranch worked, so he'd had the comfortable couch and chairs installed in his office for that purpose.

Melody settled among the cushions of the couch then pulled several files and a clipboard, along with a pair of reading glasses, from the bag she'd carried in. "As you know, the institute sent me here to conduct a quantitative and qualitative analysis of phyto-plankton in the water. I've taken samples and established cultures of the various dinoflagellates, including a certain variety of Pyrodinium bahamense as well as a Gymnodinium breve. On their own, these elements would present cause for concern, but if they were to combine, a huge problem could develop."

Even if her words had made complete sense to him, Kell knew he wouldn't have been listening. He was too busy thinking about the way her neck curved when she glanced down at her charts and how her black-framed glasses made her look even more sexy than she already did.

When she paused, he grabbed onto the last of her words, hoping his question made sense. "Do they... um...like to get together and create a problem?"

She seemed puzzled, but she answered him. "It's rare that they cooperate, if that's what you mean, but my samples are not yet conclusive." She pulled out a color-coded table and three pages of single-spaced text. "As you can see, a seawater reference spectra with chlorophyll and suspended solids would be helpful, but..." She continued her explanation and Kell drifted off, his mind taking him to a wide bed with Melody in it.

When she repeated his name for a second time, he realized she'd asked him a question, but he had no idea what it was. Instead of responding, he stood.

"You know, charts and reports don't mean much to me, Mel. I think I'd understand the whole situation a lot better if you came to the beach with me this evening and started over with your explanation down there."

"I can't do that." Shaking her head, she got up as well. "I have to see that my boss knows about these findings, and I won't be able to call after hours—"

"Won't he be there tomorrow?"

"Well, yes, he will, but—"

"Why are you scared of spending time with me, Mel? You act like I'm going to kidnap you or something." He smiled at her in a teasing way.

"Look, I have a lot to do and very little time to do it in. I came over here today because I need help and I need it quickly. I don't have time for parties on the beach."

A momentary qualm over the lie he was about to utter was not enough to change his tactics. "Then you'll just have to wait until next week," he said, his voice regretful. "I can't do anything until then. I'm booked solid."

In the sunlight pouring through the window beside them, Kell could see the freckles under her makeup. One night, under the stars on the beach, he'd counted them, kissing every one.

She considered his words a moment, then said, "If that's my only option, I guess I'll have to come back tonight. I really want to talk to you and this can't wait until next week. What time do you want to meet?"

Kell wanted to high-five someone. Instead he tried to look thoughtful. "How about six-thirty or seven?"

She nodded and they made their plans. Ten minutes later she walked out the door. Feeling like the teenager he'd once been, Kell quickly crossed his office to the window that looked out over the parking lot, his eyes tracking her progress to an older, dark-colored Volvo. She climbed inside with a graceful motion and started the car, but instead of driving away, she sat for a moment. He had the impression she was staring straight at him yet he didn't know why. Maybe it was just wishful thinking.

A VISIT TO Whispering Dawn had not been on Melody's agenda that morning, but when she'd finished reading her latest reports, she'd known she needed help. Kell had seemed like the logical choice. If what she suspected was true, he'd be the best person to turn to for advice. He had a good head on his shoulders and was well-respected, plus he knew a lot of people in Courage Bay. She'd driven to the ranch as soon as she could get away.

And now she'd agreed to meet him that evening. She and Kell had ridden down the beach almost every evening the summer they'd been together. It had been an easy way to exercise the horses, but more than that, it had given them another opportunity to spend time with each other. Kell had been her sounding board back then, too. Was she falling into the same pattern again?

Absolutely not, she told herself.

Reaching the end of the driveway, she turned left to go back into Courage Bay. Kell was the only person she could think of who could tell her what she needed to know, at this point. She could easily keep their relationship on a professional level. She wasn't one of those desperate Courage Bay women Bitsy had mentioned who were out to snag him.

All Melody wanted was to do her job.

She repeated those words for the rest of the day. By the time she left the office that evening and headed for Bay Villa, she'd almost convinced herself they were fact. Then, after dinner, she started to change clothes and her reasoning fell apart. If she was looking to Kell for advice, why did she give a damn what she wore? After trying on and then discarding three different outfits, she deliberately yanked her oldest pair of jeans and a T-shirt from the closet. Running a brush through her hair, she added fresh lipstick then left.

Kell's sister, Jackie, stepped out of the ranch's office just as Melody drove up. She greeted Melody warmly, her eyes sparkling with friendliness. Underneath their gleam, though, Melody saw the shadows. She couldn't imagine how painful it must have been for Jackie to lose her husband.

"Kell told me you were coming and to keep an eye out for you." Jackie hugged Melody briefly. "It's so good to see you."

Melody had always liked Kell's sister. "It's good to see you, too. I was sorry to hear about your loss, though."

"Thank you, Melody... It's been tough, but I'll make it." Jackie's expression darkened briefly, then, with an almost visible effort, she seemed to clear it. "Kell's waiting for you out at the arena. I just stopped by to say hello, and now I'm off to work. You guys have a good ride." She started walking away. "Give me a call, okay? We'll do lunch."

Melody nodded before heading for the sidewalk that circled the office. When she rounded the corner, she immediately spotted Kell. He was currying the big buckskin gelding he'd been riding on the beach, while a smaller, dun-colored mare patiently waited nearby for her turn. Kell had changed into his uniform. The pants were pressed with knifelike creases, and his white shirt gleamed in the gathering dusk.

She reminded herself of the professional distance she wanted to maintain. As she drew closer, he raised his head and their eyes met over the horse's broad back.

"You actually came," he said. "I didn't think you'd show up."

"I said I would," she replied, a hint of defensiveness coming into her voice before she could stop it.

Dropping the reins, Kell walked around the horse's shoulders to where Melody stood. "I didn't mean to hurt your feelings when I said what I did the other day. I hope you didn't take it the wrong way."

She shrugged. "You have a right to say whatever you want."

"Not if it hurts someone."

"It didn't hurt." Touched once again by his display of thoughtfulness, Melody smiled. "But I'll absolve you anyway." She waved her hand in front of his face as if blessing him. "There. Do you feel better?"

He captured her fingers and Melody froze, the warmth of his touch closing around her heart as tightly as his grip.

"That certainly helps," he said, his deep voice rumbling in the heated evening air. "But I can think of other ways you could make me feel a whole lot better."

Melody felt her chest compress, and she looked up at him. "I…I think that's the best I can do for now."

"'For now'?" He smiled slowly, drawing her gaze to his full lips. "That's fine with me. I'm a patient man. I can wait."

CHAPTER FIVE

KELL USUALLY TOOK Butter in a trailer to patrol the beach, but when he had the time, he let the gelding gallop there instead. Wheeling his horse around, Kell was about to suggest that very thing when Melody tugged the mare's reins to the right and took off. He'd forgotten she knew about Whispering Dawn's private bridle path.

He tried not to watch as she rode ahead of him, but finally he gave up and let himself enjoy the view. In the years they'd been apart, her body had added curves in all the right places. He still knew the old ones, though, and since he'd seen her again, he'd dreamed of them all night, every night, his hands drifting over her skin, his lips tasting hers.

She'd made a damn good-looking mermaid.

Twenty minutes later they came off the path at the southern end of the beach, the sea breeze cooling their faces and the animals. Despite the heat wave that gripped the area, several scattered groups of people were enjoying an evening by the water. Kell pulled up beside Melody and said something about the temperature to get his mind off how beautiful she looked.

She lifted a hand and wiped her brow. Her white T-shirt stuck to her skin, pulling her breasts upward under the thin material. "It's not helping the situation, that's for sure. When the weather's cold and rainy, the plankton lie dormant on the sea floor. Warmer weather makes them multiply like crazy."

They let the horses trot until they reached an isolated area of the beach. There they dismounted, then looped their reins over a large piece of driftwood. Melody walked to the water's edge and sat down in the sand.

Kell couldn't take his eyes off her. The sun had slipped over the sea's edge, the dying light cloaking Melody in gold just as the moon had done last week with silver.

He spoke without thinking. "Do you know how beautiful you are? You were pretty as a teenager, but now you're downright gorgeous." He leaned over and kissed her gently before pulling back.

An instant flush darkened her cheeks, turning them to bronze. "We're here to talk about the water, Kell, not revisit old times."

"I know that," he said, "but can't I compliment you?"

"That was a little more than a compliment."

"Yes," he said, "I guess it was. But why not? You deserve more than just a compliment. You're so lovely—"

She held her hand up. "That's enough," she said. "We need to talk about the problem, not me."

He began to protest, but she started off with the scientific jargon again. After a bit, he held up *his* hand, stopping her before she got too wound up. "Tell me in plain English."

She paused, looked thoughtful for a minute, then started over. "I've isolated two different types of organisms in the water that pose a potential threat. One causes paralytic shellfish poisoning, or PSP, and the other causes NSP, neurotoxic shellfish poisoning. I've never witnessed both species functioning concurrently in a single area, and that's very troubling. Either one is bad by itself, but if they were to come together, it would be terrible."

"Tell me why."

"We'll have a lot more dead and poisoned fish," she said bluntly. "And the potential for some dead and poisoned people, too, if they consume the fish. In addition, if the two organisms combine, the toxin could become airborne. It's a remote possibility at best, but for someone who was already susceptible, breathing the air—as well as eating the shellfish—would pose a major risk."

"What can you do to prevent that from happening?" he asked.

She dragged her fingers through the wet sand, the slow evening tide washing over them. "One, we wait. If a storm comes through with high enough winds, it would push the algae farther out to sea, where it would disperse naturally *and* harmlessly. That method depends on luck and time." She took a deep breath. "Or, two, I can try to find out what's really out there and why the organisms might want to combine. If we go this route, we get results a lot quicker and fewer fish would die."

"You said they haven't combined yet. What would make them do so in the first place?"

"I don't know for sure, but there are several theories floating around. Some biologists think it has to do with protection. When anything in the wild feels threatened, it's going to do what it has to for survival. That includes joining forces with like-minded organisms to present a united front."

"What's in the bay that could be so harmful to them?"

"I don't know." Her eyes darkened. "But I suspect

it isn't anything we'd find there naturally. More likely, someone's dumping something into the waters that they shouldn't be."

IN THE GROWING DUSK, Melody saw that Kell looked worried. "That's a serious assumption. Are you sure?"

"No, I'm not sure, not at all." She rose. "But I can't always give these matters enough time to be absolutely certain. I had to make a fast decision…and that's what I've done."

He stood up slowly. "I thought you brought me here to help you."

"I did," she said, "but not with my decision—I've made it already and had my boss alert the agencies that need to know. What I need help with is where to look for possible pollutants. You know the businesses and people in this area. Who do you think could be involved with something like this?"

"How do you know pollution is the problem?"

"I don't…but it's the logical conclusion."

"Why?"

"HABs are increasing at a rate we've never seen before. The atmosphere is growing warmer and more fish are dying all the time."

"But how much of that is due to greater awareness

of the problem? Just because more HABs are being found doesn't necessarily mean more exist. Maybe your detection methods are better now than before."

Melody hid her surprise. Not everyone caught that subtlety. "You make a good point," she admitted. "We *have* improved our methods of finding outbreaks, but in the end, we still have to deal with them, regardless of their cause. Scripps sent me here to fix things, and one way or another, that's what I'm going to do. ASAP."

"How?"

"I'm going to close the beach," she said matter-of-factly.

Kell laughed lightly and Melody tensed.

"What's so funny?" she asked.

"You're kidding, right?"

"Of course I'm not kidding," she said stiffly. "I don't joke about things like this, Kell."

He looked incredulous. His gaze scanned the shoreline in both directions. To the east, a group of people sat around a fire, several small children playing nearby. In the other direction, toward town, music from a seafood bar and grill drifted over the sand. The outdoor patio was full of diners. In between were scattered families and couples, finishing picnics and taking one last walk along the shore.

"Look at all these people, Mel," he said slowly. "You can't just put up some little signs and say, 'Sorry, folks, come back next year, I'm closing the beach.'"

"Yes, I can."

"Melody, this is the height of tourist season! Some of these families have driven for miles and saved all year for this."

"And I feel sorry for them, but I don't see what this has to do with the problem, Kell."

"What about all the local people who'd be affected? Courage Bay isn't a big city. We depend on these tourists. What a lot of businesses make during the summer months is all they have to sustain them the rest of the year. If they don't show a profit in June, July and August, the chances are good they'll go under come December."

"I'd hate to see that happen," she countered earnestly, "but some things are more important than money, Kell. They'll understand."

"I doubt that very seriously." He paused. "Why not wait? You said that was an option…."

"I did," she conceded, "but there's probably more types of algae out there that I haven't even isolated yet. I'd rather take some action. Waiting to see what happens is not the way I operate."

"Even if it's the best way?"

She felt her cheeks go hot. "I happen to believe postponing action isn't the best way."

His whole demeanor seemed to shift. "This could pose a real hit for Courage Bay. Are you sure you want to wreck the economy like that?"

"'Wreck the economy'?" She stopped, confused and upset. "Is that how you see what I'm doing? You think I just want to ruin Courage Bay?"

"You've always hated this place." Kell stared at her with a steady look. "I don't know, Melody. You tell me. What would *you* call closing down businesses and putting people out of work?"

MELODY BRISTLED visibly. "I think you're being a tad dramatic. You make it sound like I'm about to burn and pillage the whole damn place."

"No," he answered, "I know that's not what you're planning, but I also know you don't understand Courage Bay the way I do. Closing this beach in the middle of summer could be devastating. We'd need years to recover."

"And what about the bay?" she shot back. "Don't you care about it? There'll be no tourism or fishing industry at all if the bay is poisoned."

He wanted to argue, but Kell could see from

Melody's expression that he'd be wasting his breath. Somewhere along the way, she'd developed a steel-like resolve. Despite their opposing views, Kell found himself admiring her—in his opinion, people didn't stand by their convictions these days. Melody obviously didn't have that problem.

They returned to the horses and rode back to Whispering Dawn in silence. At the barn, after she dismounted, Melody politely thanked him for the ride and turned to leave.

"Melody—wait…"

Walking over to stand close to her, Kell noticed that her whole body seemed to tense and her eyes took on a sudden wariness.

"Don't leave like this." He put his hands on her shoulders and squeezed gently.

"We're not going to agree, Kell. Don't try to change my mind."

"All right, I won't," he said simply. "But why not leave the beach open and give the situation another week? I promise I'll help you any way I can after that."

"It's too late," she said. "I've already put things in motion." Suspicion made her voice husky. "I learned a long time ago not to bargain with people, Kell. It never works and someone always ends up unhappy."

He nodded, his voice regretful. "You're probably

right. Compromises seldom work." He raised his hands and cradled her face. "But sometimes we have to try. The rewards might be greater than we can even begin to imagine…."

WITH THAT PRONOUNCEMENT, Kell lowered his head until his lips found hers. Dropping his hands to her shoulders, he pulled her closer.

She wanted to protest but the message got lost somewhere between her brain and her hands. She could no more have pushed Kell away than she could have sprouted wings and flown.

Which, in a way, was exactly what she felt she was doing. It had been many long years since they'd touched each other, but no amount of time could have obliterated the wild rush of desire that now lifted Melody up and threatened to carry her away.

His hands moved lower and he pressed her into his body. Melody instantly responded by arching her back and moaning into his open mouth. His tongue sought hers and found it, the action bringing her memories of their heated past.

She found herself gripping Kell as tightly as he held on to her. Beneath the uniform, his muscles were tight and hard. She knew what he looked like without his clothes, but she also knew her memories were of an adolescent, not a man. As he rubbed himself against her, she felt his hardness grow, and the teenage vision disappeared. Replacing it was an image that made her want Kell with an even stronger desire. It was the desire of a woman who knew what she wanted, not that of a shy teenager who was afraid to voice her needs.

She wondered briefly how far they would go, then the decision was taken out of her hands.

From behind her, someone coughed lightly and said, "Hello?"

CHAPTER SIX

MELODY SQUIRMED out of Kell's embrace and straightened her clothing, her face burning as she turned to see who'd spoken. A well-dressed, middle-aged woman stood beside a girl of eleven or twelve. Two sets of identical blue eyes stared in fascination at Kell and Melody.

"I'm Mrs. Rineheart," the woman said after a moment. "And this is Taylor. We're really late but we came by to talk to someone about riding lessons. If you're busy, though..."

"Mrs. Rineheart, of course," Kell said smoothly. "One of the trainers told me you would be here this evening, but I scheduled you for seven with Stephanie."

"I was," she answered. "We got held up a bit." She threw a curious yet friendly glance at Melody, who wished for a hole to crawl into. "We can return later—"

"Absolutely not," Kell reassured the woman. As

he spoke, a teenager dressed in a uniform stepped out from the barn. "In fact, here comes Stephanie right now. She'll give you a tour of our facilities, and if you have time—" he looked at the trainer "—a complimentary half-hour ride, too. On Silky, please, Stephanie." He turned to the young girl at the woman's side. "You'll love Silky," he said with a grin, "She's a great filly. Has a strong head, but you look like you can handle her."

The girl's face lit with excitement. There was no way her mother could refuse the offer, even if she'd wanted to.

Smiling graciously, Kell turned the potential client over to the trainer and led Melody away, the awkwardness of the situation glossed over as if it had never happened.

His hand on her elbow, Melody sent a sideways glance at Kell as they walked toward the office. The small-town kid who'd been left the ranch had definitely turned into a businessman, urbane and quick. The thought resonated as she recalled their argument at the beach.

Kell was sharp. And just as important, he *did* understand Courage Bay in a way Melody never would.

If other people felt the way he did about closing the beach, she was going to have a real stink on her hands.

Obviously rattled by Kell's kiss, Melody felt confused. A second later, she pushed any uncertainty away. She'd done the right thing, the only thing, that she could do. There simply was no other choice to make.

Kell opened her car door then bent and kissed her once again. His lips felt even softer this time, more persuasive. She was almost dizzy when he raised his head.

Melting back into the car, she sat limply, then watched as he walked away.

MELODY GOT to the office early the following morning, and without even dropping her purse, headed straight for the doughnuts and coffee Bitsy usually brought in for their breakfast. She needed to stock up on all the sugar and caffeine she could get her hands on. Today would be bad, but tomorrow, when news of the beach closing broke, would be a nightmare. The corner of Bitsy's desk was empty, though. Melody started to moan as Bitsy came out of her office. "Where's the coffee—"

"We're going to breakfast with Lisa. I didn't pick up anything this morning."

"Bitsy! I don't have time—"

"No excuses," Bitsy instructed. Physically turning Melody toward the door, she grabbed her keys and shoved her outside. "This is the only time Lisa could make it and I promised her I'd get you there. She'll kill me if we're not at the diner in ten minutes."

Melody protested all the way to Bitsy's red convertible and Bitsy ignored every word. "You have to eat," she said. "Everyone needs breakfast."

"But I've got work to do!"

Bitsy started the engine. "So what?"

"'So what!'" Melody repeated. "So what? It's important, that's what!"

"Well, this is important, too. Especially to Lisa. She never gets to do anything for herself."

They were flying down the road before Melody could say more. Below them, the bay gleamed, the sheen of light on the blue water broken only by a single line of fishing boats. With the breeze in her hair and her friend by her side, Melody suddenly thought, "What the hell?" She'd already called Dr. Martin and he was taking care of the paperwork right now. The you-know-what was going to hit the fan tomorrow regardless of what she did today.

She and Bitsy were both laughing by the time they arrived downtown. Bitsy drove by Courage Bay's main fire station and waved to the cute firemen, then they parked and walked down the street to the diner. Lisa was waiting for them.

All three of them ordered bacon and eggs with

pancakes on the side. Once the waitress left, Lisa grinned widely at her two friends. "Last night I just happened to call the girl who helps me out with the kids sometimes. Taylor Rineheart is such a precious little thing, isn't she? And her mother is *sooo* friendly…. You'll never guess what they told me."

They were pointedly ignoring Melody. At first she was annoyed, then she realized they were teasing her. She felt her face flame as she recognized the name of the mother and daughter who'd witnessed her kiss with Kell.

In unison, Bitsy and Lisa turned to Melody and raised their eyebrows.

She couldn't help but laugh. Her friends joined her, and as the waitress returned with their loaded platters, they bombarded Melody with questions, insisting she tell them more.

"There's nothing more *to* tell!" She poured syrup over her pancakes, then stabbed the stack. "It was a kiss, that's it. I am not getting involved with Kell again. That's history."

And if it wasn't, then it would be soon. She thought for a second about letting her friends know she was closing the beach, but quickly dismissed the idea. She wasn't going to ruin their perfect breakfast.

"It's history," she repeated. "Really—"

Lisa and Bitsy exchanged a glance, and their skeptical expressions were so alike, Melody dissolved into laughter once again, despite her gloomy thoughts.

They talked and ate then talked some more, catching up on old friends and new ones, too. Finally Melody pushed her plate aside.

"I'm going to pass out if I eat one more bite," she declared. "But I can't believe how much I've enjoyed this! Do you two meet all the time like this?"

Bitsy shook her head and put down the orange juice she'd been sipping. "We haven't gotten together in ages," she confessed. "But we should more often."

Lisa signaled the waitress for coffee. "I don't have the time," she said, turning back to the table. "And I definitely don't have the money. I hate to ask my mom to do extra baby-sitting. She keeps the kids all day long as it is. The only reason I could come today was because I couldn't go to work anyway. Gerald has one of his endless colds and I have to take him to the doctor again. I swear, that kid's nose is always dripping."

Her life sounded hard. Melody leaned closer, her elbows on the table. "What do you do? I don't even know where you work."

Lisa looked embarrassed and her cheeks grew

pink. "I work on a fishing boat, Melody. I'm the cook, the nurse and the janitor all wrapped up in one. Sometimes I do deck work. I didn't get to go to college and this was the best I could do. Jobs—even ones as hard as mine—are hard to come by in Courage Bay without an education."

Melody felt a nudge of apprehension. If the beach closure was long-term, it was entirely possible Lisa could be affected. Melody prayed that wouldn't happen, but as she thought about the consequences of her decision, she grew even more concerned.

Working on a boat was back-breaking and not for the weak. Melody knew this because she'd done an internship on a one-hundred-foot shrimper. Her only task had been to collect specimens all day, but the boat's crew had worked endlessly. The weather, the job and the sea all took a toll. Without thinking, she glanced at Lisa's hands. They were callused and tough-looking, the nails broken to the quick.

"It's a dead-end job and I know it'll never amount to anything else," Lisa said, looking down at the table. "I won't ever be successful like you, but—"

"Don't apologize, Lisa. There's nothing wrong with working on a boat," Melody interrupted her quietly. "And nothing says you have to have a college degree to be successful, either."

Lisa glanced up at Melody. Bitsy studied her, as well, her gaze speculative.

"You've already made a success out of your life," Melody continued. "Just look at those two beautiful children of yours. They're so lucky to have you as a mother. Nothing means more than that." Melody shook her head, her throat tightening. Lisa's life had been incredibly hard, but her children were clearly her first priority. What would Melody have given to have had a parent like that herself?

She pulled herself together. "If there weren't mothers like you who love their children and put them first, this world wouldn't stand a chance."

Nodding slowly, Lisa seemed to think about Melody's words. "I guess I never considered it that way before, but I think you're right. I mean, I love them and everything, but when you're butt-high in dirty diapers, you can't always see the bigger picture."

The image Lisa's words created broke the seriousness of the moment, and the three women gave in to laughter once more. They paid the bill, then they headed outside. Lisa was anxious to get back to her sick toddler, and Melody to return to work. Bitsy was the only one who wanted to linger. Melody took one arm, Lisa the other, and they dragged the redhead down the sidewalk toward their respective cars. Before they left, they hugged and promised themselves they'd get together again.

Melody entered her office, determined to settle down to work the minute they got back. But she couldn't get the absurd image of Lisa, wading through a sea of diapers, out of her mind.

It was good to visit with old friends.

And it was almost—*almost*—fun to be back.

KELL'S PHONE rang at six-thirty the next morning. The sound woke him from a dream he was having about Melody. When he picked up the receiver and brought it to his ear, he thought he might still be dreaming. Her voice, husky and soft, sounded as if she were lying next to him in bed.

"I'm calling to give you advance warning so you can be prepared."

"Sounds ominous." He propped himself up on one elbow in his bed. "Is a storm headed this way?"

"You could say that."

Kell smoothed the sheets, visions of Melody's blond hair spreading over the pillow at his side. "I think one already came through the other night. A gorgeous lady kissed me and I still haven't recovered."

"This isn't the same thing." There was an edginess in her voice.

"What is it, Melody?" he asked, fully alert now.

"This morning's paper is announcing the beach closing. The signs are up, too, and by noon today, everything will be shut down. Dr. Martin's already notified the state and regional authorities."

He drew in a sharp breath. "I wish we could have talked about this again."

"I know you do, but like I said the other night, bargains always leave someone unhappy. If we'd discussed the situation further and someone found out, they'd only get upset because you didn't stop me."

"I'd be receiving more credit than I deserve if anyone thought I could do that."

"I don't know, Kell. Your powers of persuasion have always impressed me. But in the end I had to do what I had to do. I hope you can understand."

He started to answer, but realized she'd already hung up.

WHEN MELODY arrived at the office, Bitsy met her at the door, a copy of the newspaper in her hand. With a shocked expression, she thrust it into Melody's face. "Is this true?"

The disapproval in Kell's voice had cut Melody

deeply, and now Bitsy's did the same. Melody glanced at the headline and sighed. "Yes, it's true. We've closed the beaches and put out a fishing ban."

She had known her decision would be an unpopular one, but last night she'd realized something. Until now, Courage Bay had been untouched by pollution and the beach had never been closed. It seemed impossible, given the problems faced on the east coast and especially overseas, but the waters here had never been affected before. The articles in the paper had been limited, with little explanation of what might happen as a consequence of the HAB. More than just the economy was going to be hurt; the pride of Courage Bay might suffer, as well.

She tried to explain. "Bitsy, I came here because there was a problem with the bay. I found out what that problem is and now I have to fix it. You've read the articles and seen my work—"

"Of course I have," her friend argued, "but nobody thought you'd go *this* far."

"I don't have a choice—"

"You don't understand, either! It's hard enough around here to find employment as it is!" Bitsy's green eyes filled with anger. "Do you have any idea what this means to everyone?"

"I know exactly what it means," Melody said patiently. "If I don't do this, the fish in the bay are going to get sicker. There's even a chance all of them could die."

"What about people's jobs?"

"I can't worry about that right now," Melody answered.

Bitsy stared at her with disbelief then stalked back to her desk to pick up a sheaf of pink message slips. She held them out to Melody with a cold look. "You damn well *better* start worrying about it, because you've got to explain the problem to all these folks," she said. "They're the ones who've called so far this morning."

Melody took the slips and went into her office. As the day progressed, things only got worse.

The phone never stopped ringing. Melody talked to the newspaper, the local radio station and even a TV reporter from San Diego. Kell called, too, but she refused to talk to him. She didn't have the time to spare, and for that she was grateful. She wouldn't have known what to say to him.

The next two days were a repeat of the one before except that there were *more* angry messages and *more* upset people wanting to scream at her. Melody told herself she was doing what was right and forged ahead. Just as she had before the announcement, she continued to take her water samples at different depths and locations early each morning. Back in the office, she plotted the points and studied the tests herself, then shipped the vials to Scripps for further analysis. Monitoring the levels of the HABs and studying the samples for change took all her time. She stopped to eat but little else. The anger of the community grew until even the local fishing guide she'd hired to take her into the bay to do her sampling, a gregarious old man who'd known her grandmother, turned surly and unfriendly.

It was Saturday morning before Melody found a free second to ask Bitsy if she'd heard from Lisa. Bitsy glared at her. "Why do you even care?"

Too exhausted to argue—or explain—Melody simply stared at Bitsy. Their relationship had become so strained, Melody was no longer sure it could recover. She hoped that wasn't the case; the thought of losing her renewed friendships hurt more than she would have thought possible.

"Maybe it'd be best if you went on home for the day," she said softly. "I think we both need a break."

Bitsy didn't put up an argument. Gathering her things, she started toward the door, but before she could get there, it burst open. She actually had to jump out of the way or risk being hit.

A wild-eyed, disheveled Lisa charged in, Lily crying in her arms, Gerald barely able to keep up as she strode toward Melody. When she stopped, the little boy almost stumbled before catching himself at the last minute.

"Just who in the hell do you think you are?" Shaking with anger, Lisa clutched her baby to her chest and put her other hand on Gerald's head. "You can't waltz in here after all these years and ruin this community!"

Speechless with fatigue and disappointment, Melody felt herself sway slightly. She'd had so many people upset with her over the past week that Lisa's anger didn't shock her the way it might have, but it hurt all the same.

"Lisa, please. I'm not trying to ruin—"

"You're right! You aren't 'trying'—you already have." Hearing his mother's angry tone, the little boy began to wail and wipe at his runny nose.

Melody sent the child a worried look then faced Lisa again. "I had to do this, Lisa. More fish will die if the HAB gets worse—"

"As far as this family's concerned, worse is already here."

Uneasiness washed over Melody. "What do you mean?"

"I got laid off yesterday! I have two kids, no husband

and now no income, thanks to you. I hope you sleep better tonight knowing you've saved the fish! I'll be down at the Food Bank, begging dinner for my kids."

Lisa sent a look toward Bitsy that made it clear she considered her a traitor, too. Without another word, she clutched Gerald's hand and stormed outside, slamming the door so hard the building seemed to shake.

Bitsy seemed to take pity on Melody and patted her on the back, but the gesture felt perfunctory. She didn't stick around to offer more comfort, but quietly said goodbye and left. Too stunned to do anything else, Melody fell abruptly into the nearest chair.

When her tears came a few minutes later, they were as hot and salty as the bay she was trying to protect.

CHAPTER SEVEN

LATE THAT NIGHT, Melody sat on the veranda that ran the length of Bay Villa and watched the sun slide beneath the clouds that were threatening the horizon. They looked as if they held rain, but she knew their promise was a false one. The drought wouldn't be broken this evening. Lightning might flare and thunder roll, but that would be all.

Sipping from the glass of wine she'd poured for herself, Melody thought of the dolphin she and Kell had rescued. He'd recovered from his wound, but an infection had set in and he was still being treated.

Thoughts of the animal brought thoughts of Kell. As soon as she'd managed to stop crying following the encounter with Lisa, she'd called him and asked him to come out to Bay Villa.

She wanted him to know that no matter how he felt, she knew she'd done the right thing. Somehow she had to make him understand. At the very least, she needed *one* person to see she was doing her best.

Rising from her chaise, she glanced nervously at her watch then walked to the edge of the patio. She took another sip of Burgundy, and two seconds later, Kell's deep voice rolled over her. "This looks like a movie setting…."

She turned to find him standing on the opposite edge of the flagstone patio. His comment encompassed the sprawling old house and beautiful view beyond, but Melody thought she could say the very same about him.

Poised against the flame-red sky, Kell's dark silhouette contrasted sharply with the fire-lit bay behind him. With his wide shoulders and tall, powerful build, he could have stepped straight off the screen. Kell's good looks would have made any woman swoon.

Melody was no exception.

He crossed the space that separated them, his eyes never leaving her face.

"What's wrong?" he quietly asked. "You sounded upset over the phone."

"I'm exhausted," she confessed. "But I feel like I need to explain my reasons for closing the beach a little better. I don't think I did an adequate job the other day and I'd like to make sure that at least you understand."

He stood before her in silence, then said, "You're a big fat liar."

"That's not a very nice thing to say." Her voice was faint.

"Okay. I'll take back the big and fat part."

"But not the liar?"

He didn't answer. Instead, he leaned over and kissed her deeply, his mouth molding to hers, his arm sliding down her back. She tensed for a moment, then let him have his way, her body pressing to his as she wrapped her arms around his neck. After a bit, he tilted his head back and stared into her eyes.

"You didn't get me out here to talk," he said huskily. "You called for an entirely different reason."

"That's not true—"

"Yes, it is," he said.

"You're being ridiculous."

"No. You are. Face the truth for once, Melody. Face it head-on."

Melody stilled, but inside her, a storm began to gather. This wasn't going the way she'd planned, but as usual, Kell had taken control. Her breath caught in her chest and her pulse started to pound. She lifted her hands, still entwined with his, and put her palms on his chest. Beneath her touch, nothing gave way—she could have been pressing her fingers against steel.

"You don't understand. I asked you here so we could talk—"

"You don't want to talk to me, Melody. You want the same thing I do." He paused. "You want us to spend the night together and make love like we used to."

Her lie crumbled to dust as the truth of his words exposed her rawest emotions. He was right. She didn't want to talk. She'd called him because she needed someone's arms around her. She needed comfort. She needed closeness. She needed...him.

MELODY MELTED as Kell wrapped her into a tight embrace. Ever since she'd come back to Courage Bay, he'd dreamed of doing this very thing, and despite her continued rebuffs, he'd even made a hopeful stop at a drugstore for condoms the other day. When she'd called, he'd been shocked, but he hadn't turned her down because he couldn't. They saw the world through different filters, but Kell loved Melody and he had to accept the fact that he always would.

Lowering his head, he angled his lips to fit over hers. He meant to hold back and be gentle, yet the second their mouths connected, he lost sight of that goal. Desire welled instantly inside him, deep and powerful, and he knew he wouldn't be able to finesse this. He was a man and he wanted her. The teenaged fumblings and awkward moves they'd shared all those years ago were long behind him. He deepened the kiss and made his intentions clear, his hands dropping to her buttocks as he brought her to him.

She raised her arms to circle his neck, her fingers threading through his hair. A murmur grew in the back of her throat, a murmur Kell hadn't heard in years but one he recognized immediately. He let the kiss build a moment longer, then he bent over and picked Melody up. Their mouths still locked, he headed for the loggia that ran the length of the stuccoed home.

The double chaise was where it had always been, the cushion just as soft.

Kell laid Melody on the padded lounger then lowered himself to her side. They'd seen more than one sunrise from this vantage point, Melody slipping from her bedroom to meet him by the pool.

Their kiss resumed and Melody took the lead this time. Her mouth pressed against Kell's, she unbuttoned his shirt and slipped her hand inside to caress his bare chest. Her fingers left a trail of sparks and Kell felt every one. Raising herself over him, she peeled his shirt from his shoulders and dropped it to the floor beside them. Without taking her eyes from his, she lifted her arms and pulled her T-shirt over her head.

He stared at her in the dusky gloom, then reached up to touch the edge of her bra, the sky behind her splitting with jagged streaks of distant lightning. The cleft between her breasts was deeper and fuller, her curves more generous than they had been when she was younger. With a twist she undid the clasp then shrugged out of the scrap of silk. He took her breasts in his hands and she shivered lightly as his thumbs caressed their swollen sides.

A dry hot wind picked at the vines wrapped around the loggia's columns and rattled the twisted leaves. Her skin was softer than he remembered. Then he wondered if it had been that way all along and he'd simply failed to notice, too young to appreciate the details back then. Kell closed his eyes and let his fingers drift lower. Everywhere he touched her was smooth and supple.

When his hands met the resistance of her belt, Kell opened his eyes and pinned his gaze on hers. Slowly and carefully, he undid the leather and released it. She shed her shorts and her lacy panties, then helped him out of the rest of his clothing. Everything went into the pile on the floor.

Kell lost track of what happened next as his world

shrank to a single point. Moving Melody beneath him, he kissed her lips, her hair, her face, his mouth traversing her body then coming back up. She kept her eyes closed until he entered her, and then she opened them.

The emotions in her gaze grabbed him and wouldn't let go. Every inch of heartache she'd ever caused him, every disagreement they'd ever had suddenly disappeared. All he could see in her eyes was love. He kissed her then groaned, the rhythm between them building to a climax that shook him to his core.

If there had been any thought that separation had diminished the connection between them, it fled in the face of Kell's passion. His love for Melody had not only survived, but grown.

She was his first love, and as he thrust himself into her, he knew she would be his last.

MELODY LED Kell through the darkened house to the guest bedroom where she'd been sleeping. When she'd first arrived, she'd considered taking her old room but quickly abandoned that idea after going upstairs. Her grandmother had redecorated it when Melody had moved in, and it still held the same girlish furniture and old familiar wallpaper. One look and she'd fled the room. The memories it held—of crying herself to sleep night after night and wishing for the return of her family and her former life—weren't as easy to escape.

Weaving down the hall, past the sheet-draped furniture and shuttered windows, Melody dropped Kell's hand as they reached the end of the corridor. "The bath's through there." She pointed to her left, then tilted her head toward a door on her right. "I put my stuff in here. Come on in when you finish."

He nodded in the darkness, but before she could move away, he reached out and gripped her arm, pulling her to his side. His voice was low and husky, his breath warm against her check. "Don't disappear on me, Mel…."

She didn't know if he meant now or later. She made her voice light, as if it didn't matter. "I'm not going anywhere," she said. "When you come out, I'll be right here."

Gripping her shoulders, he kissed her, hard, then turned and vanished into the bathroom. Her mouth felt the imprint of his as the door slammed behind him. Lifting her fingers to her lips, Melody leaned weakly against the nearest wall.

What had she done? What had *they* done? If she'd somehow thought making love to Kell would dispel all the old ghosts, all the old memories, she'd been badly mistaken. Giving in to her need tonight had done just the opposite; it had resurrected the past and given it new life. Now it would never die. Not in this lifetime. Not for her.

Pulling Kell's shirt tighter around her shoulders, Melody pushed away from the stucco and walked into the bedroom. She sat down on the edge of the bed and tried to decide what to do.

But her mind stayed blank.

She didn't have a next step, a Plan B, a flowchart.

There was no formula or methodology to handle this dilemma and she found herself at a loss. All the tools and techniques she'd developed over the years to deal with her work and her life abandoned her as if they'd never existed.

She didn't know what to do.

Like an overflowing fountain, her brain filled and refilled with images of the hour she'd just passed with Kell. His hands against her skin. His lips on her breasts. His body over hers.

He padded into the room and came over to where she sat, dropping to his knees before her. "Where are you?" he asked. "In the future or in the past?"

She shook her head and reached out to cradle his

face. "I don't know where I am. I feel like Alice must have when she slid down the rabbit's hole." Leaning over, Melody kissed him. He tasted like sea spray and sex, and incredibly she felt her desire rise again.

He sensed her reaction, or maybe he simply felt the same thing. Either way, it didn't seem to matter. Melody let him push her down on the bed and they started all over again.

IN THE MIDDLE of the night, the darkness surrounding them, Melody finally talked. Kell sensed that sharing this conversation with him was somehow more intimate to Melody than the sexual connection they'd just made.

"Bitsy told me you had gotten married but it didn't work out." She lifted her head from his shoulder and looked up, her eyes locking on his in the dark. "What happened?"

"Nothing happened," he said. "And that's why we divorced. We only got married because we had reached that point where you either marry...or break up. Unfortunately we made the wrong choice."

"I was engaged once," she said quietly, her gaze turning to the ceiling.

"What happened?"

"Instead of getting married, he decided to go to Borneo."

"Why on earth would he do that?"

"He had a job offer he couldn't refuse. He was a biologist at Scripps, too, and it was the chance of a lifetime."

"You didn't want to go with him?"

"He didn't ask—so neither did I."

Kell smoothed a lock of hair off her forehead. "I'm sorry."

"Don't be." She raised herself up on one elbow and looked at him. "After he left and I stopped feeling sorry for myself, I realized the relationship would never have lasted. It was for the best."

Despite her words, Kell could see the hurt in her eyes. It was the same kind of bruised pain he'd seen when she'd talked about her parents that one time. "Did you love him?"

She threaded her fingers between his and placed their hands on his chest. "I thought I did."

"But…?"

"But he never made me feel like this." Her gaze took in the bed then came back to Kell. "Never like this."

Slowly Kell turned her hand over and brought it up to kiss her palm, giving himself some time to think. He didn't want to scare her, but he had to know if she felt for him what he felt for her. "What do you think that means?" he asked.

"I think it means I have a problem."

His heart clutched and Kell reached out to pull her closer. Burying his face in her neck, he kissed her throat. "Worse things could happen," he murmured.

"Like what?" she asked.

He pulled back and looked straight at her. "You could run away from me again. That was no picnic the first time, at least not for me."

"I was scared." She hesitated a moment before continuing. "I didn't want to depend on someone else for my happiness like my mother had, then see everything shatter when that person went a different way. I wanted to live in a bigger world than Courage Bay, and I had goals and the ambition to achieve them."

"Why didn't you tell me that?"

"I couldn't," she said simply. "I was afraid you might change my mind, and I knew if I stayed, I'd end up with nothing more than anyone else who lived here." She drew a deep breath. "I thought we would get married and have kids and I'd spend the rest of my life in some minor position that didn't matter to anyone outside of Courage Bay."

"And what's wrong with that?"

She was silent for a moment. "Not one damn thing," she said finally. "I was just too young and foolish to realize it at the time."

CHAPTER EIGHT

BY MORNING'S LIGHT, Melody watched Kell sleep, his long form stretched out on the bed beside her.

What had happened between them during the night was incredible, but where did they go from here? Did she love him? Did he love her? And if the answer was yes, what should they do about it?

Melody didn't want to give up everything she'd worked so hard to gain. She'd sacrificed way too much, including her love for Kell, to relinquish her job and her success at Scripps.

Likewise, Kell would never leave Courage Bay. He had a thriving business with a history to it— Whispering Dawn had been part of the area forever. Even the name of the ranch meant something to Courage Bay residents, supposedly referring back to an indigenous Indian woman, Dawn-Flower, who'd fallen in love with one of the first settlers, an ancestor of Kell's. Melody couldn't ask him to give up his heritage any more than he could ask her to give up her career.

She continued to ponder the dilemma until the phone beside the bed rang, shattering the quiet and her thoughts.

Bitsy answered Melody's hello without a greeting of her own. "I'm at the hospital with Lisa and I thought you should know what's going on."

"What's wrong?" Melody demanded in alarm, and Kell opened his eyes at her frantic voice. "Are you sick? Is Lisa okay?"

"It's Gerald, Lisa's little boy. Last night, she got some fresh shrimp off one of the guys at the dock. He'd caught it a few hours before—right in the middle of the bay. She fixed it for dinner, and afterward, Gerald started throwing up." She took a shaky breath. "He hasn't stopped since."

THEY GRABBED their clothes and ran out the door. As Melody explained what had happened, Kell decided he'd never seen her so pale or so upset. By the time they hit Madison Avenue, the street that led to Courage Bay Hospital, she'd composed herself but she was still clearly rattled.

"Can this be fatal?" He sent a glance in her direction, his hands tight on the steering wheel.

"Yes." Her one-word answer was anxious, her expression even more so. "Especially with a child. Their immune system isn't as developed as an adult's, and on top of that, Gerald's was already compromised. He had a cold the other day when I met Lisa and Bitsy for breakfast, and Lisa said he has them a lot."

"This is what you were afraid might happen, isn't it? This is why you needed to close the beach."

He could feel her stare as she turned to look at him. "Yes." She paused. "But I sure as hell hate being right."

Kell shook his head. He hadn't understood her argument any more than she'd understood his, and suddenly he wished he could go back in time and erase everything he'd said. Sure, Melody hadn't understood the commercial toll that closing the beach would bring, but how could she? If you'd never owned your own business, you couldn't possibly understand all the ramifications.

Turning his truck into the Emergency entrance, Kell prayed they weren't too late.

MELODY ENTERED the E.R. at a dead run.

Grabbing the first nurse she saw, she said, "I'm Dr. Harper. Where's the Montgomery family?"

"In room 4." The woman turned as she answered and began to hurry the opposite way. "Come with me and I'll take you to them."

When they got there, the tiny room was full of people. Two doctors, Bitsy, three nurses, Lisa, her mother... Everyone was focused on the toddler stretched out on the examining table. Melody's heart tripped as she saw the rash covering his skin and his lethargic manner. Her worst nightmare had become real.

"What are you doing here?" Lisa said angrily as Melody entered. "Who let you in—"

"I came to help," Melody said. "I thought there might be something I could do."

"You've done enough already."

Lisa started around the table, but one of the doctors stepped between her and Melody, halting her progress. "Who are you?" he asked, turning to Melody.

"I'm Dr. Harper. I'm from the Scripps Institute."

The doctor was an older man with gray hair. Recognition flared in his eyes. "You're the one who closed the beach?"

"Yes, I am," she answered. "And this—" she nodded toward Gerald "—is exactly why I did it. May I listen to his chest?"

With a nod, the doctor handed over his stethoscope.

Melody warmed its metal disk with her palm then gently placed it against the child's tiny chest. The little boy's breathing was shallow, his intake too rapid. He alternated between furiously scratching at his rash and lying drowsily on the table.

She took the tips from her ears and handed the instrument back to the doctor.

"He's clearly had a reaction to the shellfish he ate," the doctor said, accepting the stethoscope Melody held out. She thought he looked worried, and his next words confirmed her suspicion. "I can try the shotgun approach, but if you could tell me more about the specific toxin involved, my chances of picking the right drug to combat it would really improve. We could even the odds some."

"Have you done any cultures? I can give you a much better answer with those in hand."

"I took them to the lab ten minutes ago." A woman in scrubs spoke up from the back, her voice familiar.

It was Jackie, Kell's sister. Her eyes, mirrors of Kell's, were dark and filled with concern.

"How long will it take?"

"Twenty minutes, thirty at the most."

Melody nodded and the doctor on the other side of the table stepped closer. He looked like a teenager.

The embroidered name on his coat read Dr. Soo Keong Kwoh.

He spoke quietly and politely. "I've seen this before, in the coastal waters off Manila Bay. My roommate in college was part of a team that did remote sensing reflectance during an algal bloom outbreak in 1999."

"I know the study," Melody said with sudden excitement. "They classified the bloom types according to the singular value decomposition method by using satellite data, right?"

"That's correct. They also did sea-truth water sampling and in-situ reflectance spectra using a portable spectroradiometer."

From the corner of her eye, Melody saw Lisa and her mother look at each other with puzzled expressions. But Melody couldn't risk taking the time for lengthy explanations now.

She put a hand on Gerald's plump leg as it began to shake. "How much shrimp did he eat, Lisa? It's really important you tell us the details."

"Not that much," she said sharply. "Two or three, maybe four at the most. I boiled them and peeled them."

"Do you have any left?"

"No. We ate all of them." Her expression crumpled as her defensiveness turned into distress. "I—I didn't have the money to buy anything at the grocery store and I had to feed the kids."

Murmuring softly, Melody closed the space separating her from Lisa and folded her arms around her friend's shaking shoulders. Patting her on the back, Melody felt her heart break at her friend's pain.

Lisa began to cry, returning Melody's hug almost desperately, her words coming out between sobs. "A guy I knew on the dock told me he'd eaten from the same catch the night before and he didn't get sick, so I figured it'd be okay."

"It probably was," Melody said, "for him and for you, too. But Gerald still has his cold, doesn't he?"

"Y-yes."

"That's one of the reasons he got sick. His immune system is weak because of the cold, and bugs like this love to attack when they think they can win."

"Is he gonna die, Melody? Did I kill him by feeding him that shrimp?"

"Look, you were doing the best you could. Now we have to work with that—"

Lisa pulled back abruptly, her eyes brimming. "You...you didn't answer my question, Mel. Is...is he going to die?"

Melody met her friend's tearful gaze and spoke with more determination than she felt. "No, Lisa, Gerald's not going to die. Not if I can help it, he won't."

MELODY HEADED for the hospital's lab, Dr. Kwoh at her side. "My friend found Pyrodinium bahamense in Manila Bay," he said in a worried voice. "Do you think that's what we have here? They lost a lot of people in Manila Bay who ate shellfish contaminated with that. Some died."

"I've seen bahamense in the bay," Melody said, shaking her head. "But until the cultures are done, I can't say for sure. At least no one else has gotten get sick from this particular batch."

They'd sent a security officer from the hospital to find the fisherman who'd sold Lisa the shrimp. He'd given her the last of it, thank goodness.

"Frankly, I've been more worried about the bahamense combining with the Gymnodinium breve I've seen. If those two came together—"

"The toxin would become airborne," he filled in for her. "Then we'd have people getting sick—"

"Just from breathing the air."

His frown deepened. "Do you think that's what has happened?"

"I certainly hope not," she answered. "This is bad enough."

Without speaking further, they pushed through the double doors of the lab. Dr. Kwoh introduced Melody to the staff, and minutes later she had a microscope and a lab coat.

KELL WALKED across the yard to Butter's cubicle in the stable. The gelding neighed softly and nosed Kell's head.

He had left the hospital a little after five that afternoon. A mare had been coming in from San Diego and he'd needed to be at the ranch to oversee her arrival. Since then, he'd called the hospital every hour. Melody had been too busy to talk, but Jackie hadn't seemed hopeful. Her worried tone had said more than her words.

Quickly Kell saddled up the big gelding and in minutes they were on their way. They broke from the bridle path and trotted past the tall sea grasses, headed for the beach.

A quarter moon hung over the eerily still water. To someone who didn't know better, the endless expanse looked like a lake instead of the ocean. There were no waves, and a hushed breathlessness kept even the sea oats from stirring. The beach looked as if it were waiting for something.

Clicking his tongue and lifting the reins, Kell guided Butter to the path that cut through to the shoreline. Signs gleamed in the darkness, warning swimmers to stay out of the water until further notice and telling fisherman not to eat what they caught.

He'd never prayed before while he was on patrol, but Kell did so now. Melody needed all the help she could get, and so did Gerald.

Kell added a quick one for himself, too. He was in deep trouble.

He'd fallen in love with Melody all over again, but he couldn't ask her to stay here. Not after tonight. He'd seen her in a different light, seen the talented scientist she'd become, and now he understood why she'd left in the first place.

She had too much to offer the world to be stuck in a backwater burg like Courage Bay. He couldn't be that selfish no matter how badly his heart would ache when she left.

SHE ISOLATED the species at a quarter past three in the morning.

Picking up the phone, Melody dialed her boss, waking Dr. Martin so he could double check her work using the Scripps database. He did so while she waited, and ten minutes later, she gave Gerald's doctor the information. He took it on the run and headed gratefully for the hospital's pharmacy. The cause of Gerald's illness was Gonyaulaz catenella, a well-documented PSP Melody had yet to see in her samples, and it appeared to be the only HAB involved. Her fears of the phytoplanktons joining forces were unfounded. For now.

An hour later, exhausted and completely drained, she pushed through the double doors of the E.R. and stepped outside. Lisa was standing on the sidewalk, staring at the sky, her arms wrapped around herself as if it were fifty degrees instead of eighty. Bitsy waited nearby. When the doors swished open, they both turned to see who had come out.

"I isolated the strain," Melody announced as she walked toward them. "The doctor took the information and came back with a 'cocktail' of sorts. He started the IV before I left. It could be wishful thinking, but I believe Gerald's already looking better."

"Oh, thank God…" Lisa took two steps to a nearby bench and collapsed, her shoulders heaving. Melody and Bitsy tried to soothe her, but she continued to cry, her relief almost tangible in the hot night air. After a while, she looked at Melody, her eyes shining in the darkness.

"God, Melody…I'm so sorry I said those horrible things to you back there. This has all been my fault. If I just hadn't gotten those shrimp... I don't know how I can ever make it up to you—"

"Stop right there, Lisa," Melody said sternly. "You didn't understand how sick the bay was, but I didn't understand the impact of closing the beach, either. We were each just doing the best we could."

"But I feel so stupid! If only I'd understood what you were doing...."

"How could you have known? It's my fault for not doing a better job of explaining—to you and everyone else."

Lisa continued to castigate herself, but Melody stopped listening. She was thinking instead about what she'd just said. Many of the residents of Courage Bay depended on the bay for their livelihood, but much of their knowledge of the waters and the marine life it supported came from experience and tradition. The community lacked the sophisticated marine biology centers and labs that larger cities had. Courage Bay had access via the Internet, of course, but learning should be hands-on. And it should also have an element of fun. She narrowed her eyes, thinking of the possibilities as excitement took hold.

Lisa's voice pulled Melody from her thoughts. "I

know you're right, but I'll never forget what you did this evening, Mel. You saved Gerald's life and I'll owe you forever."

Melody's eyes filled with tears. "You don't owe me anything, Lisa. Just be my friend—that's all I need."

She stepped closer, and along with Bitsy, the three women embraced one another on the bench, crying.

A second later, Melody pulled away. "I have to go find Kell," she said.

Dabbing at their eyes, Lisa and Bitsy looked up at the same time, their expressions curious.

"I have to tell him something, and it's fifteen years overdue."

CHAPTER NINE

"WHAT'S THE MATTER, buddy? Don't you want to call it a day and head for home?"

Dawn was about to break, and they had finished their last trip down the beach. Kell's official patrol had ended hours earlier, but he knew he'd be too restless to sleep. Tugging Butter's reins to the right, Kell was now ready to leave, but the gelding had stopped abruptly, his stubborn resistance to Kell's gentle tug bringing man and beast to a sudden halt. Kell pulled harder but it made no difference. Butter refused to move.

Kell gave in and let the horse take them in the direction he wanted.

A few minutes later, he understood why.

A lone figure sat on the still shore, her curves outlined by the waning moon, her blond hair gleaming. Kell tensed, but this time he knew he wasn't seeing a mermaid.

Urging Butter into a canter, he reached Melody's side quickly.

She looked up at him and said simply, "Gerald's going to be fine. We figured out which algae was in the shrimp."

"Thank God!" Dismounting, Kell dropped Butter's reins and wrapped Melody in a quick hug, sitting down beside her in the sand. "I bet Lisa's relieved."

"You could say that." Melody smiled, then looked away from him to stare out at the water. "All this trouble and heartache from tiny little organisms that only have a single cell…. And it'll all be over in a matter of hours."

"What do you mean?"

She waved a hand toward the beach. "Don't you see how calm the water is? An offshore front is about to move in. There's no way the NSP and PSP can merge under those conditions. It'll blow everything out to sea and disperse it."

"What about the source of the toxins?"

"I have no idea." She hesitated for a moment, then turned to him. Her eyes were huge and dark and filled with something he couldn't quite define. He wanted to take her back into his arms and kiss it away, yet he held back. He wasn't sure she wouldn't shut him out.

"You were right about closing the beach, Kell. I didn't understand the impact it would have on the local economy."

"Maybe that's true, but you didn't have a choice, either," he said quietly. "You had to do it or more people could have gotten sick."

Her voice held relief. "I'm so glad you understand. I didn't want to hurt the people of Courage Bay or anyone else, but—"

"But you had to do the right thing, even if it was an unpopular decision."

"That's just it, Kell. My decision *shouldn't* have been an unpopular one. If I'd done a better job of explaining what was going on, everyone would have understood. I realized that after I talked to Lisa tonight. If she'd been more informed about the HAB first, she would never have risked eating those shrimp."

Her eyes lit up as she began to speak. "What Courage Bay needs is a facility that explains about the science of marine life, how people interact with the sea and how the animals interact with us. Think what it might mean for the city if we built an aquarium or an educational center. As an added benefit, it would draw more tourists and that would mean more money. We could use those funds to combat future problems the bay might have!"

Kell felt his chest swell but he wouldn't let himself hope. Not yet. "Are you aware of what you just said?" He continued before she could answer. "*We* could do this and *we* could do that—*for* Courage Bay. Do you want to help the city?"

She grinned. "I hadn't thought of it in those terms, but it sure sounds that way, doesn't it?" When he shook his head and frowned, her expression sobered. "Wh-what's wrong?"

"I can't think about that unless I get one thing straight." He took her hands in his. "I love you, Melody. That's a fact and it's never going to change. But I can't ask you to stay here—this has to be your decision and yours alone."

"Oh, Kell, it's exactly what I want to do! And I'm very sorry I hurt you all those years ago. I was just a kid, too scared to realize I had other options. Coming back to Courage Bay and seeing my friends again has opened my eyes." She took a deep breath and let it out slowly. "I've been searching for something my whole life and it was here all along, but I ran from it."

"I knew you were looking for something," he said. "But I didn't know what it was."

"I didn't either until tonight. I wanted a career—I felt was important. I wanted to contribute and be productive. I wanted to do something meaningful with my life. But you were right when you told me the thing that gives life meaning is love. And I had that all along. Right here. With you."

Kell felt as if an elephant had jumped off his chest. He restrained himself, though. Cupping her cheek in his hand, he said, "I can't tell you what it means to me to hear you say that. But how can you give up the life you've made for yourself in San Diego and be happy?"

"I'm not giving up anything," she said decisively. "I'm going to bring my world here! Think about how great it would be to have a facility right here in Courage Bay like Scripps, only bigger and better and—"

Kell's heart flooded with emotion. He pulled Melody to him and kissed her deeply, his lips silencing hers with tenderness. Easing back a second later, he warned her, "You need to be sure, Melody. I can't handle losing you a second time. Do you want to think about this first?"

"Okay." Her eyes turned serious. "Kiss me again and I'll think about it...."

He pressed his lips to hers one more time, but she pulled back almost immediately.

"Okay," she said. "I've thought about it."

He grinned. "And...?"

"And I love you, Robert Kellison. And you love me. We'll work out the details tomorrow."

Two days later
Courage Bay Sentinel

Officials in Courage Bay have announced the reopening of the beach and the bay's nearby fishing areas. Unexpectedly severe weather dispersed the organisms that had been recently detected, forcing the closure of the beach and its surrounding waters.

Dr. Melody Harper, former Courage Bay resident and well-known research biologist with the Scripps Institution of Oceanography in San Diego, told city officials last night that had the two potentially deadly phytoplanktons in the bay merged as she feared they might, the results could have been disastrous.

"Courage Bay dodged a bullet this time. It's imperative, however, that the local community and Scripps work together to locate what may be forcing this algae into a symbiotic relationship. If this is nature's work, then we need to manage it. If pollution is involved, we need to uncover it. More research is needed, but just as important as that is the need for more education."

Dr. Harper has opened what will be the first satellite office of the Scripps Institution here in

Courage Bay. Local businessman Robert Kellison will be leading the community effort to help finance the project. Dr. Harper plans on dividing her time between San Diego and Courage Bay, eventually making the office a permanent facility from which she will monitor the entire western coastline.

Two months later
Courage Bay Sentinel

Mr. and Mrs. Robert Kellison were united in matrimony this evening in a sunset candlelight celebration held at Bay Villa, the former home of Mrs. Ida Mae Clan, the bride's maternal grandmother. Attendants for Mrs. Kellison included Lisa Montgomery and Bitsy Sandoval, longtime friends of the bride. After a short honeymoon in the Virgin Islands, the couple will reside at Whispering Dawn, Mr. Kellison's ranch. As a wedding gift to the community of Courage Bay, Dr. Harper-Kellison has donated Bay Villa to the city to be used as a center for aquatic and marine education. Ms. Montgomery and Ms. Sandoval will run the center, which will include an aquarium with touch screen information and examples of local sea life.

Two years later
Courage Bay Sentinel

Robert and Melody Kellison are delighted to announce the safe arrival of their daughter, LeAnne, five pounds, six ounces, and son Lucas, six pounds, five ounces, on July 21, 2006. Thanks to the wonderful staff at Courage Bay Hospital.

*Ordinary people. Extraordinary circumstances.
Meet a new generation of heroes—the men and
women of Courage Bay Emergency Services.*

CODE RED

*A new Harlequin continuity series begins August
2004 with SPONTANEOUS COMBUSTION
by Bobby Hutchinson*

*Firefighter Shannon O'Shea is lifted from the
rubble of a burning building by an unknown
fireman, his protective gear shielding his identity.
She's convinced her mystery rescuer is John
Forrester, the newest member of their team. But
when John denies it, Shannon becomes suspicious.
Nothing about John seems to add up…
Here's a preview!*

CHAPTER ONE

SHE FELL FORWARD HARD from the momentum, but at least the dog was fine. The moment he felt the weight lift from his body, he scrabbled toward her, dragging his crushed hind leg, barking and choking from the smoke.

"Poor baby." Shannon's heart was racing and she was puffing hard from the effort she'd expended. She wondered for an instant how much air she had left. The smoke was growing denser by the minute.

"Gotta get us out of here fast, fella," she muttered. A rapid, horrified glance around told her that the fire had accelerated, and above her head flames were leaping from one wooden beam to the next in a macabre, gleeful dance.

"Let's go. C'mere, dog." Shannon grunted as she lifted the animal into her arms, then crouched and did a crab walk back in the direction she thought she'd come. Her equipment weighed sixty-eight pounds. The dog was easily another sixty. Skinny as he was, he was big-boned and rangy, but at least he didn't resist.

She did her best not to bump his damaged hind leg—she wondered for an instant if he'd bite—but he only yelped in agony as she hoisted his forepaws farther over one shoulder, doing her best to support his broken limb and steady him with one hand, and still hang on to her flashlight.

"Now, where—oh darn, oh lordie—"

She'd turned in the direction she thought she'd come, but a wall of flames sent her staggering back. She looked in the other direction. Oily, roiling smoke made it impossible to see. The powerful beam from her flash barely penetrated the darkness, and the noise of the fire had accelerated into a rushing, eerie roar that sounded at times like some demon chortling with glee.

We're in trouble here, pooch. I don't know where the lousy line is anymore. I came around some sort of doorway—

Shannon felt panic begin to nip at her brain, and she resolutely shoved it away. *A trapped firefighter who panics is going to die.* There was a way out of this, there had to be. She just had to find it. She turned in a 360-degree circle, searching, and now she was also praying silently.

Dear God, help us. Get us out of here, please show us the way—

But the flames roared closer.

Please, God, we need a miracle here—

At that moment a nearby beam gave an ominous creaking groan as fire snaked up its length. In another few moments it would collapse, and unless she got out of the way, it would crush her and the dog beneath it.

She pulled her mask away.

"Hello, anybody there?"

She hollered again, as loud as she could, but there was no answer.

Heat seemed to envelop her on every side, and as she clamped the mask on again she imagined that her air was running out. The stink of smoke filled her nostrils, and she gagged and choked. The terrible, awesome sound the fire made built into a crescendo.

Of all the fires she'd been on, now she was about to die in a stupid vacant warehouse, rescuing a dog?

Don't panic. She tried to calm herself, to stay in control and figure out what she ought to do next. But instinct and reason both told her that she was trapped, that she and the poor animal in her arms were going to die together.

And then from the wall of flames a shape appeared, a huge form in a silver suit that enveloped the entire body of whoever—whatever—was inside it.

Shannon gaped, certain that the smoke had gotten to her. She knew she was hallucinating, because ordinary firemen just weren't issued the mega-expensive silver suits.

Maybe this was the Angel of Death?

CODE RED

Meet a new generation of heroes.

Bold enough to risk their lives—
and their hearts.

Fearless enough to face any emergency…even
the ones that are no accident.

$1.00 OFF!

Your purchase of any Harlequin Code Red title.

Silhouette®
Where love comes alive™

code RED

Meet a new generation of heroes.

Bold enough to risk their lives—
and their hearts.

Fearless enough to face any emergency…even
the ones that are no accident.

$1.00 OFF!

Your purchase of any Harlequin
Code Red title.

RETAILER: Harlequin Enterprises Ltd. will pay the face value of this coupon plus 10.25¢ if submitted by customer for this product only. Any other use constitutes fraud. Coupon is nonassignable. Void if taxed, prohibited or restricted by law. Void if copied. Consumer must pay any government taxes. Nielson Clearing House customers—mail to: Harlequin Enterprises Ltd., 661 Millidge Avenue, P.O. Box 639, Saint John, N.B. E2L 4A5. Non NCH retailer—for reimbursement submit coupons and proof of sales directly to: Harlequin Enterprises Ltd., Retail Marketing Department, 225 Duncan Mill Rd., Don Mills, (Toronto), Ontario M3B 3K9, Canada.

Coupon expires August 30, 2005.
Redeemable at participating retail outlets in Canada only.
Limit one coupon per purchase.

```
52605781
```

Silhouette®

Where love comes alive™

Coming in July 2004
from Silhouette Books

Sly McEwen's final assignment for top-secret government
agency Onyxx had gone awry, leaving only questions behind.
But Sly had a feeling Eva Creon had answers. Locked inside
Eva's suppressed memory was the key to finding the killer
on the loose. But her secrets may have the power to destroy
the one thing that could mean more than the truth...
their growing love for each other....

Available at your favorite retail outlet.

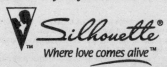

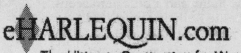

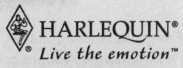

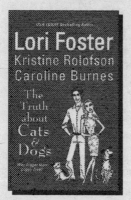
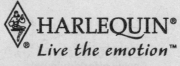

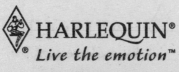